The Venom of Iona Skane

By

Bob Cregan

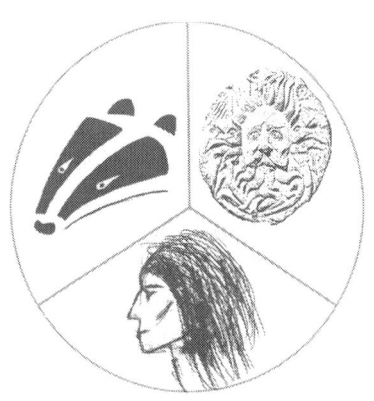

Cover, map and text is Copyright © 2015 Bob Cregan

All rights reserved. No part of this publication may be reproduced, distributed, or transmitted in any form or by any means, including photocopying, recording, or other electronic or mechanical methods, without the prior written permission of the author, except in the case of brief quotations embodied in critical reviews and certain other non-commercial uses permitted by copyright law.

For Anna, Jenny and Linda

Map of Oldmere Vale

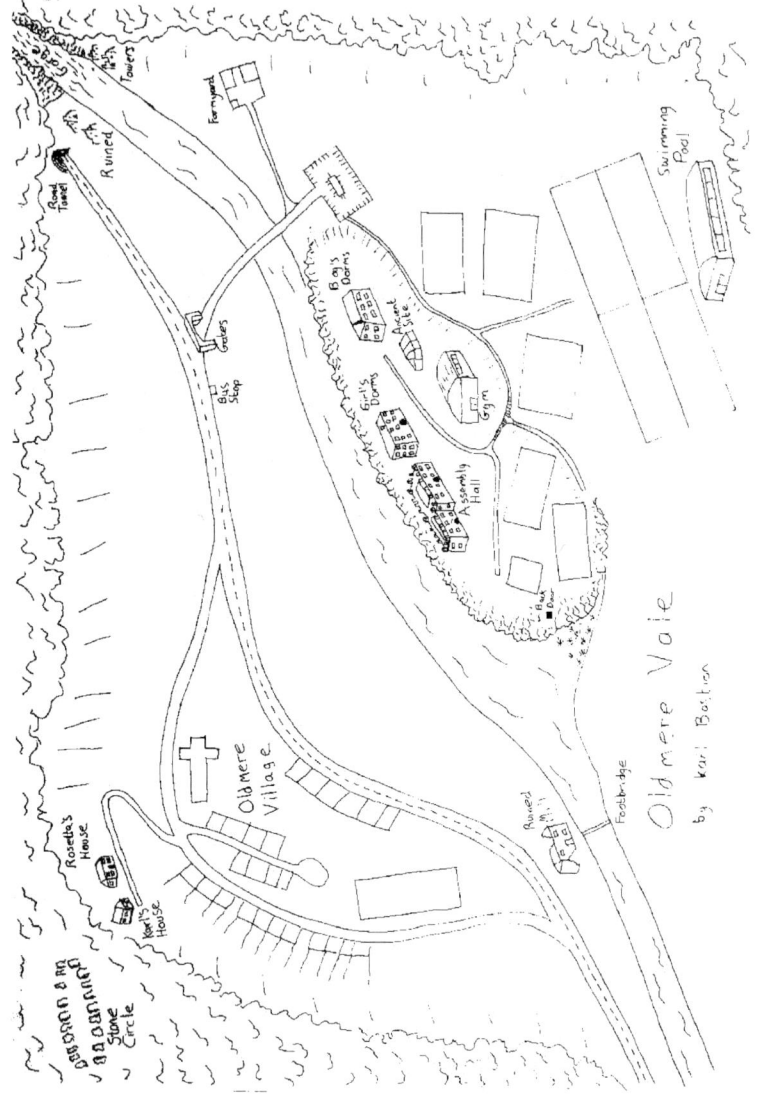

Prologue

From a diary found in the mud.

Something new has arrived in the valley. I can feel it in the rock, the mud, the flow of the river. Today the water in the lake rippled as if a squall had flashed across the surface, even though there can be no wind here and a shape was blown out from its mirror sheen. It seemed a figure of a child, though I cannot be sure for the image was gone almost as soon as it had become. And from that moment I sensed that there is now a new danger, a threat to my greatness ... but it is still vague and undirected; both my power and instinct tell me that it does not yet know of me and that is my great advantage.

I need to find it, hunt it down and destroy it, before it becomes aware, before it hunts me.

PART ONE

THE VALE OF OLDMERE

Chapter 1

Rosetta Clarence has a surprising encounter whilst lying on the roof of a playhouse.

Rosetta Clarence waited, hidden in the dappled shadows, for the badgers to come. It was on her very first day at the Clarence family's new cottage that she noticed the badger trail which was just visible through the long grass of the overgrown lawn. There was an old playhouse, half obscured in the lush foliage of a plum tree, which stood close to the trail.

The playhouse roof, she thought, would make an ideal place to watch for any badgers using the trail; the leaves of the plum tree formed a thick screen that enveloped the top of the building and the structure was built on stilts so that anyone who lay on the roof was raised well above the height of a man ... and conveniently above any sensitive noses that might be nosing for food below.

This was a likely occurrence for, as well as providing a hiding place, the tree was fruiting and had dropped a generous scatter of red, juicy plums. The fruit nestled invitingly in the grass and might tempt the badgers to linger whilst Rosetta watched them unseen from amongst the leaves, or at least that was her idea.

Looking out from between the branches Rosetta noticed that, as well as having a bird's eye view of the badger trail, she also had an excellent view of the area where she now lived, as the family cottage clung high on the steep slopes of the river valley.

Looking out from her hiding place behind the branches, she saw the valley expand out from a cramped darkness in the southwest, into the broad open shape of the Vale of Oldmere.

Even in this wide part of the valley its sides were steep – an impression that was lessened by thick woods which sprouted on the upper slopes - but they were spread far enough apart for sunlight to enter and illuminate the small and pretty village of Oldmere.

The buildings of the village clung to the Northern part of the valley. They spread down from high up the valley until they encroached onto the flat fields near the road. There were no buildings on the other side of the road, which effectively marked the southern boundary of Oldmere. The village was constructed of solid red stone and had perhaps thirty houses.

At the far end of the valley – to the east - the sides steepened further and turned to cliffs, which crowded in close to the river and formed a narrow gorge into which the river gushed. It disappeared from sight, eventually reappearing upon distant plains, which had a grey smudge smeared across them indicating a nearby town. Upstream and towards the southwest the river weaved through tightly packed hills towards its source in distant mountains.

Rosetta found her eyes drawn back to the valley, for in the centre of this wooded amphitheatre, enclosed by a loop of the river and dominating the whole area, was the impressive mass of Oldmere Knoll; a rocky outcrop which rose seemingly magically from the otherwise flat, featureless fields of the valley floor. By the river bank it consisted of cliffs, which rose to such a height that even Oldmere church, tucked into the valley wall opposite, became tiny in comparison. On its other side, the knoll fell away more gradually before rising steeply again to form the valley side.

Such an eruption would be expected to have a large mediaeval castle perched on top, and at first glance it looked like this was what had been placed there.

However closer examination showed that, though there were ancient buildings placed on the summit, there were no battlements or fortifications, and instead the structures had the look of an ancient monastery or university. The scatter of modern buildings that sprawled below the old stone lessened this effect and the car park that had been built at the foot of the knoll finished it off completely. The playing fields which rolled out over the nearby valley floor would finally make it absolutely clear to an inquiring mind that what sat on Oldmere Knoll was most a likely school, or at least it was nowadays.

However Rosetta Clarence would not be going to Oldmere School. It was a private school, famous, and its students came from the richest, or the cleverest, children in the world. Scattered amongst its old pupils there were five prime ministers, tens of government ministers from multiple nations and even one American president. Rosetta's family could not afford the fees that the school demanded. Her mother only had a small income since her father died, and even if the money was available Rosetta secretly feared she would not be able to pass the entrance exams.

No, Rosetta was due to get on a bus at the stop, situated by Oldmere School gates, and make the five mile journey to the secondary school in a nearby town, and it was there where she would have to face the fears and worries that come with being the unknown face in a class of old friends.

Rosetta dismissed that unpleasant thought and settled down once more to wait for the badgers, taking a book from her bag as she did; there were several hours to wait before dusk and she understood that badgers rarely moved from their sett in daylight.

Rosetta awoke with a twitch, and realised it was nearly dark. At first she thought her mother must be calling, and it was that which had woken her, but then she remembered that her mother and Aimee, her sister, were probably still at the doctor's. Aimee, who was three, was different from other children her age. She could not yet speak and found it quite difficult to understand even the simplest things. Her enthusiasm and good nature more than made up for that in Rosetta's eyes, and she loved her sister fiercely. However, because the doctors had not yet worked out what was the matter with her, there were still lots of visits to hospital for tests. Her mother, who knew that Rosetta hated the endless trips to London, no longer insisted that everyone went.

So what had woken her? Rosetta pushed up on her elbows to look around, but before she could complete the movement, a loud rustle made her freeze. It sounded like it came from the bottom of one of the hedges, and looking closely she thought she could see a slight movement in the prickly darkness, where the badger trail left the garden and disappeared into the undergrowth.

A nose poked out, twitching. Then a bit more came and Rosetta saw a flash of white. Soon the face of a badger became clearly visible. Its nose wrinkled and it made as if to pull back, but then it was slid bodily forward as if it had been pushed from behind. There was a scrabble and then another face appeared alongside the first one, showing where the push had come from.

Rosetta sat up slowly to get a good view, and as she did so she heard a gasp coming from over the top of the hedge - from the garden next door. Reluctantly taking her eyes off the emerging badgers - a third one was now following the first two - she looked over towards this second noise and saw a boy perched in the branches of an apple tree peering over the hedge at the animals. Excitement showed all over his face, and he had plainly not seen Rosetta, screened as she was by the branches of the plum tree.

There were now five badgers moving hesitantly across the lawn, snuffling through the grass for fallen plums, and Rosetta turned her attention away from the boy to watch them. After a few minutes, when they had satisfied their first hunger, the animals started to play; snapping at each other and growling in a good humoured way.

Except for one that is. A large badger - a male from its size Rosetta thought - took no part in the play and instead ran around in an agitated manner, every now and again stopping to rub its head against the base of the plum tree.

Rosetta glanced back across at the boy. She could tell he was short, even though his position in the tree gave no proper sense of scale, and he had black hair, worn long for a boy his age. His face was pale and was starting to show the first sign of adolescent spots.

He started to wave, having caught sight of her through the branches of the plum tree. Rosetta in turn glared back at him, and signalled that he should be still and quiet by lowering her hands as if she were closing an invisible window. Having got her message across, or so she thought, she turned back to watch the badgers who were still rolling around in the grass oblivious to all.

The peace of the scene was disturbed when a small apple struck Rosetta on the shoulder and dropped with a loud thud onto the roof of the playhouse. At the noise the badgers froze, looked around, and then made a dash for the hole in the garden hedge from which they had come.

Well not all of them, for one of the five - the large one who had behaved so oddly - seemed at the last minute reluctant to leave and hesitated by the hole in the hedge. Rosetta, who had jumped up into a crouch so she could catch one last look, found herself looking directly into the eyes of that last badger.

As she did so a most peculiar sensation overcame her and she noticed that the eyes of the badger, which one would expect to be unfocussed and blank (badgers have very poor eyesight), were sharp and concentrated. And then, as she looked into those eyes, her heart leapt and she felt a bond form; a bond that she knew that badger also felt, because those eyes suddenly blinked as if in surprise. Then to her utter bewilderment, the badger stopped, pulled itself up onto on its hind legs, and clearly said;

"Who are you humangirl? And what do you think you are looking at?"

And with that it dropped to all fours and dashed through the hole in the hedge.

The boy, whose name was Karl, sat with Rosetta cross legged on the grass and they chatted to each other about what had just happened. The shared experience had been very effective in breaking the ice and they spoke like they had known each other for years.

"I mean, you did see what I just saw ... and also heard," said Karl who was very excited. "That badger definitely spoke, didn't it?"

"Yes it did, and it also looked strange ... did you see. Its eyes were almost human. Not the same as ours to look at ... but when it looked at you, you would guess that they see the world much as we see it," said Rosetta, not mentioning the strange feeling which had overcome her. "They were not like a normal animal's eyes"

"Hmm" said Karl looking pensive. "But it was only that last one that was odd. The rest seemed to be plain old badgers ...."

"Yes but it was the eyes that got to me ... Have you seen them do anything like that before? I'm guessing you have seen them before today. You looked like you were waiting for them; like you knew they were coming."

Karl considered for a few seconds and said, "I have been watching them on and off since next door - your house I mean - became empty, but I have never seen anything odd. I mean they would come and play, like they did tonight, and then once they had eaten some plums they would go. I've never seen anything unusual before."

Then they both fell silent for, strange as it seemed, they could not find anything more to say about the talking badger; the event was so bizarre that it needed more time to think about before you felt like you could say anything about it. After a few seconds Rosetta asked Karl if he would be going to her school.

Karl it seemed went to Oldmere School; or he would be, starting from this year. This seemed odd to Rosetta; Karl's cottage was not much larger than hers and Rosetta had the definite impression that the school was very expensive. The parents of Oldmere School children were bankers or international businessmen, not people from the village.

"Oh ... Well yes you're right normally," said Karl when she asked him about it. "But the school is very old and has some very strange traditions. It was founded in 1280 by Edward I, just about the same time he conquered Wales, and written into its founding charter are lots of unusual rules that still apply even now.

"One of these is that every five years the school is required to take a child from Oldmere village on a free scholarship. The teachers come into the primary school here, and choose one of the kids. It is quite an event in the village. They hold an entrance exam in the primary school. The adults go quite stupid about it as you can imagine. Some families even move to the village just so their kids get a chance at the exam. Anyway last year they chose me."

"Wow. So you start this year?"

"Yes, but it's definitely not all it is made out to be. I'm the only child in the village who goes to the "Posh Knoll" as the school is known here, and some of the local kids hold it against you. And in the school the "Outside Scholar" can also get it in the neck. You don't sleep in the school, as your house is in the village anyway, and you come from a different background. You are kind of neither one thing or another ... you fall between the village and the school.

"Anyway after I got the scholarship, I spent a couple of weeks at the school. Just to see if I'd like it and it wasn't too bad to be honest, nothing like I'd feared, but it might be different when I start full time. Last year was just a couple of days a week for half a term."

And with that Karl fell suddenly silent pulling at the grass between his legs.

Rosetta started to say something when a voice

came from over the hedge - "Karl! Kaaarl!"

"It's Mum. I'd better go," said Karl rising to his feet.

"We should meet again tomorrow," said Rosetta quickly. "I mean ... I'll dig out my camera and we can see if we can't catch that badger."

Karl smiled and said, "Yes let's do that," and with that he climbed onto the roof of the playhouse and hopped over the hedge into his garden.

Rosetta sat for a moment thinking, and then went inside where she found her mum curled up in a wide armchair, an empty bottle of wine on the table, and Aimee cuddled up beside her. Her sister's honey hair was spread in a circle on her mother's shoulder; she was also asleep.

Chapter 2

Karl shows Rosetta the village. A fisherman behaves strangely and the badger comes again.

It was the last week of the summer holidays and both of the children had, each for their own reasons, no other company. Rosetta knew no one anyway, being a newcomer to the village, and Karl was having problems with the village children; there were some who resented his status as the new "Outside Scholar" of Oldmere School and picked on him whenever possible. Even those who were normally friendly kept out of his way in case the bullies also targeted them.

The weather was good and so most days they met as they had on that first one; Rosetta up on the roof of the old play house and Karl perched, legs swinging, on a branch of the apple tree on the other side of the hedge. The badgers, talking or otherwise, had not reappeared and so they found other things to do with their time.

Karl decided it was his responsibility, as the local, to show Rosetta around the valley. And so on most days, after some discussion as to where to go, they would grab some sandwiches from the adults and head out to explore.

It was on one of these trips, about a week after the encounter with the badgers, that Karl took Rosetta on a trip up and out of the valley.

They climbed up through cow fields, which started flat near the river and grew increasingly steep, until they reached the edge of the forest which grew everywhere high up on the valley walls. Here the ground flattened a little and wooded tracks made for pleasant easy walking.

They continued onwards until they reached a place where the trees stopped and the ground rose up steeply. This did not mean that the forest had ended, but instead indicated a treeless area which poked up out through the forest, like the bald patch on an old man's head.

And in the middle of this bare grassy area was a stone circle. Twenty large stones about the height of a tall man were laid out in a rough ring. One or two had fallen sometime in the ancient past, but most still stood tall, like sentries. There was a massive stone, which lay on its side, in the centre of the circle.

"Good aren't they," said Karl. "Five or six

thousand years old, so they say; build by the druids."

As they climbed to the centre of the circle a vast vista opened up before them, and the whole world appeared to be spread out before their eyes; looking east they could see the high ground fall away, until it reached an estuary and then out to the plains of England; to the west and into Wales, there were steep wooded valleys and further on, distant mountains.

Rosetta slowly circled drinking in the view. It was when she had nearly gone full circle, and was looking back to where they had just walked – back down into the green chasm of Oldmere Vale - that she felt it. The vastness around her, the rest of the world, disappeared and the green valley below seemed to grow until it filled the whole of her vision. And as it did so Rosetta suddenly felt exposed, like something evil was looking for her, and she knew that she did not want whatever it was to find her.

She started to feel faint as her feeling of exposure grew to the point of panic, and looking for something to hold her up she leant against the nearest of the stones, the one that sat in the middle of the circle. As her hand touched the lichen-covered granite, the unpleasant feeling of being observed vanished in a flash and the world returned to normal around her.

"Hey are you feeling OK?" said Karl seeing her leaning against the stone.

"Yes. I just had a bit of a funny turn," said Rosetta feeling a little foolish - and then, to take Karl's attention away from her weakness. "It is an amazing view."

"Yes. I love it up here. The way the hills just end and England starts; it always gives me the impression of the edge of a fortress, which is perhaps not too inaccurate.

"The area around Oldmere *is* the gateway to Wales proper," said Karl. "Unless you go the long way round by sea then you have to come through that." He pointed to the East end of the valley. "If you look there where our valley narrows and the road goes into the tunnel ... no there, look along my arm."

Rosetta put her eye close to his elbow and squinted. "Can you see those ruins, turrets, thick walls and the like? Well, they are very old, built before the Normans. Some bits are even Roman, I heard. And they were all built over the years to defend this valley ... because if you can defend the valley you can defend Wales."

"And the school? Was that once a castle? It looks like it might have been." said Rosetta.

"No," said Karl. "Before it was a school - and it has been one of those since mediaeval times - it was a monastery. Before then it was some sort of ancient religious site. No one really knows the details, but they are trying to find out. They started upon an archaeological dig late last year. They found a Roman temple and loads of other things I believe -

it was in the local paper. The school is lapping it up, all that history plays well with the parents"

Rosetta looked disappointed. "I'm amazed they didn't build a castle there. I mean you couldn't have a better spot for one." Karl smiled and shrugged.

They dropped back toward the Vale of Oldmere, Karl taking them back a different way down towards Rosetta's house. He continued to talk as they dropped down.

"These days the woods are looked after, you know clearing fallen trees and stuff," said Karl as they walked along one of the rough paths that weaved drunkenly through the woods. "But only twenty or thirty years ago they were pretty wild. Impenetrable you couldn't ... wait, what's that?" Karl had stopped, turned and peered into the undergrowth behind them.

"I thought I heard something. There was a noise. From somewhere over there," said Karl.

He pointed to an area, thick with ferns and interspersed with occasional fallen tree trunks. As he did so there was a sudden commotion in the scrub and something dashed away, its progress marked by a sudden agitation of the tops of the plants. Rosetta could see nothing clearly, but thought she may have seen a flash of grey fur between the fronds as they parted.

Karl must also have seen it, for he nodded excitedly as she said. "I think that was a badger, I saw that little stub of a tail they have."

Karl had obviously been thinking of what Rosetta had said about the school looking like a castle, and the next day as he sat in his tree he said he wanted to show her around.

"I can't take you right in to the buildings I'm afraid," he explained. "I mean I'm not even starting at school properly until next week, but I can show you around the grounds - they are open to people from the village - and take you around the outside of the buildings. I had to learn the history of the school as part of the entrance examination, so I know all about it and can give a pretty good tour."

They walked across the fields from the village to the main gates, which consisted of an impressive stone arch with the school motto written on the central span.

Custodimus, et quaerere.

"I'm not sure what it means." Karl said a little guiltily, as he saw Rosetta squinting at it.

"'We guard and seek' I think," said Rosetta. "We did Latin at my old school." she added seeing the surprised look on Karl's face. "It was not as famous as Oldmere, but a good one. We had to leave when father died ... mother could not afford to pay for the house."

Rosetta fell silent and started to play with her

necklace. Karl did not quite know what to say to this. He briefly considered patting her on the shoulder, but decided against it and instead gave her a bit of the chocolate bar he had in his pocket. Rosetta took it, bit into a square and finally said, "So how do we get in? The gates are locked."

"Oh there is a gate behind these bushes, so the villagers can come in to walk the grounds."

"They are allowed? I mean it's private property, isn't it"

"It is another one of the thing written into the schools founding charter." said Karl. "All people from the village can wander the grounds, at all times. The school gets grumpy if they do it during school hours, but they cannot stop people even then. Plenty of the villagers make a point of doing it, just to annoy the school."

They opened the gate and started the long walk up the road that swept through the deer park to the looming buildings of Oldmere School. When they came to within a few hundred meters of the car park, which sat at the base of the knoll, Karl veered left towards the trunk of a massive fallen tree. They sat on the grass their backs against it, got out their sandwiches, and Karl pointed out the various buildings in the school.

"Well the biggest building, the one that probably made you think it was a castle, well that's the Assembly Hall and library. It's built around the remains of the mediaeval monastery and is pretty amazing ... they took me around when I won the scholarship. The whole school meets there every morning. It was the church in the monastery days and is all carved wood and stone. Then at the back of the Assembly Hall, joined by a wide archway, is the library reading room. It's another big room just like the Assembly Hall, but filled with really old tables.

"The tables there are all carved, but not properly. It is mostly student's graffiti. You know 'Bob was here' that type of stuff. You'd think it wouldn't be allowed ... and well it isn't, but it is at the same time"

Rosetta merely looked at him and raised her eyebrows.

"Well you get told off if you get caught actually doing it, but not if they just find a new bit with your name on it. They say it is because they cannot be sure who actually did it unless they nabbed you with the knife in your hand. But I think the real reason is because the school has had so many important and famous students.

"The carvings are like a slice of world history, prime ministers have carved their names there, famous writers and artists also. The carvings have become part of the school tradition. But they cannot be seen to be actually encouraging it since strictly it is vandalism.

"Anyway most of the old buildings, like the Assembly Hall, are from the mediaeval monastery. That one there is the old refectory," said Karl pointing. "It's some classrooms now, and that other big one is the teacher's quarters and the head teacher's office. Oh and that tent is the new archaeological dig. The new head teacher is really interested in the history of the buildings and she commissioned some people to have a look after a student found some ancient artefact in the grounds. Now they have found loads of the ancient stuff I told you about."

Karl continued for a while, pointing out the newer buildings that held the science and computer laboratories, until he turned and realised that Rosetta had fallen asleep in the afternoon heat.

She woke later and found Karl whittling away at a section of fallen wood with a small pocketknife. He had taken the bark from a section about the size of a credit card, roughly flattened it and was now working carefully holding the knife by the blade as if it were a pen.

"There have a look at that."

Rosetta looked over his shoulder and saw a rough craving of a four-legged animal taking shape; it had a long snout and short tail. "A badger! ... That's actually pretty good." she said, looking more closely. The outline was crude, but had a definite badgerness about it.

"I'll finish it later," said Karl. "It's a good start, but I need to use decent tools. If I carry on with this penknife I'll just ruin what I've already done"

They got up and moved on past the playing fields. The aim was to go to the front of the knoll, where the cliffs rose dramatically, walk there for a while and then carry on to a footbridge by an old mill building. From there they could cross the river, and make their way home.

The western edge of the knoll consisted of cliffs which rose directly from the riverbank. Utterly ancient and very impressive, the rock shone black as pitch even in the glow of the autumn sun. Shrubs and small trees sprouted from the many fissures in the rock wall. The presence of vegetation softened the primeval feel somewhat; without them you could only imagine boiling lava and ancient reptiles.

They wandered on toward the foot of the cliff and approached a small inlet, where the river tried to split to go around the knoll but gave up and abandoned the channel to marsh and swamp.

On the far side of this inlet, sat at the base of the cliffs, Rosetta spotted a figure seated on a spur of rock, which jutted out a little into the main river. His legs dangled over the edge of the rock and he held a fishing rod. He either paid no attention to the children or could not see them, and just stared at a small crimson float that bobbed in still patch of water near some reeds.

Except you could not really say his legs were dangling, for he only had one. His left one ended just below the knee in a stump which protruded out from his khaki shorts. By his side leaning against the rock, which also supported his back, was a false leg. In a stark contrast to the bare rock all around it looked extremely high tech; it was made from a black shiny substance and had a training shoe stuck on the end. The man was clean-shaven, but had wild, brown shoulder length hair.

"Who's that?" said Rosetta, lowering her voice.

"I think," said Karl, "it's the new librarian Mr Vates. He used to be in the army, but lost his leg in an explosion, or so it is said. He came here to take over from his father who disappeared, rather mysteriously, at the beginning of the summer."

Karl was going to say more when two things happened. Firstly there was a scuffle and a splash near the edge of the river where the field ended in a low soil cliff. Something large had fallen from a bramble thicket and ended up in the river.

Secondly the man looked towards the noise, and on seeing its source lifted his head so he could peer over the reeds which lined the river bank, at which point he then saw the two children standing a little further along the water's edge. This brought about a great change in his demeanour. He sat up suddenly and looked from the children to whatever had caused the commotion in the river as if he could not quite believe what he had seen.

"Hey! .... Hey!" He shouted looking very agitated. "It's you. Stay there!" He threw down his rod, leant against the rock with one hand and with his other grabbed his false leg as if he intended to put it on.

The children panicked and ran. Karl led the way running upstream towards a bridge which crossed the river near an old stone ruin on the far bank. After a couple of minutes they boomed across the wooden planks of the bridge, reached the other side and ducked behind a wall that extended out from the main building.

Karl peered over the top of the wall his head tilted back so he seemed to be looking along his nose. "It's clear I think," he said. "I mean he has to put his leg on, and even when he has done that he won't be able run too well." He collapsed down, turning as he did, ending up with his back against the cool stones.

"He's the school *librarian*?" said Rosetta whose tone indicated that she thought that librarians should perhaps be a little more unremarkable people than the wild creature they had just seen.

"Well the librarian in Oldmere School is called the 'Custodian', and the job is not what you would expect. For one thing it is inherited. Each and every Custodian at Oldmere School has come from the same family for as long as records have existed."

"I suppose that must come from that famous School Charter," said Rosetta. "it sounds mad enough."

"Yes, it is in the charter, and it is a bit mad. The Custodian must come from the Vates family, and the Custodian's role is to look after the old library - the one next to the Assembly Hall - no one else is allowed even to go in without permission. It is one of the oldest libraries in Europe, and has loads of really ancient and valuable books. The new library, which has all the computers, technology and normal books, is looked after by another librarian who is most definitely not the Custodian."

"What, no one is allowed in ... what about the

teachers? What if you actually want to read one of the books?"

"Well most kids don't need to. But if you do, you can look it up in the catalogue and put in a request. The Custodian then brings out the book to the reading room - the one with the carved tables - and you can read it there. The library is world famous, and scholars regularly visit - you can see them sometimes in the reading room I'm told. The teachers get a guided tour of the old library when they join and after that, the same rule applies as for everyone else. They are not allowed in.

"This guy is new. His father, the previous Custodian, disappeared a couple of months ago, and he came in over the summer."

"Disappeared? What just vanished?"

"No one knows for sure, but they think he chucked himself from his office window. He had been behaving very strangely. He was getting very upset about the archaeological dig - threatening to resign and break the charter if it wasn't stopped - but the headmaster wouldn't have it and tried to shut him up. It was just after that he vanished. He didn't leave a note, but he just disappeared from his office one evening in May. The window was open and it looked like someone had been up on the sill." Karl shrugged. "Who knows what actually happened?"

As Karl finished speaking they heard a sound from the bridge, an urgent scratchy padding, which continued for some thirty seconds before silence fell. A short time later they saw a badger come running into the yard in front of the ruined building. It looked distinctly wet.

Rosetta put her finger to her lips, and they slowly slid to the floor lying as flat as they could. The badger shook itself, waddled over to the doorway to the building and went in.

Rosetta got slowly to her knees, then rose to her feet and made her way over to the wall next to the door. Karl seeing what she had in mind followed behind. As she reached the edge of door she slowly peered around the corner and saw a long streak of water leading across the hallway into a room opposite; it looked like someone had dragged a wet mop across the floor. The entrance to the room still had a door, old and the wood looked rotten, but it still looked serviceable.

"Let's trap it in there, and see," whispered Rosetta.

"What if it's just a normal badger, I mean not the one we saw... I mean heard the other day. Won't it be cruel to lock it up?"

But Rosetta had already dashed across the hall, flung herself into the room and slammed the door behind her.

Compared to the brightness in the hallway the room felt pitch black, though there were patches of brightness from holes where the stones in the outside wall had fallen out. As the door slammed behind her there was the sound of a desperate scrabbling from a corner.

"Let me in." Karl had arrived by the door. He gave it a shove.

"Wait a sec," said Rosetta, pushing back. "I can't see"

She waited and her eyes adjusted to the darkness. Before long she started to make out parts of the room. It seemed to be an old workshop, for there was a broken down bench in one corner and old iron spikes for hanging tools jutted from the wall above it. There was no window.

Rosetta looked at the corner where the scuffling noise had come from. And at first could see nothing, for the darkness sunk even deeper there, like someone had spilled some ink in the air. After a while she made out patches of white and eventually the badger came into view.

It was looking at her, not like a cornered animal, which would look past you concentrated on escape and escape only. Instead the badger was looking right into her eyes, as a human would in such a situation; as if it were judging an opponent.

"Are you following us?" said Rosetta in rush. She felt very foolish all of a sudden.

The badger snorted and shook its head slightly, and then as before, it spoke. "I am watching, guarding, and that means I must follow you, but I am not sneaking, or spying, if that is what you mean."

The door rattled some more as Karl hearing some

voices and thinking that he was missing out on something, tried once more to get in. Rosetta opened the door a crack to let him squeeze through, making sure that her body was in the way of any potential escape route as she did so. The badger tracked her every move with his eyes but did, and said nothing.

Karl slid in behind Rosetta and stood blinking in the darkness waiting for his vision to clear.

"Who are you? I'm Rosetta, and he is Karl" said Rosetta, frankly at rather a loss as what else to say in such a situation.

"My name would translate as 'Musty', that is if there were a badger language to translate from. It would be better to say my smell is my strongest characteristic and so that is how other badgers would know me; we have no language as you would understand it, and deal in impressions and memories." and indeed at that moment the children started to notice a pungent odour rising from the corner where the badger was now scratching himself.

"But how can that be?" said Karl after a moment. "If badgers do not even have their own language, how could you even start to learn to speak English?"

"Because I did not 'learn to speak' at all." said Musty, turning his eyes on Karl. "I simply ... transformed. Look I can give you my story if you want, but I would much prefer to do so in the open air. I am still enough of a badger to be very uncomfortable trapped in a small room with two humans."

Karl and Rosetta looked at each other, and then Rosetta said, "Of course, but ... do you promise not to run off before you have told it?"

"I give you my word as a badger."

The children looked at each other at these words, but opened the door and stood aside to let the badger pass. They all moved outside, and sat by the broken wall as the children had before. Musty did not run, but lay down by the base of the wall with his nose on his paws and started to speak.

"Just a short time ago I was a normal badger. My days consisted of sleeping in the set with my family; my nights hunting for food. I lived with my family. There were seven of us; my mother, four sisters and two brothers. Our sett was high up in the woods above your houses. Your garden, Rosetta, was one of our favourite places to visit, mainly because of that wonderful plum tree.

"Some days ago, we got up at dusk as we always did, and decided, in the unspoken way of badgers, that we would go to eat some plums in a garden we knew very well. We wandered down, crossed the fields and headed for the hole in the hedge that leads to your garden Rosetta. As was also normal I was first through the hole - I was the youngest and most daring in our family - and then, as I pushed, through the hedge I began to feel very peculiar.

"I felt a buzzing and itching behind my ears, and then out of the blue my head was full; new ideas streamed in fast, faster than my mind could really cope with, and I was lost in a whirl of strangeness. Eventually the spell or whatever was broken by a loud noise and the unexpected fall of an apple. All the badgers looked up and saw you Rosetta, and my family ran. This helped me snap out of whatever had taken me, for the badger instinct rose up and I just wanted to run with everyone around me, to escape.

"However at the last minute I looked back and I saw you looking at me through the leaves and in that moment I changed in two ways. Firstly I knew that I could now speak to humans; just knew it, the way that doubtless you know.

"Secondly I discovered why I was changing, why I was no longer a normal badger, no longer free to just eat, sleep and mate for my whole life. For when I looked into the eyes of that humangirl crouched up in the tree, I knew that the reason I was put on the earth was to protect her, and what is more I knew that protection was needed, that something in the valley was looking for her - something malevolent.

"So since then I have left the sett in the woods, my home - life there was all of a sudden strange to me so it was not too upsetting - and I moved over here to this building. Every morning I go over and guard your house. I am watching over you and waiting; I will be ready when it, whatever it is, comes for you."

As the story had progressed Rosetta and Karl had slowly shifted around so they both sat cross-legged in front of the badger, like small children in front of their teacher. At Musty's last words Rosetta raised her hand to her mouth and gave a small gasp; Karl just sat with his mouth open.

Musty looked from one to the other and, though the shape of his muzzle and the thickness of his fur made such judgments difficult, one could imagine from the gentle narrowing of his eyes that he was amused by the children's responses.

"And now I must go. It won't do for people to see us. I can only guard you if my existence is not known. Indeed I would have been happier if my existence was unknown even to you," and with that the badger sat up.

"Wait!" said Rosetta. "What is coming for me and why would anything want to hurt me?" there was a quiver to her voice.

Musty paused. "I don't know. I just know that it exists and it is now in this valley. I know it, you understand, this is no guess. This knowledge came at the same time as my voice and I think you will agree that that is no fabrication."

And with that he trotted around the corner, leaving the children alone and somewhat bewildered.

Chapter 3

Rosetta starts at the local school, which is not a bad as she feared. Karl has an uncomfortable experience with Marcus Vates, the Custodian of Oldmere School.

It was her very first day at her new school, and Rosetta sat at the front of the bus, afraid to go further towards the back because of all the kids she did not know. There were about ten children from the village, some who she vaguely recognised, who had got on the bus. But they were all were much older and ignored her. So she clutched her bag on her lap and looked at the back of the driver's head wondering what the school would be like when she arrived.

After an interminable journey filled with doubts, the bus dropped her by a large square building, which was slowly filling with an endless stream of children. Two teachers stood by the gate holding up their hands and calling for all new pupils to come and make themselves known.

After a short wait in a queue a teacher greeted her, gave her a map of the school, which seemed vast and, after looking up her name on a list, marked the location of her classroom. She arrived after a few missed turns and found it full of the normal bustle of school life. Within a few minutes she had found a friend, Michelle White, who was also new and before long they had teamed up, allies at least for the day; a day which all of a sudden seemed brighter and shorter.

※ ※ ※ ※ ※

When she arrived back home her spirits were high and she itched to go and see Karl; they had not had a proper chance to talk since Musty had given them so many things to talk about. However, her mother met her in the hallway, having spotted the school bus from her bedroom window, and she naturally wanted to know all about the new school and her day. Then Aimee wanted to play, an event Rosetta normally enjoyed, but which today seemed something of a chore.

So it was well past seven when she finally met with Karl on the roof of the playhouse. He, it seemed had also had a better than expected day at his first day at Oldmere School. "Most of the kids are OK," he said. "Of course most don't know I'm the Outside Scholar. Loads are just pleased to see a friendly face; half of them are not from this country even, and on top of that it is their first night sleeping away from their families."

And then from down below, from underneath the playhouse came a voice. "At least they are still the same species they were at the start of the week. I personally don't think they have much to complain about." They looked down and saw Musty sitting on his back legs looking up.

The children lay on the roof, with only their heads sticking over the lip and greeted the badger who snorted and lowered himself to his haunches.

"Good evening to you also. I trust your first day at your new school was an enjoyable one ... good. I have also had a most enjoyable day. With you at your school, and therefore out of the valley young lady I have been able to relax for the first time in over a week.

"I have not been idle though, I have used this time to think about our situation and have come to several conclusions

"It seems to me I have been wakened in order to protect Rosetta, of this there is no doubt in my mind. Also without question is that there is a danger to guard against."

At this Rosetta stuck her hand up, as if she were at school and wanted to answer a question. Musty looked up and, completing the image, said "Yes, what is it?"

"Musty, how can you be sure of this? I mean it is

very strange what has happened to you, but there have been no other strange occurrences since I've arrived in the village. All I've done is walk around with Karl, and get on the school bus once. How can I have an enemy in the valley? I know no one and have done nothing, not really."

Even as she said this Rosetta remembered the strange feeling of exposure she felt when she was on the hill near the stone circle a few days ago, but she decided not to mention it. After all it was most likely the vast open space and the height that had affected her.

"Hear me Rosetta. It is here. It lurks somewhere and it wants to find you. I know that as surely as the sun rises; as surely as the trees grow. What matters is that we are on our guard."

Karl, who had being trying not to smile - Rosetta and Musty looked so much like a bizarre pupil and teacher - spoke up.

"But, on our guard against what? I mean we know nothing about this danger.?Is it a man, woman, someone at school, in the village or perhaps it's not even a person? Something like an accident that's going to happen. We can't be on our guard against everything."

"I have already told you that I know that it is in the valley. But after some thought it seems to me that the danger is more *of* the valley, as much a part of it as the knoll itself. So I feel it will not be a person from *your* school, Rosetta, nor anyone who left the valley today. I could still feel its presence all day."

"OK assuming it true - I mean that you are not mistaken," added Rosetta quickly seeing the badger start to frown. "What can we do?"

"We can do this," said Musty. "We can meet here every day. This place is not visible from either of your houses and is a good spot - the plums are still in season for one thing" and at this comment it seemed almost that the badger gave a small wink. "At these meetings we will then give an account of anything strange that has happened. That way we may get some clues as to the nature of the menace.

"I will follow Rosetta when she is in the valley and will perhaps have a better chance of seeing if anyone is watching her. Karl can listen to village gossip. And we wait."

Weeks passed and their evening meetings passed uneventfully. Rosetta reported on her day-to-day activities at her school, as did Karl on his. Musty followed Rosetta everywhere he could, staying hidden, and saw nothing suspicious, but he still felt the Menace - the name they had given to the mysterious enemy - everywhere and he declared that his feeling of danger was a strong as ever if not increasing.

And so it went on. September passed, as did the beginning of October and, as the evenings grew darker, they were forced to meet inside the Play House; the humans muffled in jumpers, candles providing light for everyone.

Then one particularly autumnal day Karl met them, excited, and said, as the rain lashed outside, "Something has happened at school.

"It all came out today. Apparently it has been going on for ages, but because it was all one of the older kids none of us first years got to hear until the head teacher told us in Assembly this morning."

"Please," said Musty. "Can you start from the beginning and then carry on from there until you have reached the end."

"OK. Well there is this girl called Emily Watson in year thirteen who went mad last night ... well that is what it looks like. It's all so odd.

Musty blinked his eyes in a way that betrayed impatience with this explanation.

"OK well..." said Karl gathering his thoughts "Emily Watson was a model student. She just ticked all the right boxes; Head Girl, top of her class in all subjects, has been touted as a sure-fire shortlister for the Archer Prize"

"The Archer prize?" said Rosetta.

"Oh yes you wouldn't know about that. It's a special scholarship to Munsford University to do their Politics and Economics course. It's paid for by a bequest from some bigwig politician who died years ago. The course itself is practically a free ticket into Government. There have been about five prime ministers in the last the thirty years who did it. So everyone who fancies that sort of thing, politics and governmental stuff, is dead keen to win the Archer Prize. Emily Watson was perfect material; she was really clever, worked really hard and most importantly she wanted it badly.

"Well at three o'clock this morning the library Custodian - the guy we saw fishing that day - heard a loud noise coming from the archaeological dig. It's below his apartment window so he could not miss it, and he came down to investigate.

"Well he found Emily Watson with a sledgehammer - I can't get over it, her with a sledgehammer - trying to smash the locks on metal cover that they put over the mouth of the archaeological dig. She was just in her underwear, covered in mud - it was raining - and looked quite deranged. When she saw the Custodian, she just went for him screaming. She tried to swing the sledgehammer at him, but he'd been in the army for years and so, despite his leg, he dodged away and just took the sledgehammer from her. She ran off.

"Well the Custodian went to get some help and when they - it was the head teacher and a couple of other members of staff - came back, they found her back there as well. She'd found some of the special paint that the archaeologists use for marking out lines in the grass, the orange stuff, and had used it to write all over the metal lid that covered up the large hole the archaeologists had made.

"With more of them it was easy to jump on her. Loads of people saw that bit; there were people watching from the dormitories by this time. They phoned the police and her parents."

"And what had she written?" asked Musty in the silence that followed.

"Something mad - I've written it down so I wouldn't forget." He took out a piece of paper from his pocket and read

"Beware of the Morrigan. Beware the deluge. In the end all will fall."

As Karl finished silence fell on the small brightly coloured playhouse. The room, which was lit only by a small torch, seemed quite sinister. The shadows, sharp and elongated, quivered as the wind shook the house slightly.

"So," said Rosetta " what happened to Emily Watson to make her do that?"

"Who knows? Talking to people it looks like she has been a bit odd all this year, a bit wild and aggressive; not like her at all. She had a fight with her best friend a few weeks back, which was covered up and her work has been suffering. Her marks have been terrible when normally she is a guaranteed straight 'A' student. There was even some talk of cheating in tests. Well after this she's been taken out of school and is unlikely to be coming back this year. The school are not pressing charges and neither are the police. So there will be a new head girl and things will go back to normal"

"Somehow I doubt that that." said Musty, after a

short silence.

※ ※ ※ ※ ※

Karl spent the next couple of weeks trying to find out more about Emily Watson and what had happened to her, but learned little beyond what he already knew. The girl had apparently been very clever, a bit ambitious but no worse for that, and had then, starting this September, changed completely.

He noticed that people seemed reluctant to talk about Emily. It was not like they were embarrassed or angry about what she had done, but more like they were finding it difficult to actually remember things about her. The normally quick-witted became vague or muddled when her name was mentioned; this strange behaviour made his investigations difficult or impossible. It was like she was being wiped from people's memory.

Another thing that complicated Karl's life was the behaviour of the library Custodian, Marcus Vates. Normally he was rarely seen outside the ancient reading room and, as students usually did not need to access the ancient documents held in the old library, this meant he usually had little to do with the day to day running of the school. But this seemed to have changed, at least when it came to Karl.

It had started one day in October, when the Custodian appeared briefly in the main hall just before assembly in order to have a word with the head teacher. As he was leaving to go back into the reading room, he glanced over and by chance looked right into Karl's eyes. As he did so he stopped as if he had suffered a shock, and then recovering himself he turned and completed his journey back into the Old Library Reading Room, glancing back as he did so.

After that Marcus Vates seemed to be everywhere Karl went. In between lessons he lurked in the corridors; he watched the break-time football games with an uncharacteristic interest; he hung around by the dormitory entrance at the end of the day and on all these occasions he scanned the faces, searching. Karl felt strongly that the Custodian was looking for him.

Karl became expert at ducking into a crowd, or behind the corner of a building, whenever he heard the unmistakable thud of that artificial leg cutting through the general rumble of the student's feet. As a result he was sure as he could be that the Custodian did not catch sight of him on these occasions.

His luck held for two weeks, a situation helped by his status as the Outside Scholar. The librarian obviously believed the boy for whom he searched slept in the school, as the rest of the pupils did, for the bulk of his efforts were concentrated towards the end of the day and consisted of scanning the queues into the dormitory building. His other searches were more sporadic.

Then one day towards late October, in a history lesson, Karl's luck ran out. The subject they were covering was the history of Oldmere School, something Karl knew well as he had studied it as part of his efforts to win the Outside Scholarship, and so he was drifting a little as the teacher droned on to the class.

His lack of interest must have been obvious as the teacher suddenly repeated a phrase - it was his name he suddenly realised - for the second time.

"Karl Bastion! ... Thank you for your attention. Can you please let me know what pearl of wisdom I have just dropped before your unconscious snout?"

Karl decided that a lie would just make things worse.

"I'm afraid I don't know sir." he said ... and then less wisely, "but I covered school history as part of my entrance exam sir."

"Ahh I forgot ... so since you know it all, you will not mind doing me a favour. You will not know, since you were asleep, that I was telling the rest of the class about the School Charter, and how a copy may be found in the Old Library for general study.

"It would be instructive for us to view this document, and as you already know all about this area you will be available to go and collect it from the Custodian."

".... but I." stuttered Karl.

"Now, Mister Bastion. The Custodian knows it is needed and will have it ready for you."

So Karl was forced to walk with open eyes into

the meeting that he had been avoiding so assiduously for the last two weeks.

He passed through the Assembly Hall, his footsteps echoing in the empty space, and reached the wide arch that led to the reading room. Going through he turned half hoping that the Custodian would not be there.

He was disappointed. At one end of the reading room was the Custodian's desk, a vast semi-circular affair similar to the bar in a pub. This desk wrapped around a single door set in the stone wall behind, like it was a defensive wall. It was this door, made from ancient wood and rusty iron that led to the maze of shelves rumoured to be what constituted the Old Library of the school.

Marcus Vates was sat on a high stool studying some papers when he heard Karl's footsteps. He looked up, saw Karl, and put his papers down slowly and deliberately.

He did not look like a typical librarian to Karl's eyes. His long hair and scruffy look - he wore just a T-shirt and jeans - gave him more the look of a gardener than a member of the academic staff. The male teachers all wore a suit and had short, razor-tidy hair. His sharp blue eyes were locked remorselessly to Karl's own.

Leaning forward and putting his elbows on the documents he had just put down he said "Well hello. How can I help you?"

"Um ... I've come for a copy of the school charter. I think it has been booked." said Karl keeping his distance from the desk.

"Ahh ... so that would be for Mr Sherry's history class, of which you would be a member." He reached below the desk and brought out a black leather folder. "This is just a copy of course. The original charter is on parchment and is far too delicate to be handed out for history lessons. Come closer now, I can hardly throw it to you can I?"

Karl inched towards the desk and put out his hand for the folder. Quick as a snake Marcus had Karl's wrist. He was not rough, just very firm; there was no hope of Karl wriggling free.

"I think I might have seen you just before the school term. It was by the river, you were with a girl."

"I don't know" said Karl foolishly.

"Now don't be silly," said the librarian, not unkindly. "You must remember I think, for we gave each other quite a surprise. I'd just like to apologise for scaring you. You ran like rabbits." He smiled, a smile that seemed forced.

Then suddenly as if he could hold it in no longer, he said, "Who is the girl? I have not seen her at the school."

Karl managed to pull his hand away and said, "I don't know who you mean, or what you are talking about."

His eyes narrowed and he said "... Well I must be mistaken. I will, however need your name for the records." He indicated a ledger that lay open on the desk. "We don't just hand such a book to anyone you know."

Karl knew he had to give it. Mr Sherry, the teacher knew his name anyway and would give it if asked. "It's Karl Bastion."

"Oh ... this year's Outside Scholar, from the village. How interesting, and illuminating" and with that he tossed the charter at Karl, who fumbling only just about caught it.

Later that day as Karl walked down towards the school gates at the end of the day, he glanced back towards the school. As well as the lines of students heading towards their dormitories, he caught sight of Marcus Vates looking down towards his retreating figure.

☙ ☙ ☙ ☙ ☙

Rosetta got off the bus. It was dark and starting to rain. She did not notice the figure in the shadows of the school gates.

Chapter 4

From a diary found in the mud

That stupid child was a danger. I was told she was clever, but she did not have the wit to see me squatting in her head. Her ambition was her weakness; she wanted to win so badly that is was easy for me to twist her determination into something meaner. Soon it was not enough for her to just succeed. No she must be seen to do so easily, without effort. From there it is a simple step to dishonesty and deception.

In the end she fought what was happening. Yes, perhaps she was indeed strong, her integrity still intact, but it was too late and now Emily Watson is gone from Oldmere. This will be the fate of all who oppose me.

However there is still that unknown enemy, the one who can ruin all. They are still here I can feel their presence everywhere in the valley; sometimes strong and fresh; sometime so distant as to be almost absent, but always it is there. What concerns me now is that I now sense the beginnings of recognition, of understanding; it begins to awake, to prepare.

I cannot allow this creature to gain strength, not when I have achieved so much. Thanks to me the old guardian is gone, where I do not know, but he is no danger. His replacement is an untrained cripple, and no threat.

But there is always this new enemy who must be eliminated.

At the moment we blunder in the dark, neither knowing where to strike, not even sure if there is an enemy lurking in the shadows. The first to know of the other will find it easiest to break their opponent. I must be the one, I must be first.

Chapter 5

Rosetta has an unforgettable meeting, which changes everything.

It was a Saturday, the rain had stopped and the sun shone on down on a spectacular late autumn morning. Karl got up early, went into his garden then leant over the hedge and threw some soil at the window of Rosetta's bedroom. Yesterday's rain had prevented the normal after-school meeting with Musty - Karl's mother had outright refused his request for him to go out after dinner - and he needed to tell Rosetta of the Library Custodian's strange interest in her. And also of the fact that he most likely now knew she lived in the village.

Rosetta stuck a tousled mop out into the crisp sunshine. "What do you want?" she mumbled. "It's early."

"I've got something to tell you. Meet up in twenty

minutes at the play house."

Musty was also waiting, tucked away in the base of the hedge, by the time Rosetta arrived, brushing her hair and looking grumpy. The badger stayed hidden in the hedge, as it was broad daylight, whilst Karl told them of his game of hide and seek with Marcus Vates the previous week.

"You should have told me this before," Musty exclaimed. "I should have had a look at this man to see if I can sense anything about him"

"I didn't think there was anything in it," said Karl. "I just assumed he was interested in me for some unimportant reason. You know that I was in trouble for walking in the grounds that day or something. Anyway I know now and it looks like he wasn't really that interested in me, just Rosetta."

"Well we need to be on our guard and watch him carefully," said Musty. "So far he is the only indication we have of anything odd in the valley and we must not ignore it."

"Perhaps we could follow him and see if he does anth ...."

"Now wait!" Rosetta interrupted. She looked at the badger and the boy and said, "Will you two be quiet for a minute? I'm the one in supposed danger here, not that I don't believe there is danger," she added looking at Musty "but we need to be a lot more sure about things before I start doing things that will cause a load of upset and disturbance." She glanced back to the house. "The last thing my mother needs right now is for me to get in a load of trouble with the local school. What I suggest is that we don't panic about this Custodian, which after all may be nothing, and instead do something pleasant. Today is supposed to be one of the last nice days before the first of the winter storms."

꧁ ꧁ ꧁ ꧁ ꧁

After some discussion Karl suggested they go and visit the ruins at the east end of the valley. There the valley sides steepened to form a gorge so precipitous that the road was forced to burrow through a tunnel in the valley side to make it out to the plains further down the river.

"As if that was not enough of a defence," said Karl "there is a load of old watch towers, just ruins now, that guard the entrance to the valley. The river spreads out in the gorge and gets quite shallow in places so in the old days people just waded up the river to get into Oldmere. The towers are there to stop enemies coming in that way. They call that end of the valley 'Ford End' to this day."

Musty was agreeable to anything as long as he did not have to cross the river. "We badgers can swim, but that does not mean we like it, and what may be a shallow stream to you is a black chasm to me."

They grabbed some sandwiches and headed along the valley. Musty followed in the dense undergrowth provided by the hedgerows, and kept as close to the children as this method would allow.

They walked a track that ran along the high fields just below the tree line and, looking ahead, they could see where the valley walls came together, closing to a shadowy area into which the river wandered aimlessly.

As they came closer they could see that the blackness was in fact the gorge of Ford's End; formed as the valley walls grew steeper and more rocky eventually forming steep cliffs reminiscent of those on the knoll further up valley. The river broadened, sped up and started to ripple as it entered that defile. It filled the whole of the gorge in a way that, in the sunny calmness of that day, seemed quite benevolent.

Just before the gorge proper, where the valley sides were steep, scattered with rocky outcroppings and thick with trees, one could just make out the ruins of four towers. There were two on each side of the river. All that remained of each the buildings was the ground floor - a few jagged outcroppings higher up were all that indicated that they might have stood any taller. There was a small door, and arrow slits in the walls showed the warlike nature of the building.

"In the village they say that they have stood since Roman times, and some of the stonework does seem very old." Karl explained. "See the big square blocks on the bottom layers. No one knows for sure though. We could try to persuade some of those archaeologists at the school to have a look and then we'd probably have a better idea."

The nearest tower could only be reached from a steep trail that wound up through the woods, avoiding the massive piles of rock scattered pell-mell amongst the broad leaved trees. They started up the track single file, except for Musty who headed for the ferns and bracken, whose broad leaves completely hid him from sight.

It took ten minutes hard climbing before they finally reached the tower. Looking in the doorway they found that the interior was unimpressive. The remains of a small fire could be seen on the packed earth floor, as could be a few squashed drinks cans - "Teenagers from the village," announced Karl disapprovingly - but apart from that the tower was merely cold, dark and rather smelly.

As they turned to leave there was a commotion in the undergrowth and Musty ran out.

"There is a man coming up the track. He walks funny."

There was nowhere to run. Cliffs loomed, surrounding the tower, and where there were no cliffs barring their way, there was a sheer drop down to the river below. The only way in or out was up the path along which they had just come; the path which they were quite sure Marcus Vates now walked up. They were trapped.

&. &. &. &. &.

Musty moved in front of the children and made a

strange growling noise, low and rumpling, quite different from a dog. A man limped out into the small grassy area in front of the ruined tower.

It was Marcus Vates. He just stood for a second looking at the two children and Musty. He took off his hat, a wide brimmed Australian bush hat, and said, seemingly to himself. "Well it seems we have the badger girl indeed ... and the Alien boy."

He took one step forward and Musty, whose growling was becoming increasingly agitated, leapt forward teeth bared. He ran towards the man on the path, who shied away; but then inexplicably Musty stopped his feet skidding in the dirt. His growls ceased, and he looked up at Marcus Vates in a strange questioning way. He then continued forward, but at a walk this time. When he reached the man's feet he turned around, sat down and said, "You may come forward, Rosetta, Karl. There is no danger here."

Marcus Vates, already somewhat ill at ease at the animal's proximity, jumped at the sound of Musty's voice and looked down in alarm. The badger looked back at him and Rosetta knew that the bond that had formed between herself and Musty was now shared with this man; his face had softened and he bent down briefly to touch Musty on the head, something she had longed to do many times, but had never dared.

He turned back to the children and said, "Will you come forward, badger girl?"

"My name is Rosetta," she said with a defiance

she did not feel.

He looked pleased at this and said, "Well Rosetta, you trust me with your name. Will you take another step down that road and come closer?"

Rosetta took one hesitant step and Karl grabbed her arm in alarm, but she pulled away. She was somehow sure that his man was not a danger. She walked forward.

"Stop," said the man. "Now please raise your right hand, as if you were going to push me away?"

Rosetta frowned, but did as the man asked and as she did so the most remarkable thing happened. She felt a liquid feeling in her stomach, a feeling that then spread up to her head and out along her arm right up to her hand. And looking along her arm she saw her hand light up red, as if she had placed it over a light bulb. The light intensified and Marcus Vates's face was subsequently illuminated in more than one way; from the outside - for the light from Rosetta's hand spread forward to cast a golden light over it - and from within, for his face showed such a mixture of shock, relief and joy that it almost glowed itself.

Rosetta dropped her hand, and the light faded. Shocked she looked at her hand as if she had never seen it before. Marcus reached out, pulled her gently by the shoulder and called over her head to Karl.

"Quickly now into the trees. We mustn't be seen and I feel that we might be all of sudden quite visible"

He pulled the half stunned, Rosetta into the

shadow of a low hanging oak, whose rusty leaves still provided good cover. Karl followed and as he entered the canopy he saw that Marcus Vates had dropped to a crouch and was looking at them his eyes shining.

"We must be quick," he said. "Do you remember where you saw me fishing all those weeks ago?" The children nodded. "Then meet me there. Where I sat, remember, not where you were standing ... and you young one." He turned to Musty. "Don't fall in again. I don't want you dragging your wet body around where we are going"

He laughed and then said, "I will go ahead so we are not seen together ... wait ten minutes before setting off - I am afraid I'm not so quick with this blasted leg - and I will see you shortly"

With that he was gone.

They waited in silence until his uneven footsteps had faded, and then Karl said, "What was that all about?"

Musty sat up, as he always seemed to when he was in earnest. "I do not know, but he is no danger - I am convinced of that - and he knows something about all this. I say we do as he asks. What have we to lose? If he meant to harm us he would have done so by now."

Rosetta, absently rubbing her hand against her jeans as if to wipe something off, murmured to herself, "Yes you are right."

Karl watched her for a second unsure, and then patting her hand said. "So what are we waiting for?

Let's go."

In the end they remembered that they had to wait for ten minutes, and so they stood in the dappled light cast by the oak tree until Karl declared he could stand it no longer, and they set of down the track to the main valley.

Breaking out of the trees they could just see Marcus Vates crossing the flat part of the valley and heading towards the school.

"He's not going where he said he would!" Karl exclaimed. "It looks more like he is heading up towards the school."

"Perhaps he's going to get something. Let's just go where he told us to."

So they dropped down from the valley walls and headed to the cliffs at the front of Oldmere Knoll where they had seen Marcus Vates fishing towards the end of the summer holidays. By the time they arrived Marcus had disappeared into the main school and could no longer be seen, so they found a rock that caught the late afternoon sunshine and waited for him to come and meet them. Musty wriggled into a holly bush, so completely hidden that even his twitching nose was invisible.

"I cannot see how this can be any less public than meeting up in the woods," said Karl. "In fact it's worse. I mean people from all over can see us here."

Just then they all heard a whispered voice from above, and they all looked up in surprise. It took some time for them to see, but they eventually spotted the top of Marcus's torso leaning out from some hidden crevasse in the rock in the cliffs above.

He leant out a little further and said. "Go a little further along the remains of the moat until you see a large piece of masonry with an iron ring set into it. Then climb up from there. The path will be clear once you have gone a short distance."

They did as he asked, passing along the marshy area he had called the moat, and found an enormous square block lying in the mud that looked as if it had once been a part of some ancient structure, perhaps a dock; there was a ring set in the stone, worn smooth by hundreds of years of rope. They turned started to climb and after a minute or so they could see a clear route up through the rock outcroppings that formed this part of the cliff.

They scrabbled up following Marcus's voice, until after a couple of minutes they came to a large hawthorn bush which blocked their way, and squeezing between it and the rock wall behind, they came to a small passage formed from a narrow crack in the cliff.

Marcus beckoned and disappeared into the crack. Following, the children discovered that a few yards into the crack, it widened and the rock of the cliff became a stone wall; a bit further still and it was recognisably a man-made passage. Turning a corner they found Marcus stood by a rusty gate. It was made from thick iron and reached from one side of the passage to the other.

"The back door," he said. "No one but my family know of this. You will be the first outsiders to come this way for many hundreds of years. Keep the secret safe."

After they had all passed through the gate, Marcus came also, turned and locked the gate behind them with an enormous padlock. He moved passed them and with a quiet "Follow me." he walked off into the guts of Oldmere Knoll.

Chapter 6

Marcus Explains a great many things

A few yards down the passage Marcus switched on a small torch. It illuminated a low stone lined tunnel that stretched on and upward into utter blackness. Marcus moved off, stooping slightly because of the low ceiling. The tunnel forged straight ahead for a while then turned sharp left and as it did so changed its nature. The wall turned to rough rock and moved away from the children as the tunnel widened. It was obvious that they had now entered a natural cave instead of a man made tunnel.

"The Undercave, also known as the Ancient Library" said Marcus. "The salts in the rock make the air here extremely dry, and the temperature is the same all year. The old librarians used it a store for their most delicate documents for that very reason. Now of course the rooms in the main building are better for that because of central heating and so on, so the majority of the library's collection is held up there now." He swung the beam of his torch around to light up the space so the children could see.

The cave was narrow, ancient bookshelves were everywhere, some lined the walls, some piled in corners, but nowhere could a book be seen, not a scrap of paper was visible. The place looked derelict. Marcus moved on toward a dark corner, and as they approached the children saw the start of a stone staircase peeking through a rough-cut doorway. They entered and started to climb up.

The stairs seemed to go on for ever and Karl started to count the steps out of sheer boredom; he got to one hundred before he saw Marcus slow, reach for set of keys in his jeans pocket, and stop in front of a large wooden door. It was carved from top to bottom with many patterns, swirls and twisted plaits. Marcus opened the door and entered a room.

As the children and Musty entered they saw something reminiscent of one of the libraries one might find in an old manor house or stately home. The walls were so filled with bookcases that it looked like they were built using books. In the odd place, where there were no bookcases, wooden panelling lined the walls and gave the room a welcoming, warm feeling. There was one window, but it was dark outside, and so the only light came from a wood burning stove, half hidden in an ancient fireplace. Marcus lit a lamp on the desk next to the fire.

The room was filled with a soft yellow glow and

Marcus gestured towards an old leather sofa set against a bookcase.

"Sit," he said, "we have much to talk about."

The children sat down whilst Musty curled up in the space beneath the sofa, placing himself just below Rosetta.

"This room, known as the antechamber," he said "is a kind of crossroads. Through that door there is the reading room of Oldmere School, which you Karl will be familiar with." He indicated across the room to a door in the far corner. "Over on the other side is the entrance to the Old Library, which in principle only the Custodian of the library may enter, though these days anyone with a good reason may enter with my permission.

"And finally there is the door through we have just come, the door to the Ancient Library," The children looked across, and to their surprise saw only a wall of books. " ... which is disguised and secret. In the old days there were books that were considered dangerous to read - because knowledge gave power and influence many books were considered fit only for the rich and powerful - and so the library was kept hidden. Now of course we know better, but still only the Custodians of the library know of the Ancient Library. It is a secret place that has proved useful many times as a place of refuge.

Karl looked across to the entrance to the Old Library. The door was ajar slightly and some shelves were tantalisingly visible. "May I have a look in the Old Library? No one in school I have spoken to has ever been in."

"No time," said Rosetta firmly, though she was tempted herself. "We have loads more important things to deal with now." She turned to Marcus, who settled back in his chair. "What is happening here? Ever since I came to the valley strange things have been happening, and you are the only person who seems to know anything about it."

Marcus thought for a second and said, "You may well be disappointed in what I have to say Rosetta, for whilst I know some things, I am looking for answers also. Though I must admit that I will likely know more than you.

"Firstly though, can you tell me your experiences in the valley, and then I will tell you what I know"

So Rosetta, aided by Karl told him of all of what had happened to them in the last few months. "And finally there is my hand, up by the ruins just now. I mean that is so weird." said Rosetta, and Karl noticed that as she did so she flexed her right hand as if it had cramp.

"You omitted to include what happened to Emily Watson," said Marcus. "I am sure that is somehow involved in this. I'm sure Karl has told you about it as it was most odd.

"So we have some unknown force searching for you Rosetta, assuming Musty's instincts are correct which I am quite sure they are. We know it is located in the valley, and it means you no good. This fits with my experience of the valley. There are mysteries here, and over the last few months I have become convinced that not all of them are benign in nature.

"So I can add a little to the story. I can tell you things I know, things that are not general knowledge in the valley, but they may take us no further in our search for the truth or may even increase our confusion. It is possible that we only learn that there are many things to be found out ... and maybe if we are lucky where to look for them."

"I come from a very old family," Marcus began. "We Vates have lived here in the Vale of Oldmere since roman times, perhaps even before then. There is certainly something strange about the family, and the valley. You know about the founding of the school and the charter; how the librarian job is bound to the Vates family?" The children nodded.

"Well it goes a little deeper than what is told officially, and this is generally known only to family members, though it is not strictly secret. There are strong traditions in our family about the role of Custodian, beyond what is generally known outside.

"The oldest child in the Vates family has always been called "The Steward", and it has always seemed to me that there is an extra bond, like a shared secret between the people who have been a steward. They make it seem like it is a joke, but you can see them at family gatherings talking in quiet corners; there are significant glances across the dinner table. What is more, members of the family who are stewards always live in the Vale of Oldmere. They never leave and they are always the ones who become the Custodian of the Library"

"Are you a Steward?" said Karl. "Is that what this is all about?"

"Well I may be a Steward ... I don't know. I had an older sister, and when we were both young the Stewards in the family were my grandfather and my father. My grandfather was Custodian at the time. Ten years ago Grandfather died and Alma, my sister, was taken to one side and "appointed" as they call it in the family - she became a Steward and Custodian in waiting. I was the second child and was free to do as I pleased. So I joined the army and went to serve abroad, whilst Alma settled in the valley. My father as you know became Custodian.

"Then about six months ago Alma died in a car accident. Normally I would have come home straight away and been appointed - this is a powerful tradition in the family and it is a difficult obligation to refuse; the ceremony would normally have happened just after my sister's funeral. The initiation takes place in this very room and takes place over two days. However at the time of my sister's death I got caught in an explosion, over in the desert." Marcus pointed to his artificial leg. "The one that took my leg. It left me unconscious in a military hospital for three months, and by the time I awoke my father had disappeared. I came home when I could, and took up the librarian post as is demanded by the school charter.

"So you see, there is no one to tell me the secret of the Stewards. My father was the last one, and now no one knows where he is, or what happened to him."

Karl hesitated and then said, "So what is this to do with Rosetta and me? How is it linked to the strange stuff?"

"Do you know the story of the disappearance of my father" said Marcus sighing

"Well, what they said in school is that when he disappeared they found his office trashed, and blood on the window ledge." said Karl.

"Yes that is true, but there was also a note on his desk. The police paid no attention to it because it just looked like something copied from one of the old books in the library. But I know better"

At this, Marcus slipped his hand into the pocket of his tweed jacket and took out a wallet, at first sight an empty one. He opened it and slid out a single piece of paper and unfolded it upon the desk, pressing it flat with the palm of his hand. Rosetta could see handwriting, old fashioned and beautiful.

Lost, last and unappointed.
Despair not, and watch.
Watch for the brock girl,

Watch for the alien boy,
Watch by the arrowhead.
She will show the sign,
And follow,
She will show the sign,
And uncover.

The police gave it to me when I was still in hospital. I was so shocked by the news of my father's disappearance that at the time I thought nothing of it and just put it amongst some of my papers.

"Then when I arrived at the school after I had left hospital I did not quite know what to do, so I threw myself into learning the job of Custodian of the Library. At this point I just thought that all the stuff about being appointed was to do with learning how to run the Old Library, and that all the odd ceremonies were just a family eccentricity. But now I am pretty sure that there is much more.

"You see the Old Library is really just like any other library, all the shelves are numbered and the catalogue of books is held on that." He pointed to a closed laptop that sat on a side table. "Some of the books are old, but the really special ones have long gone to the British Library to be properly conserved, so there is really not much for me to do day to day, certainly not enough to make a job. So I have become convinced that there is a mystery at the centre of the Custodian job that goes beyond looking after an ancient and valuable library and some time ago I decided to try to uncover it.

"I looked at the verse found by the police and began to think that perhaps it is a clue left by my father concerning his disappearance, for I am now certain that a crime was committed that night.

"Be clear about one thing; Atticus Vates, my father, had a character such that he would never leave the school like that of his own accord. Nor would he throw himself from the window - especially because to do so would leave me unappointed. So, because there was no other evidence, I looked at the verse very closely.

"To understand my reasoning you need to know that the arrowhead is the name our family use for the point of the knoll furthest upstream, where the rocks jut into the flow."

"Where you were fishing that day!" said Rosetta. "The day you shouted at us."

"Yes. It looked very much as if it was a message directed at me - that 'last and unappointed' made that much clear. So I decided to do what the verse told me; I was to 'Watch by the arrowhead'. I don't like fishing much, but it seemed to me a good way of watching by the river. Normally I'd read, but you can't keep an eye out for anything unusual with your head stuck in a book.

"So one Saturday I sat there watching that blasted float - it never moved all day - when I saw a couple of children moving up from the school playing fields. I paid them no attention; many people walk around the school and they seemed no different."

"Us!" said Karl.

"Yes. Then a little while later I heard a splash and saw you again, but you had not made the splash. I looked across and saw a badger climbing up the bank after falling in the water. Now as you know, brock is an old word for badger and so it seemed to me that some of the verse was coming true. There was a girl, a boy and a badger behaving rather unusually - they are rarely seen in daylight - and all by the arrowhead, and so I called over."

"Shouted you mean," said Karl. "You gave us quite a fright."

"Well that became apparent when you scattered. I started to give chase, but then realised that there would be little point as I'd be too slow. So instead I climbed up the path to the gates by the back door to see if I could spot where you lived, and go and talk to you later. As I got to the top I saw you coming out from the old mill, accompanied by a badger. It walked along side you like a pet...

"A pet!" said Musty from below the sofa, where he had been cleaning his tail. "I am her guardian, not some lap dog." Rosetta smiled, for at that moment he gave every appearance of a pet dog resting after a long walk.

"Apologies master badger. That is just how it seemed at the time ... so I was now even surer that this was something to do with my father's verse. A badger would not behave like that normally - it was too much of a coincidence. So when you ducked behind a wall I waited eagerly for you to come out, but you did not. So, afraid that I would lose you, I went down from the cliff and made my way as quickly as I could towards the mill. But when I got there, you were gone and I thought I might have lost the only clue to my father's disappearance.

"So when I saw you, Karl, in Assembly that day I knew that you attended Oldmere School and I had a second chance to solve the mystery. From then I looked for you everywhere, but could not find you, until you were sent to get that book, and then I discovered you were from the village. That told me the girl from the river, would likely be from there also, and would probably go to Sebast High.

"So I watched the bus stop and saw you get off yesterday. I did not want to approach you in the dark- it would scare you once more - so I saw where you went, which house you lived in. In the morning I watched that house from the knoll, saw you leave, then followed you up to Ford End.

"The rest you know," he said finally.

"What does the verse mean by 'the sign'?" said Karl.

"Oh ... the sign is a special greeting that appointed members of the family had for each other. They would raise their hand up, and place it over each other's hearts. That's why I asked Rosetta to do that though I was not expecting that light to appear, or for Musty to start talking. There is obviously something magical, something extraordinary, happening here." He sighed.

"So now we have four mysteries; Musty and his

new abilities, Rosetta's glowing hand, the disappearance of my father and the strange behaviour of Emily Watson. They are linked I am sure."

They all looked at each other, and then Rosetta said, "Well where do we start? We don't have much to go on."

&&&&&

"Marcus followed the clues in the verse, and it led him to us." said Karl. "We should do it again. Are there any other hints we could follow?"

"'She will show the sign, and uncover' seems to be the only one that we do not yet know the meaning of." said Marcus. They all, including Musty who poked his out from beneath the sofa and twisted his head upwards, looked at Rosetta.

"Oh ... you mean me." she said, and looked at her right hand, her face twisted with worry. "You think that I should do that thing again. But I don't know how. Last time it just happened ... I mean I raise my hand all the time, every day, and nothing unusual happens."

"I think Rosetta that you have to be in a specific situation, or at a specific time, or with the correct people. Who knows? But it will not hurt to try."

Rosetta, feeling very self-conscious, stood and walked to the centre of the room just on the other side of the desk from Marcus. She shifted her feet so they were shoulder width apart and raised her right hand, as she had done so just those few hours ago.

And again Rosetta felt the strange feeling in the pit of her stomach. Again her hand glowed red, but this time the light that came from it did not light up Marcus's face in a gentle glow, but instead shot in a tight line, like a laser beam, to a spot on the floorboards to the left of the desk.

Marcus shot up like someone had stuck a pin in him. Rosetta closed her hand and put it towards her mouth in shock and instantly the light was gone. Musty rushed over to the spot where the light had shone and snuffled around his breath forcing bits of sawdust out from the cracks.

"The air here is different; there is a hole." he said. "Beneath the floorboards there is a void."

Marcus strode over, and gently tapped around with his knuckles. There was a subtle change in the sound as he passed over the area where the light had been. He knelt down and studied the area closely, his nose almost touching the wood. Taking out a pocket knife he prodded between the cracks trying to lever out any loose area, but nothing moved.

"I'll break the blade if I try to force it." he said, frustrated running his fingers through his hair.

Musty, who had continued his investigations, sat up and said, "If you look just here you might have some more success. I can smell oil, and metal coming from below the boards."

This time when Marcus pushed in his penknife

into the crack there was a click and a section of floorboard about the size of a large world atlas sprung up. Marcus lifted one end with his fingertips and pulled the whole thing out with some difficulty.

Looking down, the children saw a void, lined with lead and about a foot deep. It appeared empty. Marcus put his hand inside and rummaged around feeling in all the corners. After a few seconds his hand froze and he brought out an envelope. It was addressed with a single word; 'Marcus'.

He rose from the floor, leant against the desk and opened the envelope. After a minute or so of reading he looked down and saw a row of expectant faces looking up at him.

"It is very short," he said

Marcus

If you are reading this then you will have received my letter and found the vault under the floorboards. It also means that I am not here to tell you of things in person and my worst fears have proved to be well founded. If that is the case, then take the Folio from the vault and read it. You must then do as you see fit, for once you have my letter and have read the Folio then you will know as much as is needed.

A word of warning; do not take the folio out of the Antechamber. Once you have read it then put it back in the vault and seal it. It is the only copy and is precious, irreplaceable. To lose it would be a complete disaster.

Burn my letter after you have memorised it.
Remember whatever happens I love you as I did your dear sister.

Your loving father

Atticus Vates

He looked at the children and Musty and said, "If I read this correctly then there should be something else in that hole - it must be the vault he speaks of. It was certainly made to hold something bigger than this letter, presumably the 'Folio' that my father talks of, and that something is no longer there."

"But why is it not there?" said Karl. "The envelope was there, and your father must have put that in. Why would he then take the Folio out and not put it back?"

Rosetta, still unconsciously holding her hand, said, "Well either he took it out and didn't put it back, or someone else took it without him knowing. But why would they then leave his letter?"

"The letter was leant against the wall in a dark corner, it might be easy to miss, especially if it was dark and the person was in a hurry. They might have just taken the Folio, whatever it is, and assumed there was nothing else to find."

"But then your father would have found it was missing and changed what the letter says ... unless he didn't have time."

Marcus sighed, and Rosetta looked at his tired

lined face and was reminded that here was a man who had lost his sister, his father and been grievously wounded all in a very short period of time. He said, "If I were to guess I would say that it all happened the night he disappeared, that whoever has the book also knows what happened to my father."

"And what about the verse?" said Karl. "Where did that come from, and how does it foretell all the things that it does?"

"The verse is yet another mystery, but one I suspect that will be solved by explaining all the other puzzles," said Marcus. "I have a friend in the local police, I will see if I can find anything from the police report on my father's disappearance. It is as good a place to start as any."

"So," said Musty from the floor. "we are going hunting."

Part Two

Hunting

Chapter 1

Rosetta learns something interesting from her mother. There are investigations both physical and paper.

On the first day of the holidays Rosetta's mother had some news, which she delivered at the breakfast table.

She had been helping Aimee with her breakfast; her brown hair falling straight onto the table as she leaned her head to one side in her efforts to help her daughter. Rosetta's sister had tried hard but could never quite manage to hit her mouth and needed her mum's guiding hand every time she raised her spoon to her face. She smiled a messy smile at Rosetta as her mother, finished for now, turned to her other daughter.

"I haven't mentioned this before because I didn't want to get your hopes up."

Mrs Clarence paused - she was plainly not sure how her news would be received - and then said, "The lawyers have finally finished with your fathers will, and it appears as there is enough money to send you to the local school."

"What I have to change again?" said Rosetta thinking of which school her mother might mean. "I'm happy where I am - I'm just making friends and getting used to things."

"I mean," said her mother significantly, "the very local one."

Rosetta gave a small intake of breath realising her mother's meaning. "You mean Oldmere School? But that is really expensive, I mean the kids there are super rich; there's no way we could afford it.

"I have looked at the money," said her mother firmly, "and we can. In fact you have a place starting next term if you want it ... don't decide now. I want you to think about it carefully."

"But what about the entrance exams?" began Rosetta.

"They have spoken to your old school, and will take you for a couple of terms. Then if they think you able enough, you can take their exams. I get the feeling that if they think you good enough then the exams can be a formality.'

Rosetta fell silent, and thought about how she felt about this development. There was no doubt that the school had some amazing facilities. A swimming pool for example - she had been in the swimming squad in her previous school, and missed it - and the pool was just the beginning. Everything Oldmere did seemed to be of a high standard. The students who graduated, nearly all went to the best Universities, and generally went on to do loads of exciting and interesting things.

On the other hand, she was making good progress at Sebast High school. She generally was near the top of her classes and had some good friends. Would that be the case in Oldmere, where every child was the son or daughter of some millionaire? There could be some frightful snobbery in these types of schools, or so she heard, and Karl had mentioned that people from outside might suffer. What is more she would be one of the very few pupils who did not sleep at the school; she could only think of Karl from the village, though there may be others from nearby. That would also make her different and possibly unpopular.

"I could ask Karl from next door about it," she said. "When do I have to decide."

"You have about a week. I managed to get you in because a girl had to leave at short notice, due to of illness I think, but they do need to know fairly soon."

And Rosetta, remembering Emily Watson, decided that perhaps there was another reason, that it might be a good idea not to go to Oldmere School. But on reflection she thought it might be best to keep that information from her mother.

"What!" said Karl. "You're coming to Oldmere?"

"I don't know. I've got to decide over the next few days. I quite like Sebast."

Karl looked a little crestfallen, and Rosetta remembered that it was hard for him being the Outside Scholar. He would probably enjoy having someone else from the village to talk to in the School.

They were all - Karl, Rosetta, Musty and Marcus - sat around the antechamber. They had agreed to meet as often as they could so they could plan their investigations. It was a Saturday and they had arranged to make a thorough search of the antechamber to see if they could find any evidence relating to the disappearance of Marcus's father; things that perhaps the police had missed because they thought it unimportant. Like the piece of parchment left on the desk. The search had been somewhat interrupted by Rosetta's news however.

"I for one do not want you to go to the school Rosetta," said Musty. "I know that whatever searches for you is located in this valley. I rest easier knowing that at least when you are at school you are well away from here and safe. If you come to Oldmere School then you will be in constant danger."

"That is true," said Marcus. "But it is also true that if she is in the school we will be able to keep a close eye on her, and she will be able to help us uncover the solution to the many mysteries we have here. We must remember we cannot just sit, do nothing and expect to make great discoveries. We must be active in our search."

At this Musty gave a big snort, indicating what he thought of that strategy. Marcus gave a small smile.

There was small silence then Rosetta said, "I will come I think. I can't just stick where I am just because I'm scared to try something new. I think I'd regret it in the end. It is too good an opportunity to miss." This sounded so reasonable that as far as the others were concerned it signalled the end of the conversation. But inside Rosetta knew that was not her real reason for her decision. In reality she was thinking of the look of hope on her mother's face, so often absent these days, when she had told her daughter of her possible place at Oldmere School.

※ ※ ※ ※ ※

The search of the antechamber was frustrating. Karl was half-hearted - convinced that the police search would have discovered anything that there was to discover. Musty knew that a badger's nose was worth a hundred human searchers, no matter how sophisticated their equipment, and told Karl that endlessly. Marcus and Rosetta doggedly went through the motions, though both were convinced that the effort was most probably wasted; there was really nowhere for any clue to hide. The antechamber was kept very tidy. The bookshelves were the only place in which a fallen item could have fallen unnoticed during the events of Atticus Vates disappearance and they had not been disturbed, at least as far as Marcus could remember from the police report.

So it was to everyone surprise when Karl said, "Hey what's this?" and started to pick and pull at one of the slots in the wooden floor.

They all clustered round as Marcus used his pocket knife once again to dig into the cracks in the floorboards. This time there was no secret panel to uncover, but he did dig out the stem of a plant topped with the remains of a blue flower. It was mangled from its journey through the crack and quite dried out.

"What's that?" said Rosetta, studying the stem with interest.

"That's odd," said Marcus. "My father never had flowers around. He had quite a strong reaction to them. Sneezed like anything."

Marcus offered it up to Musty's nose to see if he could identify it from its odour.

Musty sniffed it and drew back his ears flat against his head. "Stop holding that!" he said. "It smells dangerous; it is poison."

"Poison," said Rosetta. "Are you sure?"

"I fear it," said Musty. "My badger side knows it, and fears its touch."

"OK when it comes to things like this I would

trust a woodland creature like Musty more than any human being," said Marcus. "Put it on the table Karl."

Karl did so, and as he put it down he thought he felt a tingle start in his fingers, though it was so faint he was not sure if he imagined it.

So, using a pen to push it from the table, they slid the mysterious item into an envelope.

"I'll take that to Miss Spore," said Marcus. "She is the biology teacher and an amateur botanist and might well know what type of plant that is, and if indeed it is dangerous."

They put the envelope in a drawer and continued their searches, though with no success and after half an hour they gave up and went home.

The next day Rosetta told her mother that she had decided to go to Oldmere School and as a result the next couple of days became a whirl of activity. There were several things that had to be bought, school uniform being just the first. So it was the next weekend before Rosetta was able to get away and meet with the others.

When she arrived she found everyone, except Musty who was cleaning his tail on the floor with an air of feigned disinterest, bent over Marcus's desk reading through a large pile of paper which seemed to have come from an official looking folder that lay nearby.

"It's the police report." said Marcus looking up and smiling at Rosetta. "My contact in the police came through. I've had a look at it last night and was just telling Karl what I found."

Rosetta collapsed onto the sofa and said "Well why don't you tell both of us?"

"OK," said Marcus. "You'd better sit down Karl, this may take some little time.

"The report makes interesting reading. Firstly it makes clear that my father's disappearance did not come out of the blue. He had apparently been behaving oddly for some time. It is implied in the report that this is the sign of some sort of mental instability, and it is this which might explain his disappearance."

"But you disagree?" said Karl.

"Yes. I have never met anyone more sensible, less prone to flights of fancy than my father. He would never let anything get to him in the way the police think that it did. If he was concerned or angry it would be because there was a real problem, or at least he thought there was.

"The police interviewed everyone in the school about things that may have happened in the weeks just before he disappeared, and the following picture emerged.

"It was about this time that the head teacher had announced the start of the archaeological dig. For years everyone knew that there was something interesting buried in that area of the school, but had done nothing about it. There was an old Celtic Christian cross half buried and loads of old stone, and humps and bumps. What is more people walking their dogs reported that their animals would behave oddly near that area; barking or howling or acting scared. Like they could smell something in the ground.

"But then earlier this year - around May or April I think - a pupil found some small artefact that greatly excited the local archaeologists. Something that meant that there was potentially a very important ancient site buried here at the school

"The Head had the idea to properly investigate the area using the local archaeological group. Oldmere students could help with the excavation and if they found anything significant then the school could make something of it in their advertising. Foreign students - well their parents at least - love that sort of thing. The heritage and history of this area has a great fascination.

"It sounded like a great idea to everyone; everyone except my father that is. He created a great fuss, objecting to it in every way he could. He said that the site was obviously an ancient Christian church - using the old cross as an example - and that to dig it up would be some sort of sacrilege. He tried to get the local church involved and, when that failed, he tried the local council, with no more luck

"He fell out with the Head Teacher because of it. In the end, when she went ahead anyway he threatened to resign which really got everyone worried. You must remember that if he did so it would break the school founding charter until they could get some other member of my family to take his place as custodian."

"Surely the school would not have to close? I mean - just because of an ancient charter," said Rosetta.

"Probably not, but he could make big trouble - lawyers would get involved and we all know what that means." Rosetta nodded remembering the trouble over her father's will; Karl just looked blank. "Anyway by the time my father went missing the situation was that the archaeologists were already several feet down and Dad was just about to hand in his resignation"

"That just sounds like he was making a stand to me," said Karl. "I mean if you really believe in something then you have to do something like that."

"But you see the thing is that he didn't believe. I mean my father was not a Christian, not by any normal understanding of the term. He was quite dismissive of the whole religious thing - not against it by any means - but on a personal level it was just irrelevant to him. So for him to threaten resignation with all the possible repercussions made me think that ...

"Perhaps the Christian origin of the site was not the real reason he was upset," finished Rosetta.

"Yes, knowing him as I did that is what I would assume," said Marcus and he fell silent.

"What about the head teacher?" said Musty from

below. "Your father was causing a lot of bother. Perhaps she just got rid of him. He was causing her a lot of trouble."

Marcus gave a bark of a laugh. "I don't think Miss Eastville would be up to such behaviour. Anyway the outcome would be just the same as if he had resigned - there would be no Custodian. My sister would most probably have been told to refuse the job, and cause a fuss like he did - it would be just like my father to think ahead like that.

"But the stuff about the archaeology was not the only strange thing about my father at this time. He started to behave in other uncharacteristic ways. He started to become very strict about the rules regarding who could enter the antechamber and the Old Library. Prior to that any of the teachers could just come into the antechamber if they wanted to talk. But around this time, he made people knock at the door to the Reading Room, and he would go out to meet them - even the head teacher. No one was allowed in here, and if he caught anyone trying he would become quite angry. It may be nothing; he might have been doing it just to annoy the headmistress ... Who knows?"

"What does the report say about the actual night of his disappearance?' said Rosetta?

Karl flicked through a few pages in the report and said, "He was missed at assembly. They checked the Custodian's flat, and eventually plucked up the courage to come in here without his permission. What they found gave them some concern. There had been a struggle. The desk was overturned and all the books from the shelves were scattered around the room. At this end of the room they found the window open and blood on the floor, which was found later to be that of my father. There was no other sign of him. Look there are some pictures of the scene in the report."

The pictures showed the room as described by Marcus. Karl studied them closely and said, "Is there an electronic copy of these?"

"Yes, there's a memory stick somewhere," said Marcus and digging around in the papers he eventually found it and gave it to Karl, who asked if he could use the laptop.

"You see that picture," said Karl pointing at one of the hard copies. It covers the area where I found that strange plant. The pictures the police use must be very high resolution, if I can just get it zoomed in then we might be able to see ..." Karl fiddled with the computer some more and then said, "yes. Look it's there."

They looked at the laptop screen and saw a hugely expanded area of wooden floorboards and sticking out of the crack, where they had found the flower, was the end of a bright green stem.

"And," said Karl. "you can see that in the picture the flower is mostly sticking out; hardly in the crack at all. When we found it, it was jammed in deeply, most likely because people had trodden on it. So when the picture was taken it can't have been there for very long; it could even belong to someone who was there that night."

Everyone leant in to get a closer look and there, in the picture, was the strange flower they had found a few days before. It stuck out of the floorboards, with no damage, looking as good as when it had grown.

Chapter 2

Rosetta starts at Oldmere; strange happenings at the dig.

Rosetta's first day at Oldmere School began much as would her normal day at Sebast High. After breakfast with Aimee and her mother she waited for the knock at her front door and went to meet Karl who always walked with her to the bus stop. Today however she walked past the wooden shelter and continued on towards the school gates. The older children from her old school took notice of her this time; falling silent and staring as she walked past the small shelter in her new uniform, and in through the gates to begin the walk up the drive to Oldmere.

She looked at the school with new eyes, as she strolled up the road. When Karl had described the school on their walk that day just a few weeks ago it had seemed like a museum piece; irrelevant to her daily life. But now she was about to enter and take part, to add to its history and that knowledge made her look at the building with a new awareness. By itself this new approach would have been enough to spark her imagination, but added to it was the knowledge that somewhere deep in the ancient stones there was the chance of real magic, of legend made real. And this made her stomach go queasy with excitement.

So given all this anticipation, she was somewhat disappointed to be taken by Karl to a low modern building hidden near the car park where a secretary peered at her over some glasses.

Karl gave her a nudge. "Oh ... hello. I'm Rosetta Clarence I'm due to start today."

"Ahh yes ... we've been expecting you. I am Mrs Villigier, the school secretary. Can you please report to Mr White in the room M312," she said. She turned to Karl. "Can you please show her the way Mr Bastion."

Karl nodded looking pleased, leading Rosetta out. Once they were out he said, "Brilliant, you're in my class. Old Vigilant - I mean Mrs Villigier; everyone calls her Vigilant because that is what she is like - is also from the village, and she'll have put us together deliberately. There are three year seven classes."

"What's the class like?" said Rosetta suddenly feeling a little overwhelmed.

"OK," said Karl. "They're a good bunch. The girls are a little standoffish ... but that's to be expected," he added quickly seeing Rosetta's look. "Anyway it won't be a problem. Just find your feet however you can. It's always a little awkward if you aren't a boarder. The talk in the morning is always about what went on the night before, which can make it difficult to join in, but by eleven o'clock everyone has forgotten what happened and it doesn't make any difference …"

Room M312 was high up in one of the older outbuildings and gave the impression of an old barn; the rooms on the lower floors were quite normal, but on the top floor it had obviously been decided that, rather than try to fit two floors into the available space, they would just make do with one large one, and as a result the ceiling soared up to over twice the height of a man.

This was rather unfortunate for Mr White because their teacher was very small, and as a result looked lost is such a vast space. He was there as they walked in, marking books at his desk at the front. Karl brought Rosetta up.

Mr White looked up and said "Hello. Miss ... Clarence isn't it?" He stood up rather suddenly, though it made very little difference to his distance from the floor, and said in a quite affable manner "Welcome to Oldmere School. I'm afraid that will have to do as far as ceremony is concerned. There is normally a formal reception for new pupils, but as you have joined half way through term then it'll just have to wait until after Christmas. Your desk is that one, yes at the front. I'll be taking register soon, so you have a couple of minutes get yourself ready."

Rosetta walked towards the desk and started to unpack her new books. Something hit her on the head. She looked down and saw a rolled up piece on paper still rocking on the floorboards. She looked around expecting to see Karl grinning at her, but instead saw a small girl with pigtails making a little wave and smiling.

Rosetta realised she knew her from somewhere, and then almost at the same instant knew from where; Ursula De Mailtland, for that was her name, was from her old school and, whilst they had not been friends, had been a nice girl. Posh and a little dim she recalled. Rosetta gave a smile and a wave back before the teacher gave a "settle down" and a rumble of chairs meant that everyone had started to sit.

The morning passed, and at break Ursula made a beeline for Rosetta.

"Hi, Rose it is Rose isn't it? Have you just started today? I love it here, they do horse riding at the weekend and there is cake on a Friday after dinner!"

"It's Rosetta actually," said Rosetta. "I ..."

"Oh yes Rosetta I remember now. A good swimmer, and clever, always in the library. Can't do that here ... go to the library I mean ... very secret! You can go swimming though ... I think. Tuesday and Wednesday afternoons for our year, maybe at the weekends also."

As Ursula talked, Rosetta remembered why they had not been that close. Ursula talked a great deal but never really said anything that might stick in the mind. Karl glanced over - he was talking to a group of boys - and gave her a quick grin. Rosetta suppressed an urge to go over, and turned back to Ursula, who had paused for breath.

"So what's it like here?" said Rosetta, fully aware at the same time that such a question might well open the floodgates once more.

"Well generally good," she said, but then lowered her voice and leant in close. "but it's also a bit weird as well. There are some very strange characters here. Did you hear about Emily Watson? Yes, well that was so odd. Walking about half dressed late at night - my friend Andrea saw her wandering in the grounds as she went to the loo - and then smashing up that archaeological dig. They say it was the pressure of exams, I'm not sure if some others aren't going to go the same way ... But I mustn't gossip." She smiled and then looked a little worried as if unsure if she had just done exactly that.

"Oh please do go on," said Rosetta, looking interested, and for a change she actually was, "what do you mean?"

"Well," Ursula said with renewed vigour. "There is Olivia Rigby. She's also been seen wandering at night. I'm not sure by who though. I do know that Mary Wilson, saw her in the corridor the other day and *she was talking to herself* - it was between lessons and she must have thought she was alone - and *then* she started to whack her own head, like really hard!" Ursula made motions of punching her own head. "What's more she's just like Emily

Watson; a real high flyer, been entered for the Archer Prize and everyone says she's got a good chance of doing well. At least she did have a chance ... she might not now she's gone mad."

Ursula was good person to know, thought Rosetta as she followed everyone out for the next lesson. She was a hopeless gossip and knew everyone and everything that was happening in the school. As they passed through the corridors she caught up with Karl and told him what Ursula had said about Olivia Rigby.

"I hadn't heard about her," said Karl "but you girls can be bit closed mouthed when it comes to stuff like that. The boys seem fine. No one seems to be going mad amongst us."

"If you think we are 'closed mouthed' I should introduce you to Ursula" said Rosetta grimly. "She'd soon put you right on that."

That evening Marcus opened the door to the spiral staircase that led down to the Ancient Library. He carried a supermarket bag that made a dull thudding noise; banging against the rock walls as he limped down the stairs. On reaching the bottom he crossed the cavern, entered the passage to the cliff face and started to call out.

"Hello ... Helloooo."

"I'm just ahead. There is no need to yell, I can

smell you two hundred yards away." It was Musty. He was sniffing the air, his nose upward.

"Have you brought food? I cannot smell any."

"Just wait Musty. I've got to open the tin first," and Marcus bent down and reached into the bag bringing out a tin of cat food."

Musty came close and examined the picture on the tin closely. "This is cat food." he said with some distain. I may be working with you humans for a little while but I am not yet a domestic pet."

Marcus stopped opening the tin and hid a smile. He turned to Musty and said, "I know that. However you cannot spend your evening foraging, when you are supposed to be patrolling the school grounds."

"Patrolling?"

"Yes. We need someone to keep an eye on the school grounds at night after the incident with Emily Watson - especially on that archaeological dig - and who is better to do that than a badger? Brave, loyal and nocturnal - what else would you need in a guard?"

"Nothing!" said Musty a glint in his eye.

"You must keep hidden. A badger in the grounds might attract attention of the caretaker. Remain in the shadows. Try not to set off the floodlights - those plastic and metal things that stick out of the ground and ..."

Marcus stopped talking because Musty was now not paying any attention at all and was snuffling in the bowl wolfing down the cat food with apparent gusto.

The next morning Rosetta and Karl were unpacking their bags for History, their first lesson of the day, when their teacher, Mr Oldendie, announced that he had arranged a tour of the dig in the school grounds instead of the next lesson.

"As I understand it the history of the knoll is varied and particularly ancient. There are Roman and prehistoric remains to be seen, and perhaps something unique to Oldmere. We shall have to see," he said with an excited lilt to his voice. "Douglas Level, the leader of our local Archaeological group, is going to take us around tomorrow."

The next day at eight o'clock the whole class stood shivering outside the dormitories, there was a strong wind and it looked like rain. Dr Douglas Level, man with a large beard and an impressive striped rainbow jumper, stood in front of them. He smiled amiably, despite the weather and started to explain about what the archaeologists had been up to.

"As you can see we have dug a big hole in your schools lawn, about 10 metres by 10 metres; about half of a tennis court. We did this because your head teacher wanted to know the story behind the ruins that stand there, or more importantly those that are buried beneath the ones on the surface. Now the reason that she thought that there might be something of exceptional interest here was because of a pupil who kept her eyes open. A girl found a statue here, one that indicated a pre-roman druidic site. This is very rare, very rare indeed, and we were extremely interested to find out if druids had once lived on the knoll. There are already some indications in the valley. There is a magnificent stone circle on the surrounding hills that some think may be Celtic in origin, for example. But we needed to investigate the knoll to see if this was also a druidic site.

"In order to do this we dug a hole, until we left the soil of modern times and came upon ancient layers. And from there we dug down further, but more carefully. Now as you move down through the earth you pass through all the stuff that has been left by previous generations, and in effect you move back through history as you go down. What we found was quite amazing." He smiled even more. His teeth were very bad, uneven and brown, but such was his enthusiasm they became almost endearing, like they would in your grandfather.

"So what we found was this. About twelve hundred years ago, the Saxons built a Christian shrine here. You can still see the Celtic cross to this day. There was no actual church that we know of here - no consecrated ground, though of course it may be hidden under the later monastery buildings." He indicated the Assembly hall and adjacent structures.

"Now very often religious sites have been sacred for many hundreds of years, Prehistoric sites becoming, Roman temples which then become Christian churches. And it was in this hope that we dug down - down means into the past remember - to see if that was the case here." he paused dramatically flashing those terrible teeth for far too long.

"And we did find a Roman temple, not a small one either. Also it was a strange temple. We have found no place for sacrificial offerings, just an outside wall - unusually large - and inside there was something unique to Oldmere; a very large room, completely sealed - no doors that we could find - that itself contained an even more ancient religious site - we think some kind of ancient pond or lake. Of course all that remains of the room is the very bottom of the walls.

"We think that offerings thrown into this box - simply thrown over the wall - were intended for the goddess that they thought lived in the lake. And if I were a betting man I'd say the goddess was not very nice for every offering we found was in form of a curse. People dropped these curses into the shrine hoping that the god within would bring misfortune upon their enemies. I'll read you an example. At this the archaeologist pulled a notebook from his pocket and read;

"To the banished one. Give neither, health wealth or happiness to those who oppose me. I wish their

noses to blacken and fall from their faces and madness to descend upon them and their descendants. If you do this I will worship you once more as a true god."

'The Roman temple was actually devoted to Minerva, the Roman goddess of wisdom and traditional enemy of the Medusa, but the building was obviously built on a more ancient site associated with this "banished one". Romans had many gods and they saw no reason to disbelieve in the gods of the people they conquered; here it seemed that Minerva shared her temple with this more ancient native deity. None of the curses mention this ancient god by name. She is always referred to as the 'banished one', 'she who will return' or 'the malevolent one'.

So, intrigued, we dug further down in the area that once held the pool to see if we could discover the nature of the ancient site. We found that there was indeed a sacred pool, probably worshiped by ancient Celts - the people who lived in Britain before the Roman invasion, but that the pool had been drained before the Romans built their temple; there is a crack that runs down from the side of the pool which would have made it impossible for the pool to hold water. How this happened we do not know; there have been suggestions of landslips, or even small earth tremors.

"We know that the pool was sacred, because we found, at the bottom offerings made to the pool;

small items of jewellery, bronze swords and even a small torc - a golden necklace or wristband. There has been talk of human sacrifice in the newspapers." and at this his normally cheerful face clouded over as if he disapproved of such sensational reporting; the children shifted excitedly. "However this is impossible to confirm because, though we did find some small bits of human bone, skulls we think, any bodies will have rotted away long ago."

He suddenly noticed that all of a sudden there were several hands waving in the air. He pointed at a small boy in the front. "You have a question?"

"If it wasn't human sacrifice then how did the bone get into the lake?" he asked glancing across at the teacher who stood at the back of the class looking resigned.

"Well no one knows really," said the archaeologist, "and it could indeed be human sacrifice, but it could just as likely be a burial ritual ... well that is a very short history of the dig. Shall we go over and have a look at the actual hole in the ground."

He led the children from the dormitories across to an area where a large tent covered a patch of the lawn. Entering the tent the children saw a large sheet of metal stretched out over the ground, at either end of this sheet metal rails protruded out from underneath. The archaeologist bent down and unfastened a padlock that connected the sheet of metal to a concrete pile driven deep into the ground. Once the padlock was released he stood, and with the help of Mr Oldendie, gave the metal sheet a firm push with his foot; the metal sheet slid back on the rails to reveal the archaeological dig.

"Unfortunately the site must be locked - rumours of treasure are too much of a temptation for some people." said the man sadly.

The hole was not deep, only up to the children's middle, apart from the area where the lake once stood where it plunged to a depth of perhaps four meters. The diggers had not uncovered the whole of the lake but left half completely untouched hidden under the smooth lawns of Oldmere. So on the far side of the dig, the grass of the school grounds suddenly ended with a steep drop right to the rocky bottom of the ancient site.

The most obvious feature of the site was the Celtic Christian cross that still stuck out from the ground near to the edge of the hole; it still had some grass around its base and had been largely left untouched by the dig. As Rosetta's eyes ranged around the rest of the site she could see remains of what must be Roman walls, just a few inches high now. These surrounded the central lake. The overall impression she got was that the walls were there to protect whatever lay in the lake, or perhaps - she thought with a shiver - perhaps they were there to keep something from escaping.

As soon as she had this thought, the hole that once held the lake became somehow threatening even though the children were too far away to see far into the depths. She felt that she should stay away, and so it was with some alarm that she realised that the class was moving around the edge of the dig towards the hole. She hung back as much as she could and followed the crowd.

"You can see the crack in the rock which we think led to the lake being drained." said the archaeologist, pointing to a point near to where Rosetta stood. She looked down and saw a smashed pile of rock by the edge of the ancient shore. From that rock a crack emanated that spread over the lip and down into the bottom of the lake, and as she peered over to get a better look she felt that that crack must descend into the very heart of the knoll, so black was its interior.

Her head spun as she looked down, and she felt a disconnection from all around like she had stood too quickly and was about to faint. As she wobbled on the edge of the pit, she heard someone say "Look at that, how strange!", and she felt they must be talking about her. But when she looked up through the clear plastic that formed the roof of the tent she saw everyone's faces turned toward the school buildings behind her. She looked along the building and saw hundreds of crows. They lined every windowsill and perched on every inch of the roof ridge. It may have been her imagination, but she felt that every single one was looking right at her.

In the deep shadows of a drainage ditch, unnoticed by everyone, Musty watched with every fibre twitching. He had stayed after his night-time patrol to watch the class and make sure that Rosetta was safe. He was glad he had for, as he watched the class look up towards the crows, he knew without a doubt that she was not safe, that something had noticed her. He lingered as the class broke up, heading off to their lessons and noticed that the crows had mirrored the actions of the children and scattered.

※ ※ ※ ※ ※

With the start of term and the winter darkness the children found it hard to make their meetings in the antechamber. So it was only Musty and Marcus who met the evening after the children's tour of the archaeological dig.

"I felt it strongly," Musty said. "She leant over and looked down deep into the pit and second later the crows came, from nowhere seemingly. The feeling was unmistakable to me. Before then the danger lurked out of sight, but now I know it, and it has something to do with that pit."

Marcus lay on the sofa, he had removed his artificial limb leant it against the wall. He massaged some ointment into his stump, his face wincing every now and again when he hit a tender spot, but generally his face showed only concern.

"I'll get a note to her, and warn her to keep away from the dig." he said, putting his stump onto a towel placed over the sofa. "We'll need to keep watch also. I can do it in the day. This building overlooks the site nicely, but I can't see through the tent walls. At night it will have to be you."

"I can watch. But what if I see something?"

"If it is of immediate danger then you will have to act, perhaps warn the children or whatever you think is right. Otherwise just watch, do nothing." Musty growled at this unwelcome instruction, but Marcus gently grabbed his muzzle, looked into his eyes, and said, "It is unwise to hunt something if you do not know what it is. Before we do anything we must find out what we are dealing with."

Musty eyed him intently for a while and then with a snort indicated his reluctant agreement.

Chapter 3

From a diary found in the mud.

She is here on the knoll! I sensed her in one of the classes close by. I know now she is a girl, one of the pupils here, but not which one.

I do not fear her now. I sense she is still not fully-grown, nor is my existence even fully known to her and yet she is afraid ... so afraid. The merest hint of me, and her mind pulled back. My power grows with each passing day and before long, if my servants succeed in in their missions, I will have reached the full extent of my old majesty. Then ... then I will be ready to leave here, this pitiful backwater, and the world will know me once more.

Until then I must be patient. The world is not as it was; people are not so ignorant, or fearful as they once were; my servants are not so easily led as they would have been in ages past. I must cajole and deceive before they will do my bidding. Apart from her of course; my chosen one. Her mind and mine fit so well that in the end we will be one creature, one desire and will be immortal, matchless. But until then my games must be subtle; I must be delicate before I crush without mercy.

My plans progress, my servants will find the girl. She will die and I will triumph.

Chapter 4

People start to behave most strangely at Oldmere School.

After a couple of days Mr White sat down with her and went through what she had made of her first few days.

"And finally," he said, after they had discussed lessons at some length. "Are there any extra-curricular activities you would like to get involved in? At Oldmere we think that such things are as important as all the lessons. Mind and Body Miss Clarence!" these last words exploded from Mr White with such vigour that it made Rosetta jump a little. Mr White grinned at her reaction.

"Well," said Rosetta after she had recovered. "I was a good swimmer at my last school, and you have got a pool here I understand."

"Yes we have. That should not be too much of a

problem. I think there are some spaces. It's not the most popular activity is swimming - too many early mornings for most people I think ... Looking at the schedule we might be able to fit you in tomorrow - can you do 7am?" Rosetta must have looked surprised at the time, for he laughed and said, "The seniors have to do 6 'Clock - so consider yourself lucky. Is that OK? Yes ... good I'll tell Miss Float to expect you."

"7 O'clock!" Karl was amazed. "You'll have to leave home by 6.30 to get to the pool by then. You're on your own I'm afraid. I won't be able to make that I'll still be unconscious at that time, so you'll have to walk over by yourself. Should be no problems with the unknown creature at that time though." He made a scary face and curled his hands into pretend claws. "Will your Mum let you walk there by yourself though? You know what parents are like"

Rosetta's mother did let her. When Rosetta asked her, she stopped her ironing and looked at her appraisingly. Then she said as if Rosetta had passed some sort of test, "Well that's good. It is on Tuesdays and Thursdays you say? Well then I don't see why you can't walk over to the school by yourself. But ..." and she emphasised the phrase by raising her iron. "You've got to be sensible with the roads and everything."

Rosetta agreed, and so she was in the swimming club.

On her first day of swim training Rosetta was surprised to find Musty waiting in the hedgerows as she left the house after a quick cup of tea.

"You don't think we'd let you walk by yourself at this time?" he said, as he waddled next to her across the dark fields. "Karl told Marcus yesterday and we decided that I'd better accompany you."

It was a clear morning, the stars were still visible despite the dawn's pre-glow and the long grass was crunchy with frost as they walked along the fields below Rosetta's house. They crossed the road at a dash and went their separate ways by the school gates; Musty headed towards the secret entrance to the Library and Rosetta headed up the road, across the playing fields towards the swimming pool block which nestled on a small rise near the valley wall.

A group of children waited in a huddle outside the pool on a small covered platform that doubled as a pavilion for the cricket pitches. The back wall of this area consisted almost entirely of a line of windows, which must look out over the pool, for they were very steamed up and shone with a fierce light from within. Rosetta smiled nervously at some faces that she recognised and went over to the window to have a look at the pool.

Despite what Mr White had said about swimming being unpopular, the pool was crowded. There were about six people per lane. Rosetta noticed with a thrill of anticipation that it was a 33 metre one, not as good as a full 50 metre, but better than what she was used to.

As she leant, pressing her forehead against the glass, both hands either side of her face, Rosetta felt an uncomfortable and horribly familiar feeling start up in the pit of her stomach. She looked over at her right hand and saw a glow starting within that had nothing to do with the bright lights of the swimming pool.

She quickly pushed her hand into the pockets of her puffer jacket looking around to see if anyone had noticed. She stepped away from the glass, and as she did so a door opened at a far end of the building. A voice came out of the entrance, shouting in a strange nasal tone. "Hurry up, come in and get changed." Rosetta risked a glance down at her pockets to see if the light was leaking out and to her relief saw that they looked black and uninteresting. She inched her hand out a little and was relieved to see that it looked normal.

She lined up behind the other children and they shuffled into a corridor that ran parallel to the pool and led to the changing rooms at the back. A teacher stood at the door counting them in. When she saw Rosetta she signalled for her to wait and when the last of the children had come in she came and spoke to her.

"I'm Mrs Float," she looked directly at Rosetta daring her to comment on her name. Her voice was very nasal and a bit distorted. "You must be Miss

Clarence. You need to know two things about me and if you get those on board then we will get on well. Firstly I'm 80% deaf, which means the chances are I can't hear you unless you are looking directly at me so I can see your lips. Secondly 80% is not the same as 100% and if I do catch you saying anything about me behind my back then you are out - no second chances."

She smiled at the look of alarm on Rosetta's face. "Don't panic, I have never had to do it yet. Get changed, and wait by the side of the pool for the seniors to get out - there isn't room for both of you lot in the changing room."

Rosetta got changed and waited by the head of the pool. The seniors were just swimming backstroke to warm down before getting out and heading to the changing rooms, when Rosetta felt the strange feeling in her stomach once more and did not need to look at her hand to realise that it would be starting to glow. She started to panic. She was only in a swimming costume and had no pocket in which to hide her glowing hand.

Looking about she saw a toilet door down a short corridor. Without waiting for permission she made a dash for it, got in and closed the door behind her. Looking down she saw her hand's glow was fading just like it had outside. She leant against the sink and looked up into the mirror, not knowing what to do, and what she saw made her take a step back. Her eyes, normally nut brown, had gone a most unnatural shade of luminous green - though even as she looked the colour was fading.

There was a knocking on the door. It was Mrs Float.

"Are you alright in there? Clarence! Are you well?"

Rosetta thought quickly - there was no point in explaining to Miss Float with the door closed - so she pulled her goggles on, they were blue tinted and would cover up any remaining green tinge in her eyes. The light from her hand was hardly noticeable now. She took a deep breath and opened the door.

"Sorry Miss Float. Nerves you know. I'm OK."

"Good," said Miss Float looking relieved. "Now come through, I've put you in lane four until we see how you get on."

With some trepidation Rosetta moved into the main pool area as the older children moved off towards the school. She glanced down trying to see if her hand was going to flare up again, and desperately thinking of what to do if it did. But her hand remained normal, and as she got into the water with the rest of her group, she wondered what on earth was happening to her.

⁂

At the same time Rosetta was just finishing her swimming - it had gone well and she had a feeling she might be in with a chance of the junior team - Karl had arrived at the school to have breakfast with the rest of his class. Straight away he sensed that something was wrong.

Instead of working their way through their breakfast with their normal quiet intensity, his group were talking with an excited air that told him something exciting had happened that morning.

He sat next to Sammy, a weasel boy who always knew everything, and asked "Is something up?"

"I'd say there is. One of year thirteen has gone missing overnight "

"What! Just gone?"

"His bed was empty this morning. No sign of him anywhere. Some of his civilian clothes are missing. They say he's been behaving oddly recently as well."

"Oddly? Sounds a bit like that Emily Watson?" said Karl.

"Yes. It is a bit like that. His name is Jonathan Kahn. He is clever like her - really, really excellent at piano - and he has recently started to just behave like a complete bozo. Back chat to teachers, not doing his homework and pushing smaller kids around."

"Yeah," said a boy further along the bench. "He tried something with me a couple of weeks ago. I was just coming back from maths and he was coming the other way. He crossed from one side of the corridor to the other just so he could barge into me, then he claimed it was my fault and started to push me about."

"And," said Sammy. "It's not his style at all

normally. He just loves his piano and practices endlessly. Wouldn't say boo to a goose."

Karl was pondering this when the five-minute bell for assembly rang. Everyone stuffed their last pieces of toast, grabbed their bags and made towards the Assembly hall still discussing the mysterious disappearance of Jonathan Kahn.

Karl met Rosetta in the corridor, her hair still wet from the swimming. She was eager to tell him of her strange experience in the swimming pool; he needed to relate the disappearance of Jonathan Kahn. Neither was satisfied in their desires however for they were both swept forward by steady push of the crowd heading for the Assembly Hall.

The Head Teacher looked grim as she faced the audience from the low dais that stood at one end of the room. She did not look her normal tidy self; her bobbed hair was a mess and her face was tired and careworn. Her clothes, normally immaculate, looked like they had been thrown on in a hurry.

"You will no doubt have started to hear rumours of a missing child," there was no small talk; Miss Eastville went straight to the point, again an unusual occurrence in one of her assemblies. "And it is true that we are looking into the whereabouts of Jonathan Kahn, who was not in his dorm this morning. If anyone in the school knows anything about his disappearance can they please let Mr Green know as soon as possible. Any information will be treated as confidential, and any misdemeanours that come out will be treated leniently. The police have been informed and will be searching the ... "

Miss Eastville paused because the doors at the back of the Hall had banged as if something had fallen against them. It happened again, more violently this time, and then the door handle started to turn with a terrible slowness. The door opened and a terrible sight met the eyes - and noses - of the children nearest the back of the hall. A black creature, which might have once resembled a schoolboy, staggered into the hall. If you looked carefully you could just make out that he was wearing an orange T-shirt and, bizarrely, summer shorts but it was hard to distinguish any details because of the layer of filth that covered him from head to foot. He stank like an open sewer.

"What's happening? Who is that?" said the head urgently, for she could not see the boy through the hundreds of children who stood between her and the Hall doors. She did not have long to wait for the answer to her questions however, for such was the terrible smell emanating from the boy, everyone near rushed away making him suddenly quite visible to all of the teachers at the front of the hall.

The boy stood swaying and looking a little dazed. His bleary eyes skimmed over the lines of children until they rested on the stupefied face of Miss Eastville. He took a hesitant few steps toward the front of the hall; waves of the most terrible stink caused people to back off, turning their faces away as they did.

Everyone was frozen. The boy was such a terrible assault on the all the senses; it was such an inappropriate visitation upon the normal polished and pristine Assembly Hall that no one felt able to do anything but watch as he slowly made his way up toward the front of the room.

As he approached closer to Miss Eastville he started to speak. "Ivedoneitwrong" he muttered.

"Jonathan," said Miss Eastville as he approached. His words seemed to have broken the impasse for it was at that moment that the head started to walk towards the boy. "Jonathan is that you. Are you alright?" which seemed to Rosetta rather a foolish thing to say under the circumstances.

"I've donit wrong ... wrong," and as he said these words he tripped and fell forwards, only catching himself by grabbing at Miss Eastville's knees. The head torn between maintaining her dignity and keeping her suit clean gave a kind of twitch, which quickly turned into a push and jump as Jonathan Kahn, tired, sick and half mad vomited over her tights and polished leather shoes.

※ ※ ※ ※ ※

"I must admit that was one of the more interesting morning assemblies I have ever attended," said Marcus that evening as they all met in the antechamber after school that day. "I've seen plenty of children be sick, but never over the head teacher."

The children grinned at him, the incident had cause much chat and amusement over the school all day.

"So what happened afterwards?" said Karl. "What is the story with Jonathan Kahn? How did he get into such a state?" After the incident, assembly had been cancelled and all the children moved off to their lessons. The last Karl had seen, Jonathan Kahn was being carried off to one end of the hall; Miss Eastville had disappeared into the teacher's toilets to clean up.

"Well they phoned an ambulance to take him to hospital, and because I don't have teaching duties I was given the task of accompanying him there. The ambulance people insisted he had a quick shower before the journey, but it was still a pretty smelly journey as they insisted on taking his clothes with us; they needed to know what he had fallen in, though I think most people could guess. Jonathan was mostly unconscious at first, but he did keep on saying things like 'I did it wrong' or 'I got it wrong' like he was in a dream.

"Anyway once we got through the tunnel out of the valley he perked up a bit, though he was still very confused. He kept asking for his mother, poor tyke, and we told him that she would be waiting at hospital; she had taken a helicopter from London believe it or not. Once he heard that he shut up and just looked scared.

"We got to hospital and he got checked over.

Physically he seemed fine, but his mind was still not normal and he was saying some very strange things.

"When his mother arrived he seemed to relax at last and the whole story came tumbling out. I wanted to get out, to leave them to it but the mother insisted I stay - as a representative of the school - to bear witness to what he said. What he said is bizarre, and if I didn't know everything else that is going on I'd just say he needed a long rest from any stress, preferably cared for by professional people.

"He said that one day, when he was on his way to lessons, he had heard a voice, a woman's voice. At first he thought that is was a new loudspeaker system, but he very quickly realised that no one else could hear it. What it said to him was along the lines of the following: It said that it could help him with his piano - his mother said afterwards that he was doing his grade eight exams and had been getting very stressed about them - and that without its help he would fail.

"At first, he tried to ignore the voice, but then his piano started to go downhill. Every note was difficult and the voice would not be silenced, it talked all night; he could not sleep and eventually his school work started to go downhill as well. So he started to listen and the more he listened the easier it became to listen some more.

"He found that if he did what the voice told him then things started to go better. People who used to ignore him, listened when he did as the voice told him; people respected him. Then the voice said that if he wanted his piano to improve - to go back to where it had been before, then he needed to find a special rock. A rock that held an ancient power that would help him concentrate on his practice and enjoy his playing. This rock was buried under Oldmere School. All he needed to do was dig it out.

"And so this poor boy was led by this voice to that outbuilding next to the school gymnasium. It is easy enough to get into. It just holds some broken down exercise equipment and is not locked. And it was there where he started to dig. He dug at night for hours until he was exhausted and could dig no more, at which point the voice would let him go to bed. This went on for weeks and in the end he had a tunnel of ten meters."

Marcus sighed and said, "What this boy achieved is quite remarkable. I have had a look at the tunnel - at least what is left of it now - and it was well constructed. He used bits of old gym equipment to build walls so the tunnel would not fall. He worked in horrible cramped conditions with little air - it made me think of Victorian chimney sweeps - and all because of this voice, which he thought he heard in his head.

"Last night it all went wrong. As he was digging he realised that he had reached one of the large pipes that are everywhere underground around the school - there are so many buildings in a small space here it is difficult to avoid them. He decided to dig underneath it thinking that the solid nature of the pipe would act almost as an extra bit of roof for his tunnel. What he did not know was that this was the main sewer that led from the dormitories further up the hill, and it was partially blocked so that all the waste could not flow down the hill. The waste - poo, wee, toilet paper and everything else you throw, or ends up down a toilet - had backed up making this pipe very heavy and so when he dug underneath ..."

"Ohh", said Rosetta, putting her hand to her mouth. "The weight made the pipe snap."

"Yes." said Marcus. "And everything fell on top of Jonathan, filling the tunnel at the same time. It must have been terrifying. He was in a confined space and suddenly had to worm backwards quickly or risk drowning in the filth gushing from the broken pipe. He must have managed to do so for the next thing he remembers is waking up near the entrance of the tunnel. He struggled out dazed wandered to the Assembly Hall, and you saw the rest.

"He has not heard the voice since the tunnel collapsed.

"After telling this story Jonathan fell asleep exhausted. His mother went for a lie down also, and I was left to wait for the head who arrived pretty shortly afterwards. I understand from her that Jonathan will be taking some time off school whilst he recovers and that his future will be discussed sometime after Christmas."

The children sat and wondered for a while what on earth was going on in Jonathan Kahn's mind to make him do such a thing when Rosetta remembered the strange behaviour of her hand at the swimming pool that morning. She told them.

"Very strange," said Marcus. "You say you made no gesture or did anything you think might have set it off?"

"No," said Rosetta. "Thinking about it, my hand lit up when the seniors were getting out of the pool, but that could just be a coincidence."

"Do you think something is hidden at the pool?" said Karl, thinking of Rosetta's discovery of the secret compartment in the antechamber.

"It doesn't seem likely," said Marcus. "The pool is only five years old and my father never went there anyway." He fell silent and looked thoughtful.

"I took that flower we found to Miss Spore by the way," said Marcus, breaking the silence. "And that is another strange thing."

"What?" said Rosetta. "Is it poison?"

"Yes," said Marcus. "It is called Monkshood and is very dangerous, but this specimen was very small and so dried out that handling it would not be a problem. But it is not that which struck me as strange."

"What then?" said Karl, looking at his fingers where he had held the plant.

"It was the behaviour of Miss Spore," said Marcus. "You won't have come across her yet as she teaches the older pupils, but she is almost a caricature of a scientist; very rational and precise. I have never seen her be anything but business-like and accurate.

"Well when I showed her the plant she was her normal self ... said it was monkshood, though she called it something else at first. Aconite I think. Anyway then she said it was unusual because it is quite rare - it usually only grows in the mountains - and this is the second time in just a few months that she has had to warn someone in the school about it.

"Well that got my attention and so I asked who else had it. She said she had found a student with a whole vase full next to their bed. 'Enough to kill the whole dormitory'."

"Wow," said Karl. "So who was it?"

"That is the odd thing," said Marcus. "When I asked that very question she suddenly became very distracted. She walked out of the room like I wasn't there and made a cup of tea. I waited for her to come back, and when she did she seemed surprised to see me. I asked her again and it became apparent that she had forgotten the whole of our previous conversation.

"I tried again. I showed her the monkshood and the whole thing repeated. She looked surprised, said it was dangerous, and said she had found some in the school recently. When I questioned her about it she did a double take, and appeared to have forgotten the conversation again."

"And you say she is normally not absent minded?" said Rosetta.

"Not at all," said Marcus. " I even went through the whole thing again just to be sure - with the same result. It was like a chunk of her memory had been wiped."

"So we will never know who had a load of monkshood?" said Rosetta.

"It looks like someone has made sure of that," said Karl.

🦠 🦠 🦠 🦠 🦠

Musty squatted near the gym in the dark shadow cast by a security light. It was raining, but that did not bother him - the water just ran off his wiry fur, which also kept him warm. He had watched the site for three nights now waiting for anything unusual, but nothing had been forthcoming. He wriggled a little in the small hollow he had made in the long grass to ease a pain in his haunches, and then settled down for another long watch.

After about an hour his ears twitched and rolled forward as he had heard a noise coming from the dormitories. Raising himself up onto his front paws he looked around the corner of the Gym to see if he could see the source of the disturbance. He froze when he saw two figures standing facing each other in a side entrance of the main dormitory - they must be talking thought Musty, though he could not hear any words. They were wearing raincoats with hoods that formed a deep tube over their faces so he could not see their faces, but from their size and build he could tell that they were pupils from the school – girls he thought from their smell. 'But not young ones' he thought, 'they are too big.'

The two finished their conversation, if that was what it was, and turned away from the building and started down the hill. Musty slowly lowered himself back to the ground and waited for them to pass, his nose twitching; if he could not see their faces then perhaps he could grab their scent. He was disappointed for the rain washed away any smell as soon as it left them.

As they passed his hiding place they turned left and headed towards the archaeological dig. They entered the tent and disappeared from view. Musty moved forward as soon as they did so, listening for any sound that they might be coming back.

The tent flaps were flapping gently as Musty approached the dig site. He heard nothing and so he gently nosed his way under the wet material until he could see what was happening inside.

The two figures were kneeling by the hole in the grass, which was still covered by the metal screen, and in front of them, rising from the edges of the iron sheet, a green mist was pouring upwards. As Musty watched it seemed to be coalescing before his very eyes forming a something that resembled a human shape. As he saw it he knew that this was the enemy which he had been brought into existence to fight, and with that knowledge he forgot all about remaining hidden. The badger in him rose up and supplanted whatever else had been brought into existence that late summer day by Rosetta's play house. His need to protect overcame all and he leapt from under the tent flaps, teeth bared.

At this one of the figures flashed around and looked straight at Musty almost as if it already knew beforehand where he was to be found. With the same unnatural speed it raised its arm out straight with the fingers of the hand tensed and bent like a bird's claw. As this happened Musty caught a brief glimpse of pale green eyes and thick black eyebrows before he felt a weight drop onto his back, like someone had pushed down with an enormous hand. His legs collapsed under him and he found himself pushed into the ground, quite unable to move. The green mist suddenly dissipated in the breeze as it should have done all along, and as it did so the two figures got to their feet. One of them - the one who still held Musty down - sprang up like a predator interrupted. The other rose hesitantly looking across to the first, who said "Come!" and they both ran from the tent. A few seconds passed and Musty was still unable to move from his stomach, and he started to fear that he might be somehow paralysed. It was at least a minute later until he found himself free to move and able to jump up to give chase.

However when he stuck his head through the tent flap and followed the fresh scent laid in the grass, he found he could only follow it to a hidden corner in the wall of the girl's dormitory. There it vanished as if the intruders had walked right through the wall. Perplexed he made his way back to the Ancient Library, knowing it was useless to watch any more that night and thinking that he was very pleased that Rosetta did not sleep at the school.

The evening after Musty's encounter, Rosetta was called down by her Mother early one Saturday morning. She was holding a letter. Aimee crawled around the floor playing with a bright red toy snake.

"I've just received this." she said holding up the letter. "It is from a hospital in Denmark and they think that they might be able to help Aimee, or at least find out what is wrong with her. But," she said with a sigh, they want to do some tests and that means I have to go with Aimee over to Denmark. They want to do it before Christmas and that means leaving you here. Now ..." she interrupted as Rosetta started to speak. "I have arranged with the school for you to stay whilst I'm away, provided that is alright with you."

That was of course perfectly alright with Rosetta. Apart from the fact that she had always wanted to sleep over at the school for at least one night, there was also her desire to get to the bottom of what was going on there; a few nights spent in the hot bed of gossip that was the girls dormitories might well turn up something. On top of that having a pair of eyes in amongst the children at night might be very useful, and was not something they could currently do. Karl also stayed in the village at night and, although Marcus slept at school, all teachers who were not house-masters were not allowed in the dormitories at night. This meant that he was limited in what he could find out when it came to what happened in the dorms at night. His leg also meant that secret night-time activities were more difficult for him.

What she said to her mother was "I suppose only a week wouldn't be so bad."

Chapter 5

Rosetta's Few Days Sleeping at Oldmere; clues, a chase, a capture and a rescue

It was with some trepidation that Rosetta arrived on her first day of boarding at school. She carried a large rucksack that contained everything she needed for the four nights she would be staying. In addition to what she needed for legitimate activities, she had also packed some dark clothing and a powerful torch.

There had been a lot of opposition to her staying at school when she had announced her intention in the antechamber a couple of nights before. Musty in particular had been very vocal in his objections. He had started to get quite badgerish in behaviour - his ears went back and he started to half-yip and bark as he spoke, which in him was a sure sign of agitation. But in the end Rosetta won out, because simply there was nothing anyone could do to stop her.

"The only evidence we have that there is any threat to me at all is Musty's intuition. There has been nothing else to suggest that I am in any more danger that the other two hundred children who sleep in the school every night. I am not going to give up this chance just because of that." She did not mention, that if she refused to stay at the school then her mother, who would not leave her alone in the house, would not be able to take Aimee to see the Danish doctors until the Christmas holidays, which were some weeks off.

Her bed was in the year seven dormitories, and her heart sank when she saw that they had put her next to Ursula De Mailtland. Rosetta presumed that Mr White had done this deliberately to put her at her ease, as he must know they had gone to the same school before, but all it did was make Rosetta think of how difficult it would be to do any investigating at night; Ursula was bound to chatter endlessly after lights out. So sighing somewhat she unpacked, and set off to that day's lessons.

She was right about Ursula. Whilst they waited for Mr White to arrive she bounded up, looking depressingly excited.

"Isn't this great! You are sleeping next to me in the dorm. If we hide some of the fairy cakes they give you at dinner then we can have them after lights out as a kind of midnight feast. They don't mind really, as long as you don't cause any trouble or make a mess for the cleaners."

Rosetta smiled, and hoped that it would not be too regular an occurrence.

As it turned out she enjoyed the evening spent with the girls in the dormitory, it had been a long time since she had spent an evening relaxing with friends, and as they sat on an old blanket clustered around a small pile of cake Rosetta hardly thought of her mother and Aimee at all.

As well as having an enjoyable evening, Rosetta also heard some useful rumours about the older kids.

"They're out in the corridor at all times of day and night," said Gail, a plump, horsey girl from somewhere near London. "I heard them, the year thirteen girls that is, sneaking up and down the corridor. God knows what they're up to, but it's not fair on us. I'm right by the door and I can't sleep."

Listening to this Rosetta decided that the following night she might see if she could see just who was doing this sneaking, and perhaps what they were up to. So the next day, when she went to the toilet after lessons she took her black clothes with her and secreted them, together with her torch, in a cupboard that normally held only toilet paper and bleach.

That evening there was little enthusiasm in the dormitory for further talk or cake. It was obvious to Rosetta that it had been the presence of a new face in the room that had provided the excuse for the party the previous night and her fears of regular disturbances were unfounded. Tired by the late night, most of the children were in bed and asleep by nine o'clock. Rosetta lay in the dark waiting for a time when she thought everyone would be asleep. It was raining heavily and she felt strangely comforted by the noise; without realising it she drifted off into sleep.

When she woke she realised it must be very late. The rain had stopped and moonlight flooded out from behind the curtains, framing the edge of the window in silver. She pulled back her covers, put on her slippers, and headed for the door to the dormitory. The corridor shone silver with moonlight which came from the single window in the wall, which had no curtains. And as she walked she noticed that the wooden floor had a line of wet black blobs, footprints she was sure, running down the middle. They led from the entrance to the main staircase to the year thirteen dormitory, whose door was slightly ajar.

Rosetta bent down and touched the footprints to check that they were actually water when she heard a noise coming from the open door. It sounded like someone moving around in the year thirteen dormitory and the noise was getting louder. Looking around Rosetta saw that she was too far from her dormitory door to make a dash for her bed. There were two other doors on this corridor, apart from those to the dorms and the staircase. Rosetta did not know one, but the other she knew was the toilet where she had hidden her torch and clothes the night before. She made a dash, quickly slipped inside and closed the door silently behind her.

Praying that the person did not simply want to go to the toilet herself, Rosetta pressed her ear close to the door and listened. She heard the person coming up the corridor; the noise of their footsteps was slow and tentative, as if they were taking great care to be as silent as possible. They approached the door and to her horror Rosetta began to get the, by now familiar, upset feeling in her stomach. She looked down at her hand and saw that it had started to glow faintly red and, even as she watched, it grew brighter and brighter. In a few seconds it shone as bright as a light bulb and this light was sure to be visible from underneath the door.

The footsteps stopped outside the door. A voice said, threatening, "Who's there?"

Rosetta panicked and tried to think what she could do. If the person came in and saw her with an unnatural light somehow glowing from within her hand, then all sorts of trouble might come. A half idea came to her and she quickly opened the door to the cupboard and grabbed the torch she had placed there earlier. She switched it on. The light it gave out was almost as bright that from her hand. Raising the torch high in her glowing hand, and pointing it at the door she quickly turned the handle and pushed.

A figure blinked in the light, obviously blinded by the sudden blaze, and raised its hand to shield its eyes. It was a girl. Rosetta recognised her as from year thirteen, but did not know any more about her than that. She was holding a dripping bundle in her hand of what looked like clothes.

"Oh … I'm sorry," said Rosetta trying to sound innocent. "I've just been to the loo. Do you know where the light switch is? It's my first night here you see."

The girl's shockingly blue eyes widened in annoyance. She scowled half blinded by the bright light shining into her eyes and was plainly unable to see that some of that glare came from inside Rosetta's hand. She turned, muttered something under her breath that Rosetta could not hear, and scuttled down the corridor towards the unknown door further down the corridor. Quickly Rosetta hurried away from the retreating figure back to her dormitory and was relieved to see that the light from her hand faded as she did so. When she finally reached the door it had gone completely and she could switch off the torch that she had used to mask her shining hand.

She crept across the dormitory, flopped into bed and thought that perhaps she might pop home tomorrow and get her thick black skiing gloves, which could hide her hand if it started to glow again.

※ ※ ※ ※ ※

When she woke in the morning Rosetta asked a girl what was behind the door that she had seen the girl go into the night before.

"That's the drying room. For stuff that gets wet but doesn't need washing you know like raincoats and hats. You just go in and hang whatever's wet up there."

When Rosetta looked twenty minutes later, there was only one set of clothes in there that was still damp. Black tights, and a black running top hung limply on the rails. As well as being wet they were covered in straw and had strange pale stains on them, like the dye had been somehow leached from the material. Rosetta could not help but notice that they were very similar in nature to clothes that still remained hidden in the toilet cupboard across the corridor; clothes that she had especially chosen for a secret night time escapade.

Rosetta hoped to make a quick visit to her house to collect her ski gloves but, before she could do so, a girl cornered her in the corridor just after breakfast. She grabbed Rosetta's shoulder as she walked past and pushed her roughly against a wall. It was unmistakably the girl from the corridor the previous night. She looked scruffy; her hair was matted and untidy. She leaned in close, those bright blue eyes narrowed in a focussed aggression.

"I want you to remember one thing," she whispered in Rosetta's ear. Her breath stank. "If you ever say you saw me last night to anyone I will find out and come for you. What I will do to you then will not be pleasant ... so stay quiet ... say nothing. "She broke away. The whole exchange had taken less than ten seconds. Rosetta's hand felt tingly, but seemingly had not time to glow.

"Who was that?" she asked Ursula when her friend came past a second later, pointing at the retreating back of the girl.

"Her ... a prefect if you can believe it. She is going the same way as Emily Watson if you ask me. Started out well ... gone badly wrong this year." Ursula did not bother to mention Jonathan Kahn, thinking perhaps that his behaviour was just normal for a boy, but Rosetta thought that counting this girl it would make three schoolchildren going "to the bad" this year.

"And her name?"

"Oh, her name's Olivia Rigby, but keep away from her, she's trouble."

But Rosetta was already planning the very opposite.

※ ※ ※ ※ ※

Rosetta met with Karl at lunchtime, told him what had happened the night before, and explained what she planned for that evening.

"What!" Karl exploded. "Follow her! Musty will do his nut. So will Marcus"

"That is why they mustn't know," said Rosetta. "Those two keep on waiting for things to drop into their hands, just because they are scared of some possible danger to me. We need to go after whatever is making all these children behave like this before we end up with another talented person just going to waste, just because we didn't dare."

Karl looked at her with an appraising eye and then said "OK. I can't really help you though, as I'm not in the school anyway, but I could ... "and he started to sound a little unsure as if he was not convinced of what he was about to say. "I could get out of the house, come over and wait by the entrance to the boys' dormitory.

"It's a bit difficult though. I mean we don't know when this Olivia Rigby is going to go out again, and I'll have to come late or my mum and Dad will hear me. Quite often they're not in bed until eleven. So I probably can't make it until midnight, and by then it might be too late. She might have already gone off to do whatever she does... Look, I'll try to make it for midnight as often as I can. If you are not there when I arrive then I'll wait a bit and then go home. However if I can't make it out can you promise not to go chasing after her by yourself?"

"Don't you start now, you're as bad as the other two." said Rosetta irritated. "If you're not there I'll just have to be careful. Just wait by the boys' dorms as soon as you can get there. I think I ran into her about 2.30 last night, so midnight might well be just the right time to arrive to catch her going out. I won't look for you; there may not be time, just follow as best you can. If nothing happens by about 2am then just go home and we can try again another night."

"OK," said Karl relenting. "It is interesting though about your hand lighting up again. Could it be something to do with that girl?"

"I think it is," said Rosetta. "It lit up when she came close and faded again when she left. It looks like it could be some sort of early warning system, as well as the other things it seems to do."

"You mean your hand lights up when someone dangerous comes close? That would mean that there is someone like that in the senior swimming squad because it went off in the pool that time. Is Emily Watson…"

"She doesn't swim," said Rosetta. "I've checked. But there could be more than one person."

"Nice thought," said Karl.

They walked back to the village together after lessons that evening. Rosetta pretended that she had forgotten something from home, which indeed she had. There were some rather large ski gloves of her mothers, which just about fitted her these days and would prevent any light from her hands giving her away as they had done the night before. She said goodbye to Karl at his front gate.

"Be careful." he said. "I'm not saying it for its own sake. If anything happens to you Musty will give me a big bite and those teeth look like they'd hurt."

※ ※ ※ ※ ※

That night there was some chat in the dormitory

and it was at least eleven before the last torch was put out. Rosetta waited, lying in the dark until she felt that most of the people in the dorm were at least dozing, and then she casually got up and went towards the corridor as if she was going to the toilet. She hoped that any girls still half-awake would not notice that she had not returned, leaving her free to wait for Olivia Rigby to pass through the corridor. She decided to hide in the drying room, on the grounds that no one would be using it at night. So she picked up the clothes she had dropped off in the toilet cleaning cupboard, got changed, and went across the corridor to wait in the deep shadow cast by the light from a moonlit window, hidden amongst the rails of drying clothes.

It had been perhaps half an hour before she heard a tiny creak in the corridor, and it was that second that she realised with horror that she could see the line of clothes left to dry by Olivia Rigby yesterday; clothes that she was sure to come and collect any minute, and which were situated right by Rosetta's hiding place. She looked about for somewhere better to hide, and in a far corner she noticed a whole hockey team's kit, which took up a whole rack. She quickly dashed over, pushed her gloved hands as deep into her clothes and tried to make herself as small as possible as she squatted on the floor.

It was only seconds later that Olivia Rigby entered the drying room still somehow managing to look menacing in turquoise pyjamas. For a second

Rosetta thought that she might switch the light on, but she merely paused by the door waiting for her eyes to get used to the semi darkness. After a few seconds she walked over to the drying rack and started to put on her clothes. The stains that had bleached parts of the black material were even more apparent now that the clothes were dry. As she peered through the hockey tops Rosetta saw that, from a distance, and when the clothes were being worn, it was quite apparent that the stains formed a pattern. That whatever had discoloured the material had been thrown up across her stomach and up the arms in a splash that ended just below her shoulders.

Once her clothes were on, Olivia Rigby, wasted no time and purposefully walked back across the room to the door, and left soundlessly. Rosetta got up and followed, waiting a few seconds by the door to the drying room in case Olivia Rigby came back unexpectedly. Poking her head around the corner of the drying room door Rosetta saw that Olivia had left the dorm corridor and gone through the door that led to the main staircase.

She followed and opened the door a crack. Rosetta was at first confused. She had expected to see a shadowy figure going down the main staircase as these stairs stretched from the very bottom to the top of the building, various dormitory corridors forked from it as it did so, like braches from the trunk of a tree. The stairs were wide and as a result Rosetta could easily see anyone moving on the staircase from her position by the door.

Her eyes flicked about the staircase and from the corner of her eye she saw some booted feet going *up* the stairs. As they disappeared from view, Rosetta tiptoed after wondering what Olivia Rigby was doing; there was only one more floor above the one they were already on, and it housed only some storerooms as far as she knew.

Peering upwards - her head was now level with the floor above - she saw that Olivia had taken a key from her pocket and unlocked a door in the corridor. Rosetta had always assumed that this door led to something like a cleaning cupboard as its position in the building meant it could not possibly lead to a large room. Olivia opened it and went in, leaving the door ajar behind her. Rosetta followed cautiously, and when she reached the mysterious door peeked in at the open crack.

To her surprise she saw stairs, faintly lit by what seemed to be moonlight, going higher still and she felt the chill air of the night flowing down past her to the warmth of the building behind. Climbing the stairs she found that they were short and ended in a small hut that sat on the flat, lead lined roof of the dormitory building. Looking through the door that led out to the open air Rosetta could see no one and assumed that Olivia Rigby must now be somewhere on the roof on the other side of the hut wall behind her.

Going through the door to the roof and peering around the corner of the hut, Rosetta saw a figure approaching the edge of the building, and as it got there it gave a sudden skip and hopped over the rim. Rosetta nearly screamed as it looked like the person must fall to their death, but it was it was a good thing that she did not, for the figure did not fall and simply stopped as if it were hovering in mid-air; its torso and head shining in the moonlight. Rosetta realised that, unless the girl was floating, there must be a hidden ledge sticking out of the wall and it was on this that Olivia Rigby now stood.

Once she was sure of her balance Olivia Rigby turned to her right and started to walk, and as she did so the visible part of her started to drop down and Rosetta realised that there must be some stairs that led down from the roof.

☙ ☙ ☙ ☙ ☙

Karl was running late. His parents had not gone to bed until half past eleven and he had had a nervous moment when the latch on his window had made a loud clang as he opened it. His parents had woken up and he had been forced to jump into bed with his clothes on as his father checked the house. A further half an hour wait for everyone to settle meant that it was half past midnight by the time he got into position by the boys' dormitory of Oldmere School. He had been waiting for some minutes, his eyes glued to the exit of the girls' dormitory when he felt a sudden pain in his ankle.

"And what are you doing out and about at this

time, Mr Bastion?" said Musty, who has sneaked up behind and given him a gentle nip just above the top of his trainers. He looked like a teacher about to tell off a naughty child, if that was possible for a badger, and so Karl told him everything.

"So you are saying that, you have let Rosetta follow someone, by herself, at night; someone who may well be unbalanced?" said Musty snorting somewhat.

"I'm here to help. I didn't want her to go by herself."

"They could be anywhere," muttered Musty, ignoring what Karl had said. "They could be anywhere. I don't supposed it occurred....", but Karl never did learn what had not occurred to him, for Musty had stopped mid-sentence his ears twitching. "Get down!" he whispered, and such was the urgency in his voice that Karl dropped to his knees straight away.

"Up there," said Musty lifting his head towards the dormitory building.

Karl looked up and noticed for the first time, though he must have seen it hundreds of times before, an old staircase built out from the wall of the dormitory building. The structure was more noticeable tonight because there was now a figure visible in the moonlight using it to creep down towards the ground.

The staircase had collapsed some ten feet from the base of the wall and when the figure reached that point, it bent down, fiddled for a second and then pushed down a coil of climbing rope. Quick as a monkey the figure climbed down and, just as it reached the bottom, Musty gave a hiss. Karl looked up and noticed another figure starting down the stairs near the roof. The first person, now identifiable as Olivia Rigby, strode off down a path that led down the steep grassy slope towards the School Gatehouse. She passed quite close to where Musty and Karl hid, and after she had passed Musty muttered to himself "She's one of the two the other night or I've got no nose."

By the time Olivia Rigby had disappeared over the brow of the hill, Rosetta had completed the descent and stood at the foot of the rope looking around wildly. She had seemingly lost track of her quarry.

"Over here." hissed Karl half standing. Rosetta rushed over, smiling when she saw Musty by Karl's feet.

"Did you see her?" she said, and when Karl nodded. "We have to be quick or we'll lose her."

"You forget my nose Miss Clarence," said Musty. "She'll have to swim the river to lose us now. I'll go and check." and he quickly ran off down the hill towards the path, which Olivia Rigby had just walked down.

The children started to follow when they heard a voice from behind them, a girl's voice. They turned and saw a figure dressed, as they all were, in black. The figure also wore a balaclava that served only to emphasise the bright emerald eyes which shone from the eyeholes.

"Why do you interfere? Who are you two? Well it matters not, you will no longer be any trouble to me, or to this school." And with a cold laugh the figure raised its right hand, as it had done with Musty. Karl immediately felt a huge weight appear on his back and dropped to his knees. The figure started to laugh but then paused, unsure, when it noticed that Rosetta still stood tall, seeming unaffected by her actions.

As soon as the girl in black had started to gesture, Rosetta had felt, not a weight, but a lightness that started in her feet, spread up her legs and ended in her hands. Her arms flung themselves out from her sides, seemingly of their own violation and she stood there on tiptoe arms spread like she was going to embrace someone. Then suddenly, like someone had switched on a light bulb, light flashed from her hands. The gloves withstood the blast for a second, the light leaking out the bottom, but then they exploded into nothing, the material gone in a flash, leaving her hands blazing like beacons in the dark.

As they blazed the balaclavaed figure was blown off her feet. She skidded across the wet grass and landed at the foot of the dormitory wall. She raised her head and fear was visible in her emerald eyes. She got to her feet as the light started to fade from Rosetta's hands, and then without a word dashed to her right off into the hotchpotch patches of darkness amongst the school buildings.

Musty came rushing back. "Who made the light?

That girl Olivia has seen it and stopped; she might be coming back any second." he paused, when he saw Rosetta staring at her hands in disbelief. "What is the matter? What has happened here?"

"I think we have had an encounter with the second person you saw the other night." said Karl. "Rosetta.... stopped her though, and she fell there." Karl was looking at Rosetta in a very strange way. Then realising he was staring, he pulled himself together and said. "Can that famous nose of yours tell us where she went?"

Musty went and sniffed the patch of squashed grass where the figure had fallen. He said "This way!" and then ran off in the direction of that the figure had taken. With a glance behind to check that Olivia Rigby had not come back up the hill, the children followed.

As they entered the clutter of school buildings that spread down the hill from the dormitories, the air changed. A sudden chill spread, and as it did so a mist started to shimmer amongst the grass. It quickly rose and after only a few seconds it was ankle deep.

"This mist is a problem," said Musty "it is thick and is interfering with my nose. It rose too quickly - I do not like it." But he continued to snuffle in the grass, though he moved forwards slower now.

Still the mist rose higher, making the shapes of the building hazy and unfamiliar. After just a few minutes it was thick up to their waist, and they could not even see Musty. Higher up it was less dense, but it had made everything indistinct and Karl was no longer sure he knew where in the school he was.

"We must stop," said Musty after only a few more seconds. "This fog is not natural. I am sure it is created to deceive our pursuit. I cannot smell anything; the water in the air swamps any scent. I cannot see anything down here, and I doubt it is much better up there with you longshanks."

Karl nodded and said. "We should get back to the rope. They will have to get back into the school that way. All the outside doors are locked."

"Yes," said Rosetta, "but I'm not sure that I could find the way back now." And as they looked around they saw that the mist was now so thick that it was almost impossible to see the buildings around them. In the end it was Karl who suggested that they should just go up the hill until they hit the dormitory buildings.

"Those old buildings just line the top of the knoll, so we must be careful not to go to close to the cliff. However we'd have to be very unlucky to miss all the buildings, and even if we do there is a fence across all of the cliff edge.

So Musty and the children tiptoed through the impenetrable fog. It was by now so dense that a hand held out at arm's length was invisible even if you waved it, and the children had to move forward with their hands out in front of them like they were blind or in a pitch black room. Eventually Rosetta's hands touched stone. Then they turned right until they found a doorway which was quickly identified as the entrance to the Assembly Hall; the fog had confused them so they had wandered well away from where they thought they were. From there it was easy to make their way along the walls until they found the corner of the building. They followed it round and headed to the hidden staircase where Rosetta and Olivia Rigby had climbed down.

There was only grass on the floor below the broken stairs. Someone had got there before them, climbed the rope and pulled it up behind them.

Besides losing their quarry this also meant that Rosetta was stuck in the grounds out of bed and with no way of getting into the school buildings. The only hope of getting her in was to somehow get hold of Marcus, and get him to let her into the dormitory. They could not phone from where they were as mobile phones did not work in Oldmere vale, and were banned from the school anyway. After some discussion, they decided that Karl would have to go back to his house and phone Marcus from there. Fortunately the fog was now dissipating in a sudden wind, a turn of events that made such a plan possible.

So after waiting, shivering by the dormitory door for half an hour they were eventually greeted by a grim faced Marcus who simply opened the dormitory door and said, "We will talk about this tomorrow evening." leaving Rosetta to climb the stairs to her bed for the very few hours of sleep still available to her.

They did all meet in the antechamber the next night. Marcus, sitting back in a high backed armchair, listened to their story with grave attention. When they had finished he sighed and said, "I won't tell you off, for what you did turned out to be very useful. Next time however can you please let me know what you are planning so I can at least do something to help." His fingers tapped out a rhythm on his artificial leg.

"So what have we learned from this? We know with certainty that Olivia Rigby is one of the two figures that Musty saw by the archaeological dig. We also have confirmation of something we knew before. That one of these people, a girl it seems, has strange powers. The power to subdue enemies, and it also looks like she can affect the weather or at the very least create fog. I think we are agreed that last night's mist was strange and likely unnatural. We also know something new; this person cannot use these powers on Rosetta, and that if they try then it backfires.

"It also looks nearly certain that Rosetta's hands light up when there is an enemy nearby; very useful, if occasionally inconvenient.

"What we do not know is what Olivia Rigby and her mysterious colleague are up to, which is why Rosetta started out on last night's adventure in the first place. After this they are going to be very cautious. I fear we will get no other chances to follow them and find out. "

At this Musty spoke up, "Well we don't need to. Just because my nose was blocked up with water last night, does not mean that I cannot follow a trail in the grass in good weather. So early this morning I went down to where Olivia Rigby went last night. I found her trail from yesterday and could make out her movements from that. After she saw the light from Rosetta she wandered back to the rope, taking a round about route so as not to be seen. After that she must have just climbed the rope, and either she or the other person just pulled it up to prevent pursuit.

"Down at the bottom of the hill there were also old trails from previous journeys; old but still fresh enough for me to follow. So I did, and they took me to the farm buildings down by the entrance to the school. There are loads of farm animals living there and enough poo to cover the trail of a rotting skunk, but I can tell you that Olivia Rigby has been there several times over the last few weeks; there are several trails of varying ages leading towards the buildings."

Marcus smiled broadly, and said, "So thanks to Musty, we do not need to follow any more; we can just wait."

They set the trap on Saturday and arrived at the farm early. Marcus had warned the farmer that they would be there - a school project he had said - and so all they had to do was hide. Musty was sent to watch for Olivia's arrival; she would be visible for a long time if she walked down from anywhere near the school and Musty did not suffer from the human failing of impatience. Secure in the knowledge that they would be forewarned of any approach, the children and Marcus lay in the hay and settled down to wait for Olivia Rigby to arrive.

They did not even have to wait very long. After about an hour Musty rushed in and reported that a girl was approaching along the tree line on the opposite side of the farm to that which they had expected. Olivia had gone all the way around the playing field and followed the edge of the woods in order to try and remain unnoticed.

"What she is trying to do here must be important," said Marcus "to risk it so early in the day. I was expecting her to come around dusk, maybe before dinner. She certainly can't do whatever she is doing at night any more. I persuaded the caretaker to change the lock on the door to the roof yesterday so she can't get out of the building that way."

Marcus and the children hid themselves in various places around the old barn; Musty beneath an old tractor. It was not long before Olivia Rigby walked into the farmyard. She was cautious, listening carefully before she even approached the buildings, but whether she was watching for the presence of the farmer, or of someone else it was impossible to say. After a while seemingly satisfied she walked straight into the barn where the children hid and then, also without hesitation, she approached a part of the haystack which seemed rather messy and disorderly, like it had been repeatedly disassembled and thrown together again.

She started to pull away bales until, after a couple of minutes, she revealed a small alcove in the side of the haystack about the size of a wardrobe laid on its side. It was filled with large bags and metal barrels like those used to store beer. She shifted the bales strewn about in front of this recess so they formed a wall which shielded her activities from the main farmyard. She then pulled things out from the alcove and spread them out in this newly formed workspace.

Rosetta glanced over to Marcus's hiding place. Only his eyes and the top of his head could be seen, but with a short nod and glance towards Olivia he made his meaning plain; they were to move out and make their presence known. Rosetta looked over to check that Karl has seen Marcus' signal and as a result was a little late in coming out of her hiding place. Marcus was already halfway across the gap to Olivia Rigby by the time she appeared from behind an old combine harvester.

"Olivia," said Marcus raising his hands in a calming motion. Her head snapped around. Her eyes were narrowed and her face strangely intent, like that of a snake. She crouched, ready for action, and then without any further hesitation made a dash for the exit to the barn. Marcus, his leg making fast twists difficult, could only make a desperate lunge as she passed to his left. Then, just as it looked like she was going to make it to the gate, a body came flying from out of nowhere to her left, grabbed her waist and pulled her to the ground.

Karl struggled to hold her down as she tried to get up. She was several years older than him, much stronger, and it told as she staggered to her feet. By then, however, Marcus had got to her and swept her feet away with his artificial leg. He loomed over her and she almost snarled as she realised she was caught.

"Not now, not when I'm so close," she spat glaring at Marcus and Karl - Rosetta hung well back afraid that her hands might flare if she came too near.

Marcus leant over and grabbed her hand, not roughly, but leaving no chance of escape. "Let's go and see what we have here." he said, and her dragged the girl towards the barrels and sacks.

"Fertiliser, acid ... and other stuff all too familiar to me. I'm afraid Miss Rigby you're going to have to explain to me why you have all the ingredients of what looks to an old army man very like a bomb factory."

"Explain to you! I'll not waste my breath. Your puny little mind would not understand what I'm trying to achieve here. It would be like a snail trying to understand the building it crept up." She spat at the ground and would say nothing more, but merely smiled as if satisfied that at least she still had the power of silence over her enemies. To complete her non-cooperation she then refused even to stand, and collapsed her legs leaving Marcus looking slightly foolish holding her arm up in the air.

Marcus stared at her for a second, decided that argument was useless, and said, "Then we'll have to see what the head, and I fear the police, have to say about this. I can't think of anything more serio ..."

"Wait!" It was Rosetta, who was still standing several yards back. During the brief exchange a feeling had welled up in her chest. In nature it was similar to the feeling that she got when her hands started to behave strangely, but this time it was subtly different. The feeling spread through her, giving her confidence and an instinctive knowledge of what she should do next. "Wait. Let me talk to her."

"Who are you child? Why should I speak to you any more than this cripple? In fact I would rather talk to you less as I do not like your face, or clothes. You seem poor and stupid to me."

Rosetta said nothing, but approached the girl and as she did so her hands began to glow, as she knew they would. Olivia shrank from the light, but did not seem to realise that she was doing so. It was instinctive like Rosetta's hand each held a snake.

"Olivia Rigby, you will tell me what you have done here?" Rosetta's voice was quiet but exuded authority, and with those words she reached forward and grabbed the girl's shoulders. As she did so her hands, which had been glowing with a smouldering intensity suddenly gave an intense flash which momentarily blinded all those who watched. When everyone's vision cleared it was quickly apparent that something was different about Olivia Rigby. Her eyes had softened, and Marcus was no longer holding the hand of a sitting child, but was suddenly supporting the dead weight of a body that was no longer capable of supporting itself. For a second it seemed like there was a green mist which snaked around her head, but in a second it had evaporated.

"What ... what have you done to her." said Karl looking slightly panicked.

"Wait I'm sure she will recover.' said Rosetta in a calm voice that did not really reflect what she felt. The light from her hands had extinguished, as had the confidence that had come with it. But even as she spoke Olivia Rigby snorted, her eyes focussed somewhat better and she sat up slightly.

"Where am I?" she said. She seemed dazed and vague, but an evil influence was gone.

"You are at Borden Farm, in the barn." Marcus said looking at her intently.

"Oh have I finished then? I feel that somehow I must have finished." Olivia seemed to be relieved.

"Finished what, Olivia?" said Rosetta.

"Well I had to make that device," she flapped her hand in the direction of the barrels. "Something, or someone told me how to do it. The fertiliser was already here, which was what gave me the idea in the first place... at least I think it was my idea, things have been a bit funny the last few weeks."

"Can you go through those weeks for me Olivia?" said Marcus, his eyes watching intently.

"Well when I first came back to school things were alright for a few days. Then I started to feel funny. I can't remember when exactly. I started to get tired and rather... bad tempered. Then I knew that to get things back to normal I had to get rid of that crack in the Archaeological dig. Someone, I can't remember who, told me that, and also how to do it.

"You see if I made some explosive materials and pushed them into some barrels then I could put these barrels near the crack and blow it up. Then I'd be back to normal. I could maybe win the Archer prize - you see I've been letting some of my work slip recently... Not sure why.

"So I got some instructions from the internet on how to do a bomb. That was stupid though - someone told me off for doing it. The police might have tracked me. But anyway they didn't, and I had most of the stuff I needed to get it done. Someone showed me how to get out of the dormitories at night so I came here and started to make the bombs." she giggled. "Sounds bad when you put it like that doesn't it"

Rosetta took Olivia by the hand and said, "I think that perhaps you need a little rest. I think that you will feel much better when you wake up. We can take you back to the school. I think that after a sleep you will wake up back to your old self."

※ ※ ※ ※ ※

"She won't remember much of the last few weeks I'm sure, at least nothing that has anything to do with those pipe bombs," said Rosetta back in the antechamber.

"Those were a bit of a joke anyway." said Marcus. "I was in bomb disposal in the army, and I can tell you they had about much chance of blowing up that archaeological dig as would popping a balloon. It is rather like all the other strange things that these pupils have been doing; they are all amateurish. It is like whoever was directing them really did not understand what they were asking the children to do, or perhaps the children get the desire, the hunger to destroy the Archaeological dig, from whatever is affecting them, but the plans come from their mind and as a result are childish in nature. All these schemes really achieve is to get the child in trouble."

"She won't be will she?" said Karl. "Get into trouble I mean. I'm pretty sure that something was affecting her mind - it was weird."

"No I won't be telling any of the teachers what actually happened. I'll get some help to check she is OK though - I'll mention I saw her behaving worryingly or something like that. With all that has been happening with the other two pupils that should be enough to make sure she gets looked after."

"There is a good chance she will not even remember the last few weeks lessons." said Rosetta. "That alone will put paid to her chances of the Archer Prize. I suppose she is lucky to be still in the school."

"The Archer Prize.... The Archer..." said Karl to himself. "All the kids who have been affected have been in the running for that haven't they? That's not very likely to be just a coincidence is it? How many slots are there? Five boys and five girls go up to London in May for the final tests when the winner is decided. With these three gone then the list is down to seven now - Olivia won't have a hope now surely. There are about thirty or forty kids in year thirteen, so the chances of our mysterious enemy randomly attacking Archer prize kids are very small.

"So you are thinking that these kids have been targeted because they are in short list for the Archer prize? ... I must admit that the numbers do make that likely," said Marcus, rubbing his face and looking thoughtful.

"We mustn't forget the other child that is mixed up in this. The one that seems to be behind it all," said Karl "If they are in the running for the Archer prize as well, then all these kids getting knocked out would be good for them - it makes them more likely to win."

"But no one would be that mad would they? I

mean it's just a prize isn't it?" said Rosetta." I mean this person seems to have great power. They wouldn't need to use them just to win a prize? I mean it looks like they can control people, make them do things that they wouldn't normally do why bother using that just to win a prize?"

"I don't know Rosetta," said Marcus. "If you win the Archer prize then you get to go to Politics and Economics at Munsford University. That is a where every person who is clever enough - or more to the point has enough money - goes if they want to join the Government. If you have these abilities, if you can control people, then that would be an ideal place to be. Why try to become prime minister if you can just control whoever does?"

And why work to win the Archer prize to get to Munsford, when you can just get all your competitors to just self-destruct?" said Karl his eyes shining. "I mean that would explain why all these kids have been doing such stupid stuff wouldn't it? Whoever is controlling them doesn't want them to actually achieve anything. They just want to get them caught and thrown out of school."

"OK," said Marcus. "Let us assume that we are right in all this and that is what out mystery person is up to. Can we use it? Is there a way of working out who it might be?"

"They would have to be in the final seven for the Archer prize," said Karl.

"I'm pretty sure they are a girl from their voice, they have green eyes and they are probably in the swimming team," said Rosetta. None of the other three kids affected were swimmers, and my hands went off that day whilst I was waiting by the pool. So there must have been have to be someone inside the pool that day wouldn't there?"

"Those things taken together should be enough to identify them," said Marcus, now smiling. "I'll ask about the Archer prize tomorrow, and also about the swimming. Then we shall see.

"But we mustn't forget one thing. Whoever the mystery person is, there is more to this than meets the eye. All that has happened revolves around that archaeological dig. The controlled children all wanted to destroy it in some way or another. There is something in that pit that is the root cause of this and we still have no idea what it is, and no way of finding out."

Chapter 6

From a diary found in the mud.

My power waxes. I feel my strength grow. The loss of Olivia Rigby is of no consequence, beyond her removal from the Archer Prize. As each of these foolish children falls my victory becomes more certain, my path to the people of consequence clearer.

Of more import is the child, the girl with the power who confronted my Acolyte and bested her. She must be my hidden enemy; the one I have waited for these last months. I had thought that in these modern times the old powers had faded in to nothing, that once I become free I would be unmatched in my abilities. Perhaps I must reconsider this. The power of this girl matches that of some of my ancient foes.

I will set my acolyte upon her. There will be no

more frivolities, the remaining entrants in this Archer Prize can continue unmolested for now my target is this unknown girl. From the moment I knew her, I knew that she is the real threat and must be removed at all costs.

Chapter 7

Marcus and Karl find a way of finding out.

It was late the same day, and Marcus Vates lay back on the sofa in the antechamber considering the events of the last few months. He had come to the position of the custodian of Oldmere School Library with little concept of what to do once he arrived, viewing the school simply as a refuge from the pain caused by the sudden loss of his family. Wounded both physically and emotionally he ran to the familiar surroundings of Oldmere School with the sole aim of settling into the panelled comfort of the antechamber, and perform the light duties required by the school until he could rediscover what to do with his life.

Despite these intentions the mystery of his father's disappearance had taken over his thoughts, for Marcus could not help but believe that he was still alive. This was partly, he would secretly acknowledge, because the thought was a great help to him during a difficult time in his life. His mother had died when he was very little. His father and sister were all the close family he knew, and the fact that both had died at the same time left him lost and alone. He felt this more keenly because of the bond that his father and sister had shared. The bond was one of knowledge, the knowledge that being one of the anointed members of the family brought.

He had pondered the meaning of the scrap of paper found at his father's empty desk endlessly, until out of the blue the arrival of Rosetta, Musty, and all the other strangeness that came with them, had provided his swirling mind with a dual release; a puzzle to solve and the possibility of the rediscovery of his father.

It all hinged on this "Folio". Marcus felt instinctively that this item was part of the mysteries that were handed over when a member of the family was appointed. Perhaps it was a kind of handbook that would explain all, and make this strange business at the school clear; perhaps at the same time revealing some family secrets. He now had a clue he did not have before - his father's letter from the secret compartment - and he was determined to exploit it as much as possible.

He got up crossed over to his desk and took out his father's letter and read it yet again.

Marcus

If you are reading this, then you will have received my letter and found the vault under the floorboards. It also means that I am not here to tell you of things in person and my worst fears have proved to be well founded. If that is the case, then take the Folio from the vault and read it. You must then do as you see fit, for once you have my letter and have read the Folio then you will know as much as is needed.

A word of warning; do not take the Folio out of the Antechamber. Once you have read it then put it back in the vault and seal it. It is the only copy and is precious, irreplaceable. To lose it would be a complete disaster.

Burn my letter after you have memorised it.

Remember whatever happens I love you as I did your dear sister.

Your loving father

Atticus Vates

Besides emphasising the importance of the Folio the mysterious note also gave two other pieces of information. Firstly his father had sent him a letter before his mysterious disappearance, and that he had done so because he was concerned about something. Marcus had not received any such letter from his father which could possibly be the one referred to here, but that was not necessarily very surprising. It must have been sent around the time he was wounded, and that had been a time of great confusion. He had been rushed out of his desert army base to a military hospital as quickly as possible and his personal effects had only arrived a couple of weeks later in a cardboard box. He could well imagine that many things had got lost or misdirected in the jumble of events about that time.

Secondly his father's last letter instructed him to never remove this Folio from the antechamber once he had recovered it. From this Marcus felt with reasonable certainty that his father would not have done so himself, and that the Folio must still be in the antechamber, assuming it had not been stolen.

Frustrated he got up from the couch, wincing as the socket of his false leg rubbed against the scars on his stump. The letter from his father to him in hospital was the key to everything. It must contain the complete story. He could not imagine his father failing to pass on the secrets of the Custodians if he thought that he was in any danger, as he plainly had done.

Marcus racked his brain, but nothing would come, and so giving up he walked out of the antechamber. He locked it carefully behind him and limped into the Reading Room. He crossed over, winding between the tables, unlocked another door and climbed a small staircase built into the wall. This led up to the custodian's apartments; a large flat set-aside for those custodians who were not yet married. There was a small house in the grounds for those that were. His father had moved out of that eight years previously, after his children had grown up and left the family home.

The staircase came into the living room through a hole in the floor. Marcus stopped on the top step and looked around. There were still many of his father's possessions scattered about. Marcus had not had the heart to clear them out and he was just thinking that he must get around to it soon, when he noticed a small plastic bag sat on a small table that he had not opened or even thought about for some time.

It rested on a pile of old photographs, and contained a mass of his father's letters to his sister. Her husband had sent them back some time after her car accident thinking that they might be of some comfort to the old man. Marcus had not read them; he was afraid that he might find them too upsetting at the time, and since then he had just plain forgotten about them.

Now however he realised that they could contain some important clues. Both his sister and father were appointed, and he felt they were sure to discuss things in these letters that they might not in a telephone conversation. He limped over to the table, grabbed the bag and sat upon an old wooden chair to read.

The letters covered the two months before his father disappeared and seemed to be simply those of a loving father to his daughter. He was pleased to read that whenever he was mentioned it was with affection, and concern about the dangers he faced in the army. They contained nothing explicit about the situation at the school. There was not even any talk about the archaeological dig, even though the dates of the letters showed that his father wrote them about the time when he was known to be very agitated about the prospect.

Marcus found this unusual. But it was not the only strange thing he found. Occasionally the letter would break off without warning, and there would start a whole section of random numbers - sometimes interspersed with the odd word. The numbers were grouped in threes joined by a comma. Marcus looked at an example:

345,23,5 45,6,4 34,5,6 230,23,2 48,12,7 34,21,4 67,34,6 56,15,8 67,15,6 89,14,3 49,13,3 48,24,14 antechamber 173,16,5 292,3,2 13,2,2 47,15,2 67,16,12 93,12,11 321,19,1 429,29,9 90,11,4 374,1,2 462,8,5 86,9,7 82,6,8 61,12,6 20,24,13 370,27,11 63,12,5 15,31,7 57,20,7 480,2,9 92,1,4 37,26,11 460,21,12 326,7,6 120,8,14 321,22,3 396,3,9 22,1,8 330,24,4 425,5,11 128,22,12 361,13,13 24,15,14 69,17,4 12,1,2 230,30,1 77,14,8 230,15,4 412,11,9 75,12,5 90,10,8 344,5,6 128,11,10 326,25,14 127,22,15 235,19,11 27,18,10 33,13,8 57,32,9 431,17,4 246,10,2 287,4,12 155,22,11 238,8,10 Oldmere.

At first glance it was incomprehensible, but he knew what it must be; a code. The groups of numbers could be translated into letters or words - probably words he thought looking at the size of a typical passage - but to do that you needed a key; a list of what each group of numbers meant. A simple one would be that each letter corresponding to a number; 3 meant A or 7 meant C for example. But this one was obviously more complicated than that.

In secret codes, this list of meanings, the key, is usually kept in a special codebook. The book would have to be well hidden because once an enemy had that book he or she could translate any and all of the so-called secret messages.

Marcus looked about for something which might be the codebook that was used to make these messages. His sister must have had an identical copy to her father - the book obviously could not be sent along with the letters. But he thought it likely that his sister's copy was gone; her husband would have no inkling that his father-in-law might want it and would have just kept it in storage or thrown it away, rather than send it to his father on his wife's death. But his father's book must still be at the school.

He went over to the bookcase to see if his father kept the book there, unlikely as that was. However scanning the lines of books he did see something that caught his attention. It was a volume - read many times by the state of the cover - called "Cryptography Through the Ages - a history of codes and code breaking". Marcus smiled because he was sure his father must have used this to help him devise whatever code he used to talk to his daughter, and there might be some clues as to how to break it hidden within.

After an hour of reading Marcus was becoming discouraged, he had read the chapters on transposition and substitution cyphers, but had found no help there. He was halfway through the chapter on book cyphers and was beginning to wonder how he could possibly begin to make any progress on such a complicated subject, when he noticed something that made him sit up.

Under some - a very few - of the words in the book he could make out a small, delicately placed, pencil dot. They were very faint, deliberately so Marcus thought and he stopped and flicked through the rest of the book. Yes all through the book there were these dots under some of the words. He went back to the chapter he was reading, and went through it carefully. After he had finished it, he smiled and set to work.

♣ ♣ ♣ ♣ ♣

"It was very lucky that I happened to be reading that particular chapter when I noticed the dots," said Marcus to the children the next day. It was a Sunday, and they had come up to the antechamber after Marcus had sent Musty with a message to come as soon as they could. He had explained what he had discovered the night before to their rapt attention. "I would never have made the connection otherwise. "You see a 'Book Cypher' is when you code a message using a book you both own as the key; a novel or other innocent volume, not a special codebook. The numbers in the passage refer to the page number, the line from the top and the word number. If you have the correct book all you have to do is go through the book and pick out the words that make up the message. Some of the words he needed aren't in the book he was using, which is why he had to write them in in plain text."

"Yes, but we don't know what book your father was using," said Rosetta. It could be any in here or even in the whole of the Old Library.

"Yes, but when I noticed the dots in the book I was reading it occurred to me that the book I was reading might be the one that contains the key."

"What you mean 'Cryptography Through the Ages' might be actually the key?" said Karl.

"It is the key," said Marcus. "It is just like my father to make a code breaking book the key to a secret message. He always used to say to me 'Hide things in plain sight Marcus. People never see what is right in front of their noses'"

"OK so what does he say?" said Karl, sounding impatient.

"Well most of it is not very instructive. There are things like "try to make the meeting in London on Monday 24th" or "The dig is going ahead I will phone later this week" which either tell us nothing, or something and nothing at the same time. Most are very short. But there is one passage that is very interesting. Here I'll read it out."

"'Remember that the hidden office must always be closed and locked. The antechamber is not completely secure and people can make their way in if they are determined. These days I have a bad feeling and some of the signs are not good. I think that the time might actually be coming once more. We must talk when you next come to Oldmere'"

"So there is a secret room." said Karl. "And that must be where the Folio is hidden. I mean perhaps he put it there when he felt that the antechamber was no longer safe."

"That is what I think also."

Everyone looked around the room, seeing it in a new light. If Marcus was right then somewhere amongst the walls lined with books there was a room, a room that must surely hold the secrets of the Custodians of Oldmere School; but where to start?

"I have tried behind the bookcases," said Marcus. "I have pulled every book off the shelf and none opens a secret compartment. Banging on the wooden backs produces a uniformly hollow sound, so unless there is a hidden room behind every wall then we cannot use that as any reliable clue."

There was a debate about how to proceed without much progress being made; Musty had been dispatched to see if his nose could find any strange smells or unexplained draughts, but had found nothing. Marcus and Rosetta were just on the verge of persuading themselves that perhaps the entrance to the hidden room might actually be somewhere else, perhaps in the Old Library, or hidden even deeper in the tunnels of the Ancient Library.

"The cypher does not actually say it is hidden here," said Rosetta studying the piece of paper that held Marcus's handwritten translation.. "All it says is that the door must be locked because the antechamber is not secure. It could be that it is actually in a place that may be reached from here."

Throughout this last discussion Karl had remained silent looking thoughtful. Eventually he said, "Have you measured the room?"

The other three looked at him in surprise. "A room takes up space in the building. You cannot change that fact. If it juts into a next door room you will be able to "see" it by measuring the distances, or if it is stuck onto the outside of the building you should be able to see that from the outside."

"Well," said Marcus after a few seconds, during which he appraised Karl with a small smile on his face. Rosetta looked disappointed, like she wished she had thought of the idea. Musty made no comment, but was cleaning his tail a sure sign that the conversation had lost him for the moment. "That is a rather good idea. We can check the outside wall pretty straightforwardly." And with that he got up and walked to the window, opened it and leant out.

"Can someone take hold of my leg? I need to lean

out further ... no not that one Karl, my good one." Holding on to the window frame with one hand and with Karl holding onto his outstretched leg, Marcus looked left and right, up and down along the outside wall. With a grunt he swung back into the room grinning from ear to ear.

"Well, I think we may have it. If you two take turns leaning out, and if you look down and to the left you will see a large stone object sticking out from the other side of this wall," he slapped the wall near the window. "It looks like it is located below the fireplace in this room."

The children leant out of the window one by one, and saw what Marcus meant. As they looked out of the window, the stone wall of the building spread away flat and featureless except for one place, just below the main chimney of the antechamber where a large mass of stone jutted out.

They wandered over to the fireplace and looked at it with some interest. It was obviously old. Wide enough one could imagine to take a large fire and roast an animal, as would have happened in Tudor times. It had not been actively used for some time though - there was a large wood burner that now provided heating for the room in winter - and the stone on the inner wall was now clean and soot free. The iron door of a bread oven stood chest height to one side. Marcus considered it and said, "Now I don't know much about the history of the school, but I do know that this room, the antechamber has never been a kitchen and what is more it is far too small for such a large fireplace."

Rosetta was thinking hard, trying to catch up with Karl for his cleverness just before, "... and what need has such a room for a bread oven?" and with that she leant over and opened the metal door and peered inside."

At the very back of the oven she could just about see a metal ring. She reached in and pulled, as she did she heard a clunk as some mechanism engaged, and at the same time felt a tremor that quivered up her arm. After a second or so, a section of the sidewall of the fireplace moved out, gently nudging her shoulder as it did. Turning, she grabbed the edges of the door and pulled as she did so. It moved further out and swung in a tight circle, finally settling against the back of the fireplace. It left a narrow hole though which an adult could just about squeeze provided they were not too large. Through it Rosetta could just about make out a sloping passage that swept down and to the left disappearing into darkness.

"I'll go and get a torch." said Marcus.

The passage was narrow and dropped very steeply making progress very difficult for Marcus who went first. It would have been impossible for him but for a guiding rope that was attached to the passage wall which acted as a makeshift banister. The children followed more easily and Musty took up the rear. After only three or four yards Marcus said "We are here." The children craned their heads to see past him. This was more difficult than normal as he was much taller than them, and his body filled the entire width of the corridor.

Marcus reached to one side, grunted in mild surprise, turned on the light switch he had not expected to be there, and took a step forward into his father's secret office.

It was tiny. A bookcase at one end filled the whole wall. A large wooden beam, as wide as a kitchen worktop and stretching the length of the room, jutted from the wall at waist height. It plainly served as a desk, for a modern chair was pushed underneath at its middle, and papers were scattered along its length. At each side of the chair, and also pushed underneath the wooden beam, were a couple of small old fashioned metal filing cabinets. A bare light bulb dangling from the ceiling lit the area with a soft glow. The general impression was that of a prison cell, but a very comfortable one.

The children stood back whilst Marcus quickly went through his father's papers. After a minute or two he stopped, rubbing his eyes, and said, "There is too much to get through here today. I'm tired - I was up very late last night - and it would be best if we all went back home and got some rest before tomorrow."

"But tomorrow is a school day. We won't be able to come back here properly until next Saturday," complained Karl. "I cannot possibly wait that long to find out what's hidden here."

"If I find anything important I'll ask for you at lunchtime. Until then you will just have to be patient," said Marcus. "It is going to take me a while to go through all this, and I do have the library too look after as well."

So the children were reluctantly taken upstairs. It took a while to work out that the door to the secret office closed by merely pushing until a loud click echoed around the room. After a quick check to ensure that they could open it once more, the children were taken through the Reading Room - Musty went through the Ancient Library to the tunnel in the cliffs - and ended up at the main entrance of the Assembly Hall. It was drizzling in a horribly persistent way.

"Now remember to be on your guard. Keep an eye out for any children behaving oddly. Rosetta let me know if your hands so much as twinkle near another student. I'll find out about the kids still in the Archer prize when the school office opens tomm ..." Marcus stopped suddenly as he heard a sudden crack from above. Rosetta glanced up and froze in horror as she saw a large stone gargoyle slowly topple from its mount at the very top of the building. It was right above them, and started to descend, seemingly in slow motion.

Rosetta and Karl stood watching in mute disbelief, rooted to the spot mouths open stupidly. Marcus however did not hesitate. He moved forward and half-pushed, half carried the two children away from the spot beneath the falling sculpture. With a final shove the children were pushed away from danger, but Marcus, unbalanced by his final effort, fell and to the children's utter horror they watched as the gargoyle landed on the man's legs.

Marcus yelled and the children got up and rushed forward. As they came over they saw that Marcus was swearing and sitting up, which seemed odd given that he must have suffered a very serious injury.

"For pity's sake, that is the last straw!" said Marcus as the children looked at his lower body with some trepidation. "It will take forever to get a new one made up, and until then I'm on bloody crutches."

The gargoyle had struck Marcus on his artificial leg missing his intact one by centimetres. His fake leg was completely smashed however; the metal that made up the limb was twisted like scrunched up aluminium foil.

"Help me get up," said Marcus raising his arm to the children. After a bit of a struggle they managed to get him to his feet. He leaned on them, looking up and said, "Did you see who did it?"

"Did it?" said Rosetta. "Surely you don't mean that you think that was deliberate? It's an old building."

"This building gets checked every holiday to make sure it is OK for the start of term. There is no way that was an accident. Someone pushed it over."

The children helped Marcus up to his apartment. Marcus declared that he would not let the children up onto the roof to see the place where the Gargoyle had sat.

"It is too dangerous," he said. "I want you two to go home now. Go via the gate in the cliffs, not through the school. That person may be waiting for a second attempt. Go straight home and do not mess about. I'll phone the headand let her know what happened. I will not tell her that you two were nearly hit. There will be enough trouble about this as it is."

♣ ♣ ♣ ♣ ♣

At assembly the next day Marcus was there looking tired. The gargoyle had been tidied away and the main entrance to the Assembly hall was closed off with orange tape - the pupils had to stream in through a little-used side entrance to get to the Assembly hall. Later in the day a hard-hatted builder could be seen walking on the roof talking to the head and pointing to various structures

At lunchtime Karl and Rosetta went to the Reading Room and found Marcus sat at his post as normal, except now a set of crutches could be seen poking above the top of the desk.

"The builders have looked on the roof. They think that frost got into a crack in the stone and caused the gargoyle to fall," said Marcus in a low voice so that the other students scattered around at the antique desks would not hear. " They have gone around the whole of the roof and found no evidence of any further problems. So the official line is that it was an accident, but I do not believe it. I want you two to be extra careful from now on. If you come here at weekends make sure you are not alone, and preferably are with each other, or Musty.

"Also you can come after lessons tomorrow afternoon, but not tonight. I need time to have a look about that office of my father's by myself." He held up his hand as the children started to protest. "I will tell you everything that I find, if I can, but I would like to look alone to start with. Come tomorrow afternoon, and we shall see what I've found."

The children reluctantly went back from the reading room and went to lunch wondering what secrets the hidden office might hold, and if indeed it held the Folio.

"What nothing?" said Karl.

"I have only just started really," said Marcus. "There are a lot of documents. It seems that the Custodians of Oldmere are very thorough record keepers. There are records from six hundred years ago up until today. But nothing at all interesting to us, receipts for books, bills newspaper cuttings, nothing that refers to anything out of the ordinary. It looks to all intents and purposes like an ordinary office that might be in any small business except it is very old and there is no evidence of any business beyond that of running a small library.

"There must be clues to something," said Rosetta. "You don't have a secret room for no reason."

"Well the books in the book case are interesting," said Marcus. "They are all about the old religion of Britain. You know the one that existed before the Romans came, and well before Christianity. Some of the books are extremely old - taken I suspect from the Library - but there are some modern ones too. The Custodians seem to have had an interest in such matters for some time. I found a receipt for one of the books in the shelf from 1753.

"You know what that makes me think of?" said Karl. "The ancient site in the dig. The archaeologists said it was pre-Roman and that must mean it must have been part of the Old Religion."

"Yes," said Marcus. "But what the phrase 'Old Religion' exactly means is very hard to discover. The people who followed the Old Religion did not have writing, and so we know very little about what they believed. The books in the office cover a whole range from modern archaeological texts to some of the old Roman histories. It is probable that none of the various theories describe what actually happened in these islands during those ancient times. Beyond telling us that the Custodians were interested in the Old Religion I suspect those books will be rather uninformative.

I will continue to search the office for other clues, and you can come up on Saturday to help. Up until then I will be much happier if you are tucked up safe in your beds."

The rest of the week went according to the same pattern; the children would catch Marcus's eye during Assembly and he, with an almost imperceptible shake of his head, would tell them that he had found nothing. A quick visit to the Reading Room at lunchtime would confirm this. After a couple of days like this Marcus stopped the children coming.

"People are beginning to notice," he said. "People your age are not supposed to be interested in the Old Library." And indeed during their visits the Reading Room had been mostly scattered with older children and adults. "You'll just have to come at the weekend and find out what I've got then ... yes if I find anything earth shaking I'll let you know but apart from that you'll just have to wait.

So it was with considerable excitement that Rosetta and Karl waited by the door in the cliff wall - Marcus had forbidden any visits to the grounds out of school hours because of the risk that the children might be vulnerable to attack. They crouched down behind the bush that covered the entrance to the tunnel, so they might be hidden from casual observation, and waited for Marcus to arrive and open the gate to let them in.

They were shocked when he arrived to find him pale and ill looking, with Musty following at his heels somehow managing to look disapproving. "Come in," he said. He leant on his crutches, to leave his hands free as he fiddled with his keys. "I have got something to tell you. Nothing good though.

"I've been foolish," said Marcus as they went through the door to the antechamber "I have underestimated our opponent. They are clever and daring, *and* because of my stupidity they now know of the existence of the Custodians secret Office."

"Whaaat," said Karl. " How?"

"Last night I was in the Library sorting some books for lending to a foreign University. They had to be sent off first thing and that meant working late. I had just come back to the antechamber with some books and I had a fleeting impression that the door to the Reading Room was swaying slightly, like someone had gone through just a few seconds before. I had a look and saw nothing unusual and so I put it down to me being unusually tense because of all the things that have been happening this week. I finished my coffee, sat down at my desk and started to do some paperwork. After a couple of minutes I started to feel a little strange, light headed and queasy.

"And that is the last thing I can tell you about until I woke a few hours ago, still sat in my chair in the antechamber, with a terrible headache and a strange taste in my mouth. I straightaway realised that I must have been drugged by something in the coffee."

"I'm amazed you didn't smell it - the drug that is - ten miles away," said Musty dismissively. "It practically smelled worse than the foul coffee drink itself. You deserved the headache."

"Thank you Musty," said Marcus with a sigh. "Anyway I checked around the antechamber to see if anything had been tampered with and all seemed OK... until I went up to check my apartment. The whole place had been turned over and it became pretty obvious that the only thing that was missing was the translation of the bit of code from my father's letter."

"What is the point of having a secret code if you just leave the decoded message just lying about?" said Musty with a snort.

"Thank you *again Musty,*" said Marcus. "But now they must know that there is a secret office, and they have as many clues to the office's location as we did last week. We discovered it with little trouble.

"We must be very careful now. I strongly suspect that whoever did this may have had something to do with my father's disappearance. And if that is the case then they are extremely dangerous, even to me. They may do anything to discover what we know"

"And how much do we know now?" said Karl. "What have you found in the office?"

"Nothing in the papers," said Marcus sighing. "They are just a load of administrative waffle. A historian might find them interesting as they say a lot about how the Library grew and developed - you know bills, letters from collectors of rare books and so on - but they say nothing at all about the what the Folio, is and what the custodians are really up to. I've read all them and there is nothing. At the moment I'm wading through the books, the ones in the book case in the office, but there is not much even in them."

"Can I - I mean Rosetta and me - have a look at the papers?" said Karl. "There might be something you've missed ... I mean a second pair of eyes can do no harm." he added seeing the look on Marcus's face.

"Of course you are right, given the mistakes I made over the last few days I can imagine there is a good chance I've missed something." said Marcus with a sigh. "I'll carry on looking through the books and you can have a good time reading Victorian accounts."

♣ ♣ ♣ ♣ ♣

Rosetta's heart was not in it really. Marcus was right, she thought. There can't be anything amongst this lot - she eyed the pile of papers with boredom - it really was like reading a load of her mum's letters from the bank. Karl however was tireless. He read each document with close attention before eventually placing it on the growing pile of documents classed as of no interest.

She looked around the Secret Office. There was only just enough room for her and Karl to sit - Marcus had taken some of the books up into the antechamber so he could read them without bumping elbows with the children - and she thought again about how it was really far too good a place to be wasted on a plain old office.

"Look here!" said Karl. "There is a mention of the Folio here ... it's easy to miss - it's in a note at the bottom of an invoice."

Rosetta looked over Karl's shoulder at the piece of paper he had been reading. It was, like many of the papers, a bill. This was from a blacksmith for a large quantity of lead sheet. It was old written in neat calligraphy. She followed Karl's finger to the bottom of the paper and saw that there was something scrawled across there in faded ink.

'Have we enoughf monies for thyss? The Folio groweft large and is precious and I must needs enfure a solid futyre. The old playse is subect to rain and wind now the garderobe is removyed".

"It's from 1606," said Karl pointing at the date. "And if I'm reading this correctly then the writer is saying that the Folio's hiding place is no longer safe because it is exposed to bad weather - what's a garderobe? Never mind we can work that out later. So he ... or she is looking for a safe place to move the Folio to, and he is buying a load of lead sheets."

"The secret panel we found in the floor is lined with lead." said Rosetta, becoming interested. "It could be that she ... or he, was making the hiding place we found a few weeks ago in order to keep the

Folio safer. So there might have been an older hiding place."

Karl grinned at her and said, "And if Atticus Vates was worried that someone could find the Folio where it was...."

"Then he might have moved it back to its old hiding place ... assuming it still existed, and assuming he knew where it is. That is a lot of mights and assumptions - and even if they are all right it also doesn't bring us any closer to finding it ourselves."

"Maybe, maybe not. Let's see what Marcus thinks." and they ran upstairs to where Marcus was snoozing over an open book.

"A garderobe is an mediaeval toilet," he said when they had roused him. "Buildings back then didn't have running water or waste pipes, so what they used to do was make a bit of the building stick out of the wall so that there was a clean drop to the ground. Then they'd make a hole in the floor, usually with a stone seat over it so you could sit down and then, well all the waste would just drop to the ground below. They usually made them so it dropped into pits or rivers so it wouldn't get too smelly.

"So this note says that they removed one - they became unfashionable as soon as plumbing was invented - and that meant that the Folio suddenly became exposed to rain and wind."

"So your ancestors kept their most treasured possession in a toilet," said Rosetta raising her eyebrows.

"It doesn't actually say in the toilet," said Karl "it just says that the Folio became exposed because the garderobe was removed.... I'm just wondering." And with that Karl walked over to the widow. He leant out as they had done before when looking for the secret office.

"Look," he said. "To me it looks like there used to be an extra room stuck on the side of this one." He came back out and looked at the edges of the window. "And this wasn't always a window - medieval buildings didn't have them, too cold and glass was expensive."

Rosetta pushed past and looked out of the window and, now she was looking for it, she could see quite plainly a line of stones in the wall that were quite different to the others. A line that mapped out what was obviously the remnants of a room; one that had been removed like it had been sliced off the side of the building by a big knife. The outline included in its perimeter the window, which Rosetta could now see might easily have been a door to the room and it also butted up right against the wall of the secret office.

"That old room would have stuck right against the secret office. They must have been right next to each other." said Rosetta. "And so if the garderobe – assuming the missing room was a garderobe - was removed then parts the wall of the office would suddenly be exposed to the weather."

Everyone looked at each other for a second, and

then Marcus said, "I think that Karl should go down to the Custodian's office and have a careful look at the walls. If anyone deserves first go at this, then it is him; anyway there is not room for everyone down there."

Karl squeezed through the narrow entrance to the office and Rosetta could hear his voice, simultaneously muffled and echoing, coming up the narrow passage.

"I'm looking along the wall that would have been next to the garderobe - the one behind the desk. It all looks very solid to me. Very hard to imagine anything hidden here." There was silence for a few minutes until Karl spoke again, excitedly. "I've got something. It's right near the ceiling in a corner. The stones are loose."

At this Marcus, unable to contain himself any more, wriggled through the gap and made his way down the stairs.

"Thanks Marcus ... yes take that one from me. I think it is the last one. What's this? Ohhhh"

The minute that passed next seemed to Rosetta to last a year. Eventually the light coming from the passage flickered as Marcus came up the stairs and blocked the light from the office. As he came to the top she could see that he held something that lay on top of a plastic bag.

It had to be the Folio.

Chapter 8

The truth is out!

The children trudged in torrential rain across the fields towards the knoll in a state of great anticipation. Musty trailed them in the hedgerows, occasionally dashing out into the fields when some of the drainage ditches overflowed into small lakes which blocked his path. It was a week after the discovery of the Folio, a week of worry and frustration for the children. Marcus had said that he could not allow the children to read the book with him as it could contain information only meant to be read by an anointed Custodian. Whilst the children could see his point, they had an almost overwhelming urge to just go over and sit by the back door until he let them in or gave them some information. They were curious to the point of distraction. On top of this Rosetta was worried that their mysterious enemy would not be idle during this time and might somehow get hold of the Folio before Marcus had completely read it. They had been bold and clever enough to find the hidden message in Marcus's apartment after all.

So the days had passed like this and on the last Saturday before the Christmas break Marcus had eventually sent Musty over to the village to collect the children so he could relate what he had discovered.

"Don't ask me what," Musty had whispered from out of the hedge near the tree house. "He has hardly said a word during the last week so deep has he been in that book."

Making the quick dash up the side of the cliff towards the back door and the cover of the hawthorn bush that grew over the path to the gates, they were soon pushing at the cold metal bars, only to discover that the gates were locked. Musty nuzzled through the gap at the side and made his way into the tunnels. He came back holding the key, which he dropped by the children's feet.

"He is finding it hard to come down here now his leg is bust," said the badger with a snort. "And so now I have to be butler as well as sentry and messenger boy."

The book had been placed in the middle of the desk in the antechamber. Marcus sat in his normal chair, looking more refreshed than they had seen him for some time. The ancient volume looked as it had done a week ago. The Folio did not resemble a normal book. It had a large soft and ancient leather cover decorated with intricate patterns of swirls and knots. Inside there was a large mass of paper made up of all sizes, types and ages. This rather disorganised jumble was held together at the spine with a series of thin leather laces. It looked rather like a very large wallet packed with money, receipts and the detritus of everyday life. But this wallet held something quite different, as Marcus now began to tell.

"The Folio is in reality a kind of collective diary, or a notebook that the Custodians of Oldmere used to record both their thoughts and any important events that affected this hidden part of their lives. There is no other information here. No personal or family records, no comments about the history or times in which these people lived, unless they impacted upon the mission of the Custodians.

"So it is not is the detailed manual we hoped. It does not tell us about what is to be anointed or relate what happens when you become anointed. It assumes a background level of knowledge about the position of Custodian that I do not possess, and that makes it very difficult sometimes to understand what is written here. It is written for other Custodians.

"Before we start on the contents of the Folio, I need to tell you a story. It is a story told in our family for generations, which I have heard many times before. But I did not know until now that it relates so closely to what is happening in the valley today. I thought it was simply a history story passed down the family.

"The tale is first told in the Folio in Latin, and is written on papyrus. It tells the story of a Druid who was captured by the Romans as they fought their way into Wales. All members of our family know it, it is told every Christmas after dinner, and it is important you should hear it"

And Marcus started to speak, his voice changing, becoming more formal as he did so like he was reciting something learned by heart.

"This is a story from when the Roman invaders came to take the kingdom of Kymyr that is now known as Wales. There was a druid, captured by the Romans, who was to be sold as a slave. He tried to save himself from this fate by giving a warning to the centurion who had taken him prisoner."

" He said, 'Do not pass through that valley ahead, even though it may seem your best way forward, for the druids there have called up a foe who will lead to the ruin of your troops. Your armies will fail. They will turn their swords upon themselves and be blind to the existence of the enemy, who will then enjoy a great slaughter. It is only I who can prevent this, for I was one of those who called the Morrigan from the sacred lake.'"

"The Morrigan?", said Karl.
"I will explain later."

"The Centurion ignored the druid, as he thought that the druid was lying, playing for time in order to save his life, or even that the man was protecting some secret treasure hidden in the valley. So he marched his troops onward through the narrow pass that marked the entrance to the valley. As they entered, fording the steam near where the fortresses now stand, a thick fog fell, rolling down from the woods as if some kind of dam had burst from above"

"The Roman troops were enveloped by the fog and also by the spell of confusion that was woven into it. This spell made things appear in the mist - shadows in the shape of men - and these ghosts drove the Romans mad with fear. The army scattered in disarray, men swinging their swords at all that came close, be they real men or phantom shades; many were killed by their comrades; many by the black arrows that suddenly shot from out of the mist."

"The centurion lost and confused, came by pure luck upon the river, and using it as a guide he waded downstream following the flow until he eventually found that he could see once more and that the magic fog had gone. Looking back he saw a wall of mist hanging unnaturally across the gates to the valley and he knew that the druid he had captured had spoken the truth."

"So he brought the druid before him once more and said, ' If you can remove the mist and help me take the valley beyond, then not only will I free you from slavery, but I will make you and all your family citizens of the Roman Empire. You shall have

dominion over the valley beyond and shall have great power and wealth.'

" The druid agreed, but said one thing to the centurion. 'I will raise the mist and make your enemies visible, but one condition'"

"'Speak", said the Centurion.

"'In the centre of the valley you will find a sacred hill..."

"Oldmere Knoll!", said Rosetta. " Could he have been talking about Oldmere Knoll?"

"Likely he was", said Marcus. "Or so I believe. Anyway the druid's warning went thus;

'On this hill you will find three men, druids of our tribe, guarding the path to the sacred lake. You must leave them unharmed, for if your men kill them then it may not be possible for me to control the evil spirit that they raised to protect this valley.'"

"The centurion, minded this time to pay attention to the druid, gave instructions to his men that all people found on the knoll were to be left unharmed."

"And so he ordered his men to move forward as the druid started to chant a spell from behind. As he did this the wall of mist collapsed and fell away in a carpet of smoke that rolled past the feet of the advancing legionnaires."

"The Celts that guarded the valley were then exposed to view and they quickly fell to the swords of the Romans. The army stormed through the valley until they reached the foot of the great hill. Here

they stopped, mindful of their captain's orders concerning the people on the hill."

"And it might have remained so, had not an arrow fired from the heights struck the centurion in the thigh causing him to fall with a cry of pain. His men, enraged at the wounding of their captain, stormed the hill crashing through the defences until finally they reached the top."

"On the summit they found three old men, who stood in a circle chanting around a sacred lake, and in their anger they slew them all. As the third druid fell the last remains of the mist vanished, and the lake began to boil. The legionnaires closest to the water turned, madness in their eyes, and fell on all who stood nearby, Celt and Roman alike."

"And just as all seemed lost a voice was heard, a voice singing from below. It was the druid, who climbed up from the valley his staff held aloft, chanting in the language of the Celts. As his voice floated over the water of the lake, it ceased to boil and all who were mad regained their senses. He approached the edge of the lake and drove his staff into the ground near the edge crying out as he did so. There was a great commotion in the water as he did so and the water was seen to slowly disappear from the lake until all was left was a muddy hole."

"'You fools', cried the druid. 'Those druids who you have killed had raised a slave from the lake and now that slave, unbanished by those that called her, may return. I have sent her, the Morrigan of water back for now, but she will return again and again to

plague the people of this valley."

"The centurion, carried up from the base of the hill an arrow in his thigh, said 'Druid, you may have this valley. You have the authority of Rome and may do what you will in this place, but in return you and your descendants must guard this place for I fear evil now dwells here."

"Well there is a lot more ... mostly about what precisely the druid now owned in the valley - like an ancient legal document", said Marcus. " But the summary is that the druid agreed to the centurions terms, became the local governor of the region and lived happily ever after."

There was silence in the room, which Karl eventually broke "Emily Watson wrote something about a 'Morrigan' when she smashed up the dig, didn't she? So is everything happening here linked to that story?"

"Yes. My family is directly descended from that Druid. The Folio makes clear that the Custodians of Oldmere are here, not as academics protecting some ancient books, but as guards of a more literal type. We watch and wait for the return of the Morrigan and are here to protect the valley should that ever happen. Ever since the Romans, there has always been a place of learning here where the Custodians could hide in plain view. A Roman temple, a celtic shrine, a monastery and finally a school."

"Oh come on," said Karl. "How likely is that? I mean your story is just a legend. It probably has some sort of basis in truth, but in reality it is just a myth."

"It is true. According to these writings," and Marcus indicated the open Folio. "She has already come back; five times in total, and each time the Custodian has driven her back. There was one almost straight away, just a few years after the original story, another time in the dark ages, a couple in medieval times, and once in Victorian times. That last one was touch and go apparently. It had been so long since the last time she had risen that the Custodians had stopped believing, thinking the whole thing based on medieval superstition. They were nearly overwhelmed as a result. It made the national newspapers. You can look it up. People at the time put it down to some sort of mass hysteria, but the Custodian recorded what really happened.

"Every time she comes back it is the same story. People start to behave oddly; previously honest men start to lie and deceive, women murder their husbands for no reason people can fathom, and generally there is a distorted, strange atmosphere in the valley. The centre for the strangeness is always the knoll and it usually relates to some kind of building or excavation happening near the summit of the hill. When this was realised - during the Tudor period, at the time this building was put up in fact - the Custodians realised that part of their job was actually to make sure that no one started digging around the top of the knoll. By Victorian times they had forgotten and they allowed the new boys dormitory to be put up. And this year...

"They started the archaeological dig!" said Rosetta. "So your father realised and tried to stop it, but could not and so the Morrigan is back again."

"Yes it looks like it. I do not think that the person we are dealing with, the one you encountered the other night, is actually the Morrigan though. I'm not sure she can come physically to our world, not yet at least. The Folio talks of an "Acolyte" that the Morrigan chooses. One that she can possess, or control to a great extent, and that person can use the Morrigan's power to help her become completely free. So she can go out into the world and cause all sorts of trouble."

"So," said Karl. "What is the Morrigan? And how do we stop her? And what do you mean by 'completely free'"

"The Morrigan is the name given, by the ancient Celts of Britain to a Goddess. Not a nice one either. She is associated with war, strife, deception and madness. She has four aspects, each associated with one of the elements; water, fire, air and earth. She is meant to cause confusion in battle; just for the fun of it the legends say. She would turn a battle into a slaughter, forcing friends as well as enemies to fight each other if she felt like it. She is associated with flocks of ravens.

"In the story, the Druids raised her to protect the valley from the Romans and when they did so they called her aspect as the Morrigan of Water so they could use her to raise the fog. When the Roman legionnaires killed the druids that had raised her, they ensured she could not be properly banished, for only those who raised her in the first place could do that.

"As for 'completely free' I mean this; the Folio says that when the druid drained the sacred lake, the Morrigan was trapped in a sacred place, a kind of prison apparently somewhere in the centre of the knoll. When the knoll is disturbed, by building work or other disturbances then she can extend her influence out from her prison and start to create trouble in the valley. Then the job of the Custodian would be to make their way to the sacred place and re-do the rite that the old Druid used to trap her in the first place..."

"Which is what has happened before," said Rosetta.

"Yes. The Morrigan's aim is to get her Acolyte to this sacred place and to completely undo the power that traps her. What happens should that happen is not clear, but most of the old chaps here," Marcus pointed to the Folio, "seem to think that she could completely possess the Acolyte and then wander the world effectively as some kind of malevolent super human."

"So let's go and do the rite and just send her back to where she came from, and stop this nightmare from continuing." said Karl, obviously relieved that there was a solution the problem.

"But we can't," said Marcus, looking particularly

grim. "The location of the sacred place and the details of the rite are not in the Folio. They must be part of the knowledge that comes with being anointed. That knowledge was passed on by word of mouth only. It might be in the letter sent to me by my father when he realised that he was in danger. But that letter is lost. The knowledge we need is not mentioned anywhere in the Folio."

"So we cannot beat her," said Karl. "I mean if we cannot completely repair the damage done by the archaeological dig then she can just bide her time and eventually the Acolyte will find the sacred place and free her."

"Yes and no," said Marcus. "There are only two pieces of paper in the Folio from Roman times. The first details the story I've just told you, but the second is very different and is much discussed by later custodians. It is a poem, in Latin, you know some of it already. The translation goes something like the following:

Morrigans four were forged in hell
Water, fire, earth and Air
Guard the Knoll for that is first
Guard her, who will break the spell.
Know her by these signs four
A Badger is her Avatar first
The Outsider is her fraternity
She destroys deceit, finds fortune.
A Glyph she will save us all

Water is her first test
The rest will follow
Last of all she will defy.
Lost, last and unappointed.
Despair not, and watch.
Watch for the brock girl,
Watch for the alien boy,
Watch by the arrowhead.
She will show the sign,
And follow,
She will show the sign,
And uncover.

"Not very good, but perhaps the translation does not do it justice."

"The last two verses are the same as the piece of paper that they found on your father's desk!" said Rosetta.

"Yes," said Marcus. "I think he must have copied them out, and was studying them just before he disappeared. And it would not be the first time those words have been studied. The Custodians have debated the meaning of them endlessly over the centuries, and there is a general agreement that it is a prophecy written by that first ever druid. A prophecy that looks now very interesting. Don't you think Rosetta?"

Rosetta was standing with her mouth open. "You think that refers to me somehow? I mean it does mention a badger, but I mean that is not much to go on. It could just be a coincidence."

"I would agree with you," said Marcus "if it were not for what is said in the Folio about this prophecy. These words have been studied and sieved for meaning over two thousand years and there are many different interpretations as you might imagine. However some of the research has uncovered some interesting facts.

"The word 'Glyph' in the translation comes from a Celtic word. That Celtic word 'gyfrinllythyr' is translated as Glyph in the poem, because it can mean something like 'secret letter'. But what it actually refers to is a specific thing in Celtic mythology. It took out one of our Victorian Custodians to dig that out from one of the books in the Old Library.

"A gyfrinllythyr, or Glyph, is a very special type of person. Someone who is sent by the gods to bring order and truth." Rosetta started to object at this, but Marcus held up his hand. "Hear me out. There are many powers attributed to a Glyph in various texts, and not all of them agree with each other, but there are some that are common to every description.

"A Glyph is immune to the magic of others, they cannot be manipulated or tricked by any power; they are always true to themselves. As well as this they can sense deception and things that have been hidden. They can expose lies. The power comes from a Glyph when it is needed. One may lie dormant for years, or indeed their entire life; their power comes out when he or she is threatened or needed by others. And when their abilities do come out, they acquire a 'familiar' - an animal that becomes an extension of themselves. Here let me read an extract from the Roman Historian Livitus. He is describing a time when they had a Roman agent working amongst a tribe of Celts they were fighting.

"The gyfrinllythyr exposed our spy; a great light came from him and shone upon our man. The people knew the meaning of this and went to capture our spy, knowing him now for what he was. He escaped and reported to us. He told us that if we should see the gyfrinllythyr we would know him straightaway as he was always accompanied by a talking eagle, which was his familiar"

Marcus sighed and said "What has been happening to you over the last few months can be all explained by you being one of these Glyphs. You were immune to the strange power that our opponent, the Acolyte, tried to use on you and Karl. In fact it rebounded upon them when they tried. Your hands glow when you come close to one of the people affected by the Morrigan, and they are practicing a deception if ever there was one. You can even discover things that are hidden as you did when you looked that first day in the antechamber."

There was a pause and Karl spoke. "It does make sense of what has happened to you and why it only started when you came to Oldmere. Before there was no danger or need for your... abilities to come out so they never did. You just happened to arrive in Oldmere when all this stuff was starting up."

"Yes .... I suppose it might be so," said Rosetta anxiously "But I can't control it! My hands just start glowing at all times of day and night. I wear gloves when I can, but I can't wear them all the time, people think it's weird.

"I don't want to be one of these Glyph things!" she exclaimed. "I don't want to be part of some thousand year old prophecy and have bits of my body exploding whenever I go near the wrong person."

She stopped feeling foolish for her outburst, and just sat there pouting. Karl saw her face, and seemingly unable to help himself, started to smile. Rosetta glared at him, angry for a second, but then after a moment or two gave also a rather sheepish grin.

Marcus looked at them both, a strange expression on his face, and then said, "I think you will be able to control it Rosetta Clarence. You are new to this ability, and you are bound to have difficulties at first. Also up until now every time it has happened you have been stressed or distracted. Next time it comes on try to control it - go somewhere private if you can - and just concentrate and try to stay calm. I'm sure in the end you will master it."

"What about the prophecy?" said Karl. "What do the old custodians have to say about that?"

"They say lots. The prophecy has been discussed endlessly and mostly fruitlessly. We have found out more in the last few weeks than they found out over the last couple of millennia. We know what the last two verses mean, or I think we do. I am the "Lost, last and unnapointed'. The brock girl is you Rosetta and the alien boy is you Karl. Those verses are instructions to me, which I eventually followed only because my father was studying them just before he disappeared. They tell me to wait by the part of the river called ' the arrowhead' by my family and watch for you two. The rest we know.

"The rest of the verses are fairly clear, apart from the references in the third verse to 'the rest will follow' and 'last of all she will defy'. They predict the coming of someone who will defeat the Morrigan. Someone with a badger Avatar - you could just as easily translate that word as 'familiar' - and a friend who is an 'Outsider'. That is, in my view, a reference to you, Karl, as the Outside Scholar.

"Incidentally 'the arrowhead' is called that because family legend has it as the place where the old Centurion was shot by the arrow.

"So the scene is set. We know what we face."

"But we have no idea what to do," said Rosetta. "The Morrigan is out, or nearly so, and the knowledge of how to put her back is gone. All those times she escaped before - all the Custodians had to do was go to this sacred place and do some stuff and she would be back in her box. The last person to have that knowledge is your father and he did not tell anyone else before he disappeared."

"Actually he did," said Marcus. "The last entries in the Folio are of course written by my father. Amongst other things they tell of his last few months. They make hard reading for me …"

After a short pause Marcus continued; "He tried everything short of sabotage to stop the dig, but the head was completely determined to continue. He even thought for a while that the Morrigan might have subtly influenced her, but in the end he decided she was just being stubborn. And so he was rather stuck. He could not really resign, though he threatened to do so, because he needed to be in the school. But experience had shown that to allow digging at the top of the knoll could easily lead to trouble.

So he was already in a state of alarm when my sister had her accident; he was extremely upset by that. As well as the normal feeling of grief at her loss, he knew that I was the last of the family who could take on the role of Custodian – our family has dwindled somewhat over the years -and I was in a dangerous job in the army. He tried to get the army to release me so I could come home, but before he could do that I was caught in that explosion; suddenly he was alone.

"He put all this down in the Folio as he thought they might be the last ever entries made in the book. He really thought that he was going to be the last of the Custodians of Oldmere.

"To add to his feeling of isolation he found someone looking around the antechamber one night

- they escaped before he could see who it was - and he realised too late that it was likely the Morrigan had already possessed someone in the school. He states in the Folio that he wrote a long letter to me in hospital. It explained things and attempted to give me the knowledge I would need to take over should something happen to him. In effect he tried to make me appointed in a letter. As I have said I never received this letter, and its current whereabouts is unknown.

"His last note in the Folio explained he was going to move the book back to its old hiding place in the secret office, as he thought it more secure than the box under the floor, and then he was going to perform the ritual to banish the Morrigan from this world. The entry is dated the day he disappeared. I feel that he knew something was going to happen - the last words he wrote were 'Custodimus et quaerere'"

Part Three

The Morrigan of Water

Chapter 1

Floods and Chaos!

It was the next day when the rain started. Everyone woke to the blackest of black skies; impenetrable cloud hung low across the top of the valley. The weak winter sun could not penetrate the inky clouds and the darkness was such that it seemed that night had simply continued into the day.

It was mid-morning when the deluge started, and it did not stop. Endless sheets of rain lashed down on the already saturated land. Cows stood miserably under leafless trees in a vain hope of shelter; brown rivers flowed down country lanes; the rain soaked through the land until it seemed that its very bones were liquid. The soil bled water; rivulets flowed from the side of any slope and cars, lights shining in the darkness, crept through part-submerged roads.

On her way home from school Rosetta stopped on

the bridge, ignoring the downpour, so she could look at the river. It was already near flood. Its surface was just below the top of the bank, and it flowed in the twilight with a dusky blackness that spoke of freezing cold and danger.

Karl ran over his umbrella up. He held it over Rosetta and said. "If it doesn't stop in the next day or two the river will burst then we'll have an interesting time. Oh don't worry it never gets high enough to flood any of the buildings in the village, or the school, but all the fields will look like a big lake with just the roads and buildings sticking out. I'll get my canoe out of the shed and we can go exploring the fields once it's calmed down. It's quite safe as long as you stay away from where the river is - the current is too strong there."

Rosetta looked down into the swirling blackness and felt a faint stirring in her stomach. She felt this wild intensity could not be natural like it was directed. Like the weather had intent, a purpose;

"Let's go home," she said. "I need to dry out."

⁂

Karl ended up having dinner at her house that night. There was a tree down further up the valley and the road was closed whilst the council sorted it out. Karl's parents were on their way back from a trip to the town and were stuck whilst they waited for men with chainsaws. Rosetta and Karl sat on the sofa in the living room and spoke in whispers whilst Mrs Clarence beetled about in the kitchen

"So Marcus's plan is to wait until next term?" said Rosetta. "We've a whole week of school to go until the start of the holidays and I have a feeling that this acolyte person is in a hurry."

"Yeah I know, but Marcus wants to hold back. He says that we can't do anything until we know how to defeat the Morrigan. He wants to go back to his old army regiment and make enquiries about that letter his father sent. It is bound to contain details about what we should do in this situation, about how to deal with the Morrigan. His father said as much in his diary entries in the Folio. Everyone at school goes home at Christmas and we will have time here that the Acolyte does not. They'll be stuck at home eating turkey, or whatever and we will be here getting ready for when they come back. We might even get it all finished before school starts again."

"Yeah," said Rosetta, glancing at the TV. Aimee was sitting cross-legged in front of the screen watching men in fluffy suits jump around a brightly coloured studio. "But I have a feeling that they will not let that just happen."

※ ※ ※ ※ ※

At midnight the rain stopped. And the utter silence coming after so many hours of lashing rain was enough by itself to wake people from their slumbers. For a few minutes there was absolute quiet apart from the rustle of the wind in the trees. Then from the blackness at the north end of Oldmere Vale there came a simultaneous explosion of light and sound that shook every window; it woke every person. Lightening lashed out three times and on the third stroke there came a noise like a thousand aircraft taking off. It grew in intensity for what seemed an age, but must have been at most thirty seconds, until it eventually slowly faded away. Everyone in the valley lay in the darkness of their rooms wondering what on earth the morning would bring.

♣ ♣ ♣ ♣ ♣

When they woke the first thing everyone noticed was that the rain had started again, like it had never stopped. And as people peered through the rain splattered window panes they might have at first thought that, in the confusion of the night, that their imagination had perhaps exaggerated the intensity of the events of the night.

But if they looked over to the Fords End they would have blinked and even rubbed the sleep from their eyes just in case they were mistaken in what they saw. The valley had changed. Where the shoulders of the hills had moved in steeply before there was a subtle flattening. Opening the window gave a clearer view. The whole of one side of the valley had collapsed in a pile of mud, rocks and shattered trees. The ruined towers were gone like they had been in a dream.

Rosetta turned off the radio. She turned round to look at Karl - his parents had not been able to make it home because of the weather and he had been forced to stay in the Clarences' spare room - and then to the other side of the kitchen at her mother. They both looked dumfounded. Overnight their comfortable confidence in nature had disappeared.

"What do we do?" said Karl.

"The radio was quite clear," said Mrs Clarence. "The road to the North is blocked; the tunnel filled by a landslide, caused they think by lightening hitting a slope already waterlogged; to the South fallen trees and general flooding have also made the road impassable. The landslide to the North has also blocked the river and it is backing up the valley. They have no idea exactly what will happen, but they do know that there will be a lot of flooding. They cannot evacuate us all - the whole of the county is in chaos. So we have to do as we're told and go to Oldmere Knoll - it is the highest point in the whole valley."

"Why?" said Rosetta glancing at Karl. "We're high up here. There is no way the river could make it up this far."

"No, but they are going to be dropping food and medical supplies at the knoll." said Mrs Clarence. "I haven't been to the shops for a few days. So before long we'd be hungry and by then we might not be able to make it across to the knoll. No we go now whilst we can. And if it turns out that we can come back, then we will. For now we will have to assume the worst. I'll phone your mother Karl. She will be beside herself, no doubt."

They packed a bag each - Karl went next door to sort out his - and Mrs Clarence packed a clear plastic bin with as much food as she could manage, together with a camping stove, pans and a tent. "You never know what we might be facing over there," she said. "With the whole village moving over it might be quite a squeeze."

At the last minute Rosetta remembered something with a flash of guilt, and dashed out to see if Musty was waiting by the playhouse, which indeed he was.

"Get over to the knoll," she said breathlessly. "This side of the valley may get cut off by water soon. You can stay in the Ancient Library no one will notice."

Musty gave a snort of agreement, licked her boot and dashed off into the undergrowth.

The pile of bags in the Clarence's garage was quite impressive. They simply threw the whole lot into the car and were just about to move off when a man strode up. He was wearing a high visibility vest with the name of the local Rotary Club printed on the front.

"If you're going to the knoll I'd leave your car here. The river's burst its banks by the school entrance and blocked the road there. The only way into the school is via the back now, over the footbridge. I'd hurry as well. The river is blocked and the water is rising at a tremendous rate. By the end of the day the knoll will be cut off or I'm no judge. Just take what you can carry."

They unpacked the car and stood looking at the mound of equipment piled by the boot. Mrs Clarence wrung her hands and said, "What can we do. We'll never carry all this over and I need it all." She glanced over at Aimee who was playing happily in some puddles by the side of the road.

""I've got an idea," said Karl. "Come with me Rosetta; we won't be long Mrs Clarence."

He led her up behind his house to a lean-to nestled amongst the long grass. Rosetta had only glimpsed it from her garden before, and the view from the top of the playhouse did not show what was inside. There were three canoes lining the walls supported on bars. Karl went over to the smallest.

"We won't be able to handle Mum or Dads they're too big, but this one will be fine."

"We don't need anything else to carry Karl. This isn't going to help."

"No. You don't understand we can put everything in the canoe. We've got carry straps here," and he started to rummage in an old plastic carton. "So we can carry it easily hanging from our shoulders. I wanted to take it anyway - it might come in useful if the whole valley floods - but I knew we'd never get it on top of your car. But now we can use it to carry stuff as well..."

With a bit of careful packing they managed to get

everything loaded into the canoe and arranged the straps so that two people could carry it with not too much bumping against knees. They set off dragging the canoe down the grassy slope that led to the main road. Once they had crossed over and manhandled the canoe over the style, they started the trudge over the waterlogged fields towards the school.

As they did so they joined a rag-tag line of bodies, every one wrapped in brightly coloured waterproofs, which meandered towards the school from the village. Families grouped together for comfort and aid; parents carrying bundled of goods, children holding grandparent's hands; they all walked slowly through the mud and lashing rain.

At the footbridge there was a queue. A teacher stood with some prefects to make sure that there was no panic, and to tell everyone crossing over what to do once they reached the school. As each group approached the bridge the teacher came over, talked for a couple of minutes and then handed over to the prefects who then helped carry the bags over the bridge. Rosetta waited patiently in line until it was their turn.

The teacher was Mr White, who smiled at them, his wet glasses twinkling in sympathy, and said, "I'm pleased you've made it over. If you weren't here soon I was going to send a message to the school to phone your house. The water is rising very fast I'd say we've only two, maybe three hours before Oldmere School becomes an island.

"Now. Once you have got to the school go to the

main hall. There are temporary sleeping arrangements for the villagers there. The children can go into the dormitories if they want, but as the school is now officially closed - yes no lessons, we are not going to insist on *that* - and if you would rather stay together as a family, then that is fine with the school." He eyed the canoe. "You'd better leave that by the Gym. Good idea though, may come in useful!" he smiled, the water dripping from the hood of his waterproof. Go and see Iona there and she'll help you get your boat over the bridge." He moved past them to those next in line; an elderly gentleman accompanied by a middle-aged woman.

As they approached the prefect standing by the wooden steps that led up to the footbridge Rosetta slowed as her stomach started to feel empty and strange. She hung back and shoved her hand deep in her pockets, sure that they would be starting to glow. Her discomfort grew as she approached the bridge, and she felt her hair must be standing on edge such were the shivers running up and down her body, but she remembered what Marcus had said about trying to control her power.

Looking down at her raincoat she saw that from the outside there was no visible sign that there was anything unusual going on. Her waterproof was black and hid the glow well; anyway most people had their head down as the rain was driving almost horizontally, which made looking out into the world somewhat painful. But if she looked straight down the outside of her jacket she could look into the top of the pockets and could just see the glow from her hands leaking out.

She tried to concentrate as Mrs Clarence started to talk to the prefect ahead; the prefect that Rosetta was now sure was the cause of her flare up. She concentrated on staying calm, on filling the quivering hole in her stomach like she was trying to steel herself for diving into deep water from high up, and as her nerves calmed she saw the light flicker and fade. But she knew that it was held back by her will alone, and if she wanted to she could drop her control and bring it out in a second.

"Hello, you must be Rosetta," the voice was close and intense. Rosetta looked up and saw a pair of vivid green eyes looking at her, eyes she knew well from that night up on the knoll. "I've explained to your mother and..." her voiced changed and became menacing "your sister. You have a sister how nice." She paused significantly, and then continued. ""Maria and Laura will help you get your boat over the bridge. And *I'll see you at the school.*"

Rosetta could not mistake the menace in the voice of the girl; the threat to her family was practically stated out loud. Rosetta looked up to see if she could get a good look at the girl's face, but her raincoat was zipped well up well past her chin and her hood was pulled down so all she could make out were those green eyes and a few wisps of wet black hair.

Her concentration lapsed for a second and she felt her power, the power of the Glyph rise. Something must have showed, or been felt, for the girl's eyes widened in surprise and she took a step back. Rosetta controlling herself once more, stepped past the girl and said, with bravado that she did not feel, "Yeah. I'll be seeing you."

The others had, with the help of the other prefect, raised the canoe over their heads and had just started over the bridge. Rosetta, her heart pounding, risked a glance back and saw the figure of the girl, ignoring the family waiting patiently next in line, watching her intently. And as she walked away she felt the tension in her stomach fade to nothing.

She reached the canoe, which was being slowly manhandled, foot-by-foot, over the bridge. There was a prefect at the back supporting the canoe on her shoulder. Rosetta went up to her and tried to help, but really the boat was too high for her to support much of its weight. Instead she turned to the prefect and said, "Who is that prefect there? The first one by the steps."

"Her? You mean Idolater Skane?" she said with a snort.

"Idolater?"

"That's not her real name of course. Iona - Iona Skane. From up North somewhere. She got the nickname because of the old statue she found last year. Keeps it by her bed and won't let anyone touch it." The girl shifted the canoe on her shoulder as Mrs Clarence, who held the front, went down the steps. She looked over at Rosetta as she did so, "Gave you the creeps did she? She's a bit intense, but don't worry about her there's no harm in her really."

Once the canoe was over the bridge, the prefects headed back to help the other villagers waiting to pass over. Rosetta bent her knees, flung the strap over her shoulder, and straightened up to take the weight of the canoe. They set off and started the final trudge over the fields towards the black lump of Oldmere Knoll, which loomed hazily through the rain.

♣ ♣ ♣ ♣ ♣

They unloaded their stuff by the entrance to the Assembly hall, and carried the empty canoe to the gym. Once they reached the hall they saw that someone had set up a desk by the entrance. It was manned by Marcus, who seemed remarkably pleased to see them.

"They've put me in charge of the accommodation here," he said carefully writing down their names. "I'm not much practical help without my leg. I've got a new one coming from the army, but they can't get it here with all this going on. I'm putting you over there, near the reading room. It is near the toilets and other amenities."

Looking over the top of Marcus's head the children could see the hall was filled with camp beds. People's belongings lay in piles next to about half of them.

"The authorities are getting a helicopter to drop some more beds, food and medicines. They will take anyone who is sick or needs regular medicines, but they cannot evacuate us all. So most of us are stuck here until this is over, and god knows when that will be," said Marcus with a sigh. "Once you're settled you should go and have a look from the North end of the Knoll. It's pretty spectacular. Brings it home how long all this will take to clear."

The children went over to their beds and Rosetta couldn't help but notice that, whilst their beds were close to the toilets, they were also the closest to the Reading Room and gave uninterrupted access to the entrance to the Antechamber door. Marcus was obviously thinking ahead.

They unpacked their stuff and, left Mrs Clarence in the hall. Aimee was excited by her new bed, had got into it immediately and was refusing to get out . They left the buildings and went out to have a look at the valley to the North.

Closer to and from a higher spot the devastation caused by the landslide was clearly apparent. The whole of one side of the valley at Ford's End had collapsed. The river had been completely blocked and was now simply pooling in front of the wall of debris created by the landslide. The water had reached well past the gates to the school. The bus stop where Rosetta had once waited to go to school was now at least two feet under. The landslide had spread out sideways as well as flowing downwards and had blocked the road. Only a small black crescent sitting above a pile of earth showed where the tunnel had once forged its way out of the valley.

"Were in trouble now," said Karl. "The acolyte, whoever it is, is now stuck at the school as well. Marcus's plan is dead in the water. We're just going to have to cope with the situation."

"Yeah," said Rosetta glumly. "I know who the Acolyte is though; a prefect called Iona Skane." And she told Karl what had happened by the bridge.

"Iona Skane. I know her; black hair, pretty ... So we now have a name, we can ask Marcus if she is one of the finalists in the Archer Prize."

"She is in the swimming team," said Rosetta. "I remember seeing her name on the team list. She's the captain of the year thirteen squad."

"So now everyone knows who everyone is," said Karl "and on top of that we're stuck together for the next few days at least."

※ ※ ※ ※ ※

Getting to talk to Marcus was very difficult. All the rest of that first day he was busy making arrangements for the refugees from the village who came in dribs and drabs. By four O'clock they had stopped however, and word went around that the water had reached the footbridge and now the only route between the village of Oldmere and the school was by boat. They were all cut off.

The Assembly hall was only about three quarters

full - it looked like a lot of people had decided to stay with their homes in the village - which made life there moderately comfortable. Noticeboards were taken down from the walls and made into makeshift screens so that each family group was enclosed in a sort of cubical, which gave some degree of privacy to the occupants. Karl and Rosetta decided to stay in the hall rather than move to the dormitories; they felt the openness and public nature of the new dormitory gave them some sort of protection from Iona Skane, as well as giving them easier access to the antechamber and Old Library. Marcus must have been thinking along those lines also for he gave his apartments to a family who had many children, and moved down into the Hall. He put himself next to Clarence cubical.

There was only a chance for a few hurried words with Marcus before the whole of the temporary dormitory went to sleep. He laughed when Rosetta ask about Musty. "He has turned up, very wet and rather put out. He had to swim the river by the school gates and did not enjoy it."

After Karl told him about Iona Skane, Marcus became very serious. "Be on your guard," he said. "Don't wander about by yourself. We can have a proper talk tomorrow."

♣ ♣ ♣ ♣ ♣

That night Rosetta woke in the middle of the

night. Her hands shone bright as they lay on top of the bedclothes. She lay still for a second and tried to bring herself under control. She fought the feeling of uncertainty and just plain wrongness that invaded her very fibre and as she did so the glow faded as it had done by the bridge the day before. This time however it was easier, quicker. It felt like the power she had - the power of a Glyph she admitted to herself - was somehow becoming aware of her. That before she had tried to control, it had not even known her and had acted of its own accord, but now aware of its owner, it was learning to take its lead from Rosetta's will.

She sat up and looked around for Iona Skane, for she was sure it could only be that girl's presence that had triggered her power. Now her hands had faded the only light in the Hall came from the signs that illuminated the fire exits, and in this strange green glow things seemed indistinct, unreal.

As she looked over towards the Reading Room she became aware of a bright white light that lined the door to the Antechamber. Someone was in there. A quick glance told her that Marcus was asleep in his bunk so it could not be him, the only person who is officially allowed into the ancient library. She reached over and shook Karl. He did not wake. She sat up, swung round so her feet were resting on the floor and shook harder to no avail. "Karl," she whispered in his ear, but there was no response. In turn she tried to wake Marcus, her mother and even Aimee, but they were all unmoving, breathing slow and heavy.

Rosetta felt that this sleep could not be natural. Her new sense, power of the Glyph, made her aware of it. She reached out with her mind releasing the power as she did so and her vision changed. She could suddenly see a red mist hovering over the sleeping bodies, a mist that curled around their heads washing through their hair and passing through their nostrils and out of their mouths. Rosetta reached out toward the mist that enfolded Karl and saw that it pulled away from her hand like it was afraid, but if she drew her hand back then the mist returned, caressing Karl's face and hair. Thinking for a second she then placed her hands upon his chest and freed the Glyph power, releasing it into her hands.

Her hands did not glow, but she could see faint glimmers, like sparks, flashing under her finger nails and seeming to pass from them into Karl's chest. His lips glistened with power and she could see a golden glow leak from around his eyelids. The red mist shot back from Karl fast as a snake and he snorted as his eyelids flickered.

Rosetta snatched her hands back and whispered "Karl wake up. Someone is in the Antechamber." But even as she said it she somehow knew that it was no longer true. She looked up and saw a black figure dash from out of the Reading Room. As it ran Rosetta saw the red mist start to disappear. It was being drawn to the person now running through the maze of beds. She, for Rosetta was sure that this figure had to be Iona Skane, leapt over beds and knocked over chairs as she made her way to the door out of the Hall. All effort of secrecy was gone. Rosetta stood ready to chase, but it was already too late; the figure was already at the door and then disappeared into the corridor beyond.

Rosetta rushed over to the antechamber door, which was somehow unlocked, to check to see if Iona Skane had discovered anything there. But the room looked untouched and Rosetta felt that the search had been disturbed perhaps by her attempts to awake Karl. Maybe Iona, as the Acolyte, could feel when her power was interfered with.

She left the antechamber, just pulling the door closed as she could not lock it. Rosetta stood in the dark and watched as the last of the red mist faded into the air. Karl turned, once more deep asleep, and Rosetta, feeling helpless and alone turned towards her own bed. It was several hours before she too drifted into oblivion.

※ ※ ※ ※ ※

Karl woke her excitedly a few hours later.

"Quick, come when you're ready. Everyone's going to look." and with those words he rushed off out of the hall.

The hall was empty and Rosetta realised she had overslept. She got up, pulled on her clothes and followed Karl out of the main doorway. The whole of the population of the Knoll - both school and village - made their way to the edge of the cliff to see what the night had brought to the valley. The rain still fell; an endless deluge that sapped everyone's energy and spirit.

The valley was unrecognisable. Only at the very southwestern end could any green fields be seen. The river had taken the rest; a sheet of wind-blown water stretched from one side of the valley to the other. There was a ribbon of turbulence spreading through the middle of this strange lake which was the only sign on the surface of the river that still flowed in the depths. Looking behind her Rosetta saw that even the playing fields, which sat a little higher than the main valley floor, had large puddles spread evenly over them. It would not be long before they joined together to complete the knoll's new status as an island.

As she stood on the bluff of the cliff Rosetta heard an occasional dull croak from above amongst the school buildings. Looking behind she saw that on every window ledge, on every chimney there sat a black bird. The school was covered in Ravens.

Mr White who stood next to her followed her gaze and said, "They turned up yesterday. Most unusual. Perhaps their normal nesting site has been damaged by the weather. There are a lot of trees down around the county."

She watched the birds for a second and then turned back to watch the scene again only to find Marcus and Karl standing in front of her.

"Come we've a lot to discuss."

In the Antechamber Rosetta interrupted Marcus before he could start, and told him about what she had seen the night before.

"Unlocked!" said Marcus. "I'm sure I locked it last night. But then again perhaps she just made me think I had done so."

He fell silent for a bit looking very concerned and then said, "So you think that it was Iona Skane? Karl has told me all about her. If she has the power to do that - open the door somehow, make everyone sleep - then that is concerning. I'm worried that she might find a way to find the Folio or even discover the sacred place of the Morrigan." He paused thinking, and Rosetta spoke up.

"Who is she? Do you know of her?"

"I've asked around and I'd bet my other leg that she is the one we are after."

"I know she is - I recognised the eyes at the footbridge yesterday, my hand glowed and she practically admitted it."

"Yes and there are some other things that count against her. She was the one to start the whole thing going with the archaeological dig. I asked the school secretary and she told me the story. It was Iona Skane who noticed, towards the end of last year, something in the in the ground near that old celtic cross. She dug and found an ancient statue. She took it to the head. A bit of investigation told them that it was likely to be the figure of a preroman goddess - a very rare find. The local archaeologists got very excited and so did the head. Iona Skane's father, a rich man, funded the dig and that is why she was allowed to keep the statue. She was most insistent about it apparently and persuaded her father to make it a condition of the money he gave.

"Other than that, she is known to be a good student. Not quite top flight though. She did make the shortlist for the Archer Prize, but only just. Second or third in everything and hates it by all accounts. She wants to be top.

"She is moving up the ranks now though. The secretary seems to think she could be having a second wind just in time for the exams at the end of the year."

"Easy enough if you can control teacher's minds," muttered Karl under his breath.

"And take out any competitors," added Rosetta.

"I dare say," said Marcus. "But her academic achievements are not what concern me at the moment. What does is what we can do to stop her. Rosetta aside, it looks like she can pretty much wander the school at will at night. No one can prevent that apart from Rosetta who is immune to her power. And Rosetta cannot be everywhere."

"Musty can watch outside," said Karl. "We are not completely useless."

Marcus smiled and said, "Not completely. But we, Karl and I, cannot be trusted. Iona Skane seems to be becoming more powerful and there is no guarantee that she will not just take over my mind and get me to simply hand her the folio, show her the hidden office, everything. Because of this I'm minded to hand the Folio over to Rosetta's care."

"Now wait," said Rosetta. "Me hold it! It's safest in your hidden office."

"No. I'm afraid that is not true. It is safest with you Rosetta. You are the only one who is not affected by Iona Skane. If she wants it from you she will have to come and take it. The only question is - will you accept it? By right it is not your responsibility, that lies with my family, so I cannot force it upon you."

Rosetta panic stricken thought of refusing for a second, but then saw that there was really no choice. "OK I'll take it, but there are no guarantees of its safety. I'm not sure even where I can hide...."

"Do not tell us,' interrupted Marcus. "If we know where you have put it then we might, under a spell of some sort, tell Iona." and with those words he hopped over to the door to the hidden office, opened it and disappeared. He returned a couple of minutes later half-pulling himself up the passage to the office by the rope tied to the wall. He held the Folio under his other arm.

"There should be some sort of ceremony," he said with a smile, puffing slightly. "But as we don't know what it might be I'll just hand it over." And he did just that.

"Guard it carefully."

Chapter 2

Rosetta follows Atticus's advice and has an encounter which does her no good.

Rosetta sat in the toilet with the Folio on her knees considering what on earth she should do with it. It was all very well for Marcus to say that Iona Skane would have to take it from her, but the problem she now faced was that she could quite easily imagine Iona doing just that. She was six years older than Rosetta, bigger and stronger. She would not need to resort to any magical powers to rob her of the book.

The only thing to do, Rosetta thought, would be to hide the book so well that Iona Skane would not be able to find it even if she could somehow overpower Rosetta. But where could she hide it? The bed in the main hall, despite the screens placed around, was essentially in an open area. There was nowhere secret where she could hide the Folio. As for the many other places in the school things were difficult. Most of the classrooms were locked up now that the school had officially closed until the New Year, and anyway there was no guarantee that she would not be seen hiding it.

In the end Rosetta decided that the only place that she could be sure could not be secretly pilfered was, wherever she, Rosetta Clarence, happened to be; she would have to keep the folio with her at all times. Anywhere else could be searched when she was not there; any watchers or guards would be subject to Iona Skane's power and so useless. She looked at her rucksack. She generally carried it with her most of the time anyway, and so it would not attract much comment if she now kept it with her all the time. It was a large rucksack and could take the Folio's bulk without showing too much and she could push some stuff, say her spare jumper over the top, so that the book would not be spotted if she opened it in public.

She thought of what Marcus had said about his father's advice. Atticus Vates had told him to "Hide things in plain sight" and she could not think of anywhere more obvious than on a package strapped to her back.

※ ※ ※ ※ ※

The next two days passed and Iona Skane had not been seen by either of the children; Rosetta felt sure that she would recognise those green eyes should she see them again and Marcus and Musty also had nothing to report. There had been no other night time forays into the antechamber that she knew of.

"She must be about somewhere," said Marcus "or her form teacher would have reported her missing. But she is keeping a very low profile. I prefer to know where she is - I don't like it."

Rosetta, who felt the weight of the Folio in her rucksack as a constant niggle, as a worry that would not go away, agreed. If they knew where their enemy was, things would be much easier.

The weather continued as before and now the whole of the valley was under at least three meters of water and it was still rising, albeit somewhat slower; the water level had risen the river had found a way though the dam at the Northern end and it was in the process of forging a new river bed that would eventually drain the valley. The television news said that engineers were waiting to help with this process, by widening the channel with digging machines. But they could not start until the rain had stopped and the natural flow of water had drained the valley to a degree. They also said that any precipitous action now could breach the dam and cause a devastating flood downstream.

So the refugees now living on Oldmere Knoll could do nothing but wait and watch the water levels rise. The playing fields were now submerged so even the occasional helicopter visits had now stopped. There were plans to drop supplies into the main grounds, but for the time being, as there were no food shortages, this had not happened.

As the waters rose people began to notice strange phenomena associated with the sudden increase in the weight of water on the land; weight pushing down on places which had never previously been subject to such pressure. At the base of the cliffs that bordered the river, or where the river had once been, there were strange unusual eruptions of water flowing out from cracks in the rock. There was even a small explosion as pressure had built within some hidden chamber in the knoll and eventually blown out a section of the cliff, leaving a dark hole that leaked water in a steady dribble.

In addition to these natural events the Archaeological dig now had a constant pall of mist around it; water vapour could be seen rising in a steady stream from the crack in the very deepest part of the pit, like from a kettle that could only produce dank cold air. The resulting miasma also had an emotional emanation. Blackness flooded the area in a wave of depression that mirrored the fog; people avoided the white tent near the dormitories.

Except for Rosetta that is; Karl noticed that, whilst she did not actually enter the dig, she spent a great deal of time sitting at the window seat at the end of one of the corridors looking out over it. Looking out and tapping the backpack that rested next to her on the window ledge. A glance out of the window when she was not sat there showed him the view she had. And as he looked out at the tent, which contained the archaeological dig, he saw a dense mist swirl out from within. He stared at it, wondering what was on his friends mind.

※ ※ ※ ※ ※

He did not have long to wait before he found out. That night, the third since the landslide, Rosetta lay awake in her bunk, waiting. She waited until the noises from the snoozing villagers slowly faded to the heavy breathing of a deep sleep; she waited until eventually even the occasional trip to the toilet faded in frequency and she was sure that the time was right.

Slipping soundlessly from under the covers, she grabbed the rucksack from under her bed and made her way with care through the sleeping villagers, weaving between the beds and stepping over piles of belongings. She reached the Assembly Hall entrance and slipped into the girls' bathroom which were situated just on the other side of the corridor. Once inside she switched on the light, and took out the bundle of clothes she had hidden there earlier in the day. Putting them on she replaced them in her bag with the pyjamas she had just taken off, and then set off out into the night.

Once out of the door she headed straight for the Archaeological dig, tracking along walls and keeping to the shadows as much as possible. She had just reached the end of the girls' dormitory when she was stopped in her tracks by something grabbing at her trouser leg. She looked down and saw Musty's striped face looking up at her. His body was braced, all four legs locked out in front of him, ready to pull her back if she attempted to move forward.

He said nothing at first, as his mouth was full of denim. Rosetta reached down and he drew back like a dog pulling at a favourite stick.

"No Musty, will you please let go," whispered Rosetta. She looked more amused than irritated. Musty made no response apart from to brace himself even more against the ground. "Look," she continued after a few seconds. "I am here to try to end this now. I think that I might be able to if the verses in the Folio are right, and then all this will end and we can go back to normal."

"Ahn nt netting gu" said Musty through gritted teeth. "yu r not gewing thir bi yrself"

"Musty," said Rosetta. "I think you cannot stop me if I really decide to do this." As she said this she reached with her mind out to Musty's, and felt an echo of that connection she felt when they had first met, all those months ago by the Play House in her garden. "You are my familiar and I think you cannot go against me if I really will it. And this time I do." As she said these final words, she gently took his mind with hers. As she did so he let go with both his teeth and his mind, and could no longer oppose her.

This did not mean that he liked this situation however. "I cannot stop you," he muttered, "but I must advise most strongly against what you plan.

That pit over there is a trap. She hopes to flush you out, to get you alone, in the dark and then take you."

"I won't be alone, because you will be there."

They moved across the last few feet of lawn and entered the tent. Inside it was dark and cold. The fog permeated everywhere, chilling bones and sapping willpower as it did so. As she crossed into the main body of the tent Rosetta felt the power stir in her gut and she suddenly knew what to do. Raising her right hand she released the power into it. A gentle glow illuminated their immediate surroundings and drove the mist back.

"Come on," she said to Musty, and together they moved towards the centre of the canvassed area, where a metal sheet covered the excavation. Bending down Rosetta examined the padlock that held the covering in place. She grunted in satisfaction. "As I thought" she muttered, and with a sweep of her hand she lifted the padlock off and showed it to Musty. "Look the shank has been cut through and the two ends just placed together for show." She placed both hands against the front of the metal and gave an almighty push. With a low rumble the cover slid back on its rails to uncover the black hole that contained the archaeological dig.

Keeping the hand that provided the light lifted high up, she hopped into the hole and started towards the most ancient part of the excavation - the part that held the sacred pool with its crack that delved down into the very heart of the knoll.

"If you are leaking out from anywhere Morrigan,

then it is from that," said Rosetta watching the fissure. Somehow it was a deeper black than the rest; as she watched fog started to rise from it in a steady stream. Rosetta raised her hand and gathered her will, aiming to find a way to strike down, to flood her power through the crack until it reached the hiding place of the Morrigan where it could strike at her, sending her back to wherever she came from.

As she did so a terrible sound started outside the tent. A screaming caw came from a hundred throats and echoed through the night causing Rosetta to freeze and Musty to growl and raise himself up on his hind legs. The noise grew louder as the flock of Ravens, hidden and watchful on the school buildings all this time, flew down to protect their Mistress.

They dived through the door of the tent, through every hole in the fabric big enough to allow them passage and they went for Rosetta. Instinctively she dived for the floor and covered her head so as to protect her eyes. The Ravens landed upon her back and started to peck at the back of her head. They could only land for a second however before they had to fly again, for Musty would offer instant death to any that lingered too long. His teeth flashed repeatedly and bird after bird fell, some tried to move their attack to him, but to no avail. Their beaks made no impression upon his tough hide and wiry fur.

And then, as suddenly as they had come, the birds

withdrew. In the sudden quiet Rosetta looked up towards the door and saw Iona Skane. She stood by the flap to the tent and glared down at her.

Then she smiled, unpleasantly. "So you have come, and alone."

"Not alone!' snarled Musty. And he leapt towards her, his teeth bared. Iona Skane, flicked her hand and Musty flew through the air and landed heavily against the old Celtic cross that stood to the edge of the pit.

"A talking badger how novel," sneered Iona, looking at Musty, who lay still, stunned in the damp grass. Then she cocked her head, as if listening to something unheard and said, 'oh a familiar, and that must mean you my dear are...," and she turned back to Rosetta. "Rosetta Clarence the Glyph." At this she fell silent and just studied Rosetta moving her head at an angle like a bird studying a worm.

Rosetta glanced over at Musty and saw that his grey furred side still rose and fell, which meant he was still alive at least. And at that thought, just the very idea that Musty might have been hurt, her temper flared despite her fear.

"Yes. I am her, and you are not Iona Skane, but The Morrigan - demon, released from her cage and taking this opportunity to hate and destroy."

Iona's eyes froze. "Firstly," she said,"I am most definitely Iona Skane. The... angel you call the Morrigan, comes and goes. She is not me. Her power is limited as she is not yet 'out of her cage' as you put it. But we are true kindred spirits.

"One day, a year ago, I found her, under that idol there, " and Iona Skane pointed to the Celtic cross. "Or at least a relic of her. A statue dropped by an ancient worshipper. But I matched her soul, her heart, and she matched mine, to such a degree that, despite the centuries, and the spells trapping her, we became one. We were both trapped you see, her by the layers of incantations and the watchers who maintained them, me by my enemies. Those at school who held me back and pushed me to one side; those Archer prize snobs.

"So we recognised each other, joined and have removed both of our sets of enemies. There is very little now to stop us. We will complete our union and then together we will go out into the world and then you will see something amazing."

"You have not removed them all. Marcus is still there. A Custodian."

"A cripple with no training. Without his leg he can barely hand out library books to students. I removed his father, a true Custodian that one, with ease. I have not gone to such extremes with his son - why should I when he is such a failure."

Rosetta glared at the girl in front of her. She stood tall, attractive - her black hair shone - but contrasting to her outward appearance you could sense the presence of the Morrigan. From the very way she stood, to her arrogant, unfeeling words, she screamed the ugliness of her mind to all. Rosetta raised her hand, without a thought, and a white blaze came from it reflecting the anger she felt at those words.

Iona Skane flinched, and shielded her eyes as the glare lit her face. Rosetta advanced, climbing from the pit, her confidence growing as she felt the power hum through her core. "Iona Skane," she said, not knowing quite from where her words came. "You are a pawn and a fool. The Morrigan will abandon you as soon as a better vessel comes near. She is like the wind and rain, or the mountains. We are nothing to her, our deaths are inconsequential unless they affect her desires; our pain irrelevant" Iona Skane drew back and fell to the floor her, beautiful face twisted and snarling.

"You can still be released. Just take my hand and she will be gone, and you will be free." Rosetta put out her hand as if to help her to her feet and the glow became less fiery, softer. Iona Skane's face softened and you could see a glimpse of the young woman that had once been; but in a flash she was gone. Iona Skane reached inside her jacket and in a single fluid motion brought it back out again in a sweep that passed over Rosetta's hand. She felt something burn her hand, and looking down she saw that her hand was welling with blood.

Iona Skane raised the knife above her head, and laughed. "You are the fool. My mistress's power may not affect you, but you are flesh, blood and bone. You die as well as anyone else I daresay."

The blood dripped down Rosetta's hand and she looked at it in astonishment, and as she did so she started to feel a numbness, a burning in her lips and mouth, like she had rubbed a chilli pepper over them. Pain and sickness rose from her stomach and the light died in her hand.

"You feel it? Good, it won't be long then; or it might be, who knows or cares. You can stay here to die, or you could go and crawl away to some forgotten hole like that cretin Atticus Vates who suffered the same fate. I never did find him you know, he's probably at the bottom of the river."

Rosetta's legs suddenly gave way, and she collapsed. Lying on the floor she felt numbness spread from her mouth to her jaw and then down her shoulders to her arms.

Iona Skane stood up, leant over her and grabbed Rosetta's rucksack. Rosetta tried to resist, but her limbs were useless and the pack just rolled from her back as she was pushed over.

"I'll say goodbye to you Rosetta Clarence. We will not meet again." and with a quick glance at Musty who was just beginning to stir, his legs twitching with a faint echo of Rosetta's suffering, she strode out from the tent.

Rosetta lay curled on the floor, her body a haze of pain, her mind confused. She tried to move but every attempt brought waves of nausea, which completely incapacitated her. She just lay down and was ready to give up until she felt a lick on her injured hand.

Musty had wobbled over and lay down beside her. He sniffed her hand and started to lick once more. Somehow just this simple act of compassion from the small, grey furred animal beside her raised her spirits.

"Rosetta, I have failed you. That creature has hurt you. I can smell it in your blood. This is wolf's bane, the same as we found in that floorboard in the antechamber. It is a deadly poison. I need to get Marcus or I am afraid that..."

The pain and concern in Musty's voice made Rosetta think of her mother and Aimee, and the memory of their faces in turn made her determined that she would not die. Not in this way. And with the thought she felt the power flood back. She just let it go where it would.

Musty watching saw a wave of purple light wash like an endless flame over Rosetta's body. It lasted a few minutes. When it was gone, Rosetta closed her eyes.

She had time to say, "Go and get Marcus now ... good boy." before she fell unconscious.

Chapter 3

Miss Eastville is unhelpful, Marcus indisposed.

Marcus glared at Miss Eastville, who regarded him coolly.

"Mr Vates," she said. "I see no reason to take any action against Miss Skane. There has been a serious assault certainly, but there is no more evidence against this particular girl than there is against any of the other pupils still here at the school.

"What is more it is my opinion that it is far more likely to be one of the villagers involved in this than one of Oldmere School's prefects. I mean what evidence do you have?"

Marcus looked at the table, frustrated. He could not tell the head teacher that a talking badger had told him of the details of the attack. He was tempted to say that he, or even Karl, was the witness, but knew that such a lie could all too easily be exposed.

"Do you have any at all?" said Miss Eastville putting her hand to her forehead. "These are extremely serious charges. This is attempted murder, if indeed there is poisoning as you suspect."

"It may well be actual murder if we do not bring Iona Skane under control..."

"Mr Vates," she interrupted. "I cannot go about locking up children just because of a gut feeling that you have. I need to know what it is based on at the very least. Can you not please give me some sort of clue?"

"She..." Marcus thought desperately. "She has been acting suspiciously, strangely constantly obsessed with that statue she found last year, hanging around the Archaeological dig."

"She understandably is excited by her part in an historic find. There is no other site like it in the United Kingdom, and she was the one who effectively discovered its importance. I'm not surprised she is somewhat fixated by it. You cannot make a leap from perfectly natural behaviour like that to murder. You are beginning to sound like your father, who was unnaturally obsessed by the dig..." she paused, realising that this would still be a sensitive subject. "I'm sorry, but I absolutely refuse to take action on such a flimsy pretext.

"I will however try to get a police officer sent here, as there is obviously a need for one. I believe that a helicopter can make it here tomorrow to pick up Miss Clarence - yes I'm afraid that is the earliest. There is nowhere to land so they need one with a winch, and as Miss Clarence seems to be not getting worse they have not prioritised her journey. The policeman will come with the helicopter, so we have to wait until tomorrow for that also."

"If you would just let me search Miss Skane's room I'm sure that we would find a book I believe she has stolen from the library. It would prove what I am saying."

"A book? What is this now? Another accusation? And what is this one based upon? ... I really cannot see how you can link a missing book to Miss Skane with any more conviction than to the attack upon Miss Clarence."

"No, they are linked," said Marcus "I had leant the book to Miss Clarence just yesterday and now, just after the attack it is missing..."

"That is only reason to search Miss Skane's room if one believes that she is responsible for yesterday's attack, which I do not and cannot. You will just have to calm down Mr Vates and let the police do their work."

Marcus rose with difficulty. "I can only hope that Ros... Miss Clarence does not take a sudden turn for the worst. If she does I will hold you personally responsible." And with that he picked up his crutches, hopped a little as he nestled them in his armpits, and then with a body swing that somehow managed to ooze contempt made his way from the head teacher's office.

An old classroom, chosen because its large fireplace made it easy to keep warm, had been chosen as the makeshift hospital. The school nurse - an old army medic - also slept there, as she was the only medically trained person in the school. The hospital had only two patients; an old lady who had slipped and broken her ankle and Rosetta. The lady sat up in a chair by the fire, with her leg up on a leather stool, and chatted endlessly to Rosetta despite the fact that she was unconscious. Rosetta lay motionless in a bunk bed pushed up against one of the walls. The nurse sat in a far corner reading the newspaper.

The old lady looked up as Marcus came in, "Oh hello, must be the changing of the guard. That boy, I forget his name.... he's been here all the time until now. Before that it was the girl's mother, but she had to go off and look after their other daughter. The little one couldn't sit still, poor mite"

"Karl Bastion, that's the boy's name" said the nurse looking up. "Oh, it's you Captain," she said when she saw who had come in. She got to her feet in a rush. Marcus got the feeling she was fighting an urge to salute.

"Hello," he said. "How is she?"

"No better, no worse. I can find nothing wrong with her beyond that cut on her hand. I remember you said it could be poison, but I can't find any evidence of that. You need a patient to tell you about the symptoms when it comes to aconite poisoning - that's monk's hood to you and me - otherwise there is no way of telling without blood tests. This young lady is in no position to tell us anything.

And that's another thing. If she was poisoned like she is supposed to have been and she was unconscious like this, then I'd normally say she was on her way out. But that is not the case here. It's strange ... almost like she has shut down her body so as to recover more quickly. Almost like a self-imposed coma. Anyway I'm not really worried about her - like I said to the head teacher she is stable."

Marcus went over and looked at Rosetta. She lay on her back, bedclothes tucked up to her chin. Her face was pink and she her breathing was smooth and easy. Marcus looked up at the old lady with the broken ankle and said, "Did that boy say where he was going?"

♣ ♣ ♣ ♣ ♣

Karl sat on a bench by the cliffs and looked across the lake that had once been Oldmere Vale, towards his village. The water had flooded the primary school playing fields, and was now threatening the school buildings themselves, despite the fact that they were built at least fifteen meters above the valley floor. The roof of the old mill, where they had caught Musty all that time ago was now completely covered.

There was some improvement however. The rain had stopped today, and Karl hoped that this might mean that the waters would start to recede before long. He sighed, picked up a rock and threw it out over into the lake. It disappeared over the edge.

Marcus came up behind him and plonked himself on the bench. Karl glanced over and said "Any luck with Miss Eastville?"

"No. She won't believe me, not that I can really blame her. But it had to be said just the same; it might add weight to any future evidence against Miss Skane." Marcus paused and said "They are going to take Rosetta to hospital tomorrow, when a helicopter becomes available."

Karl nodded, looking at his feet. "So what do we do now? We can't just go against Iona without the backing of the head teacher, and to be honest I wouldn't fancy it anyway not without Rosetta and her power to back us up. Iona is too strong, she could just do that thing she does" - he waved his hand in a vague manner - " and we'd all be stuck to floor. I wouldn't fancy being helpless in front of her holding a poisoned knife. She's already proved she is not scared to use it."

"We have time on our side. The rain has stopped and the waters will fall. In a couple of weeks at the most the children will go home and then we can go back to our original plan so that when school starts again we will be ready for Iona Skane."

"But she probably has the Folio. I'm pretty sure Rosetta kept it in her bag, and Musty said that Iona took it. I mean it has all the secrets of the custodians; she will know it all."

"Yes," said Marcus running his hands through his hair. "But it will not tell her what she really needs to know, which is the location of the Morrigan's sacred place. Remember I have been all the way through that book, and it does contain many things I'd much rather Iona Skane did not know, but it does not contain the location of the sacred place - believe me I have read it most carefully and with just that in mind."

"So we just wait?"

"Like you say, we are helpless without Rosetta."

※ ※ ※ ※ ※

Iona Skane sat at her desk, the folio open upon its pitted wooden surface. The door to her room - prefects had private rooms just off the dormitory they were responsible for - was closed and she feared no interruption as she read through the pages with a look of intense concentration up on her face. The monkeys, as she liked to call the students which lived in her dormitory, would rather have stuck their hand into a fire than risk the anger of Iona Skane by interrupting her in her room. Most were out anyway as it was mid-morning.

Two hours passed and Iona Skane's demeanour did not change; she just sat her eyes locked forward as she slowly tuned the pages of the folio occasionally licking her fingers as she flicked the next leaf over. Then, just before midday, she stopped a small frown creasing her forehead. After a few seconds, during which her whole body moved not a millimetre, her face broke and a smile spread. And then she spoke, not as you might imagine one might when alone, but in an animated conversational tone, as you would with a close friend.

"So now, I think we might have it. Just a few things to clear up, namely Marcus Vates, and then I think I will be ready. "

※ ※ ※ ※ ※

Later that day Marcus sat in the reading room eating his lunch - something he completely banned others from doing - which consisted of rice and curried vegetables. The school chefs had started to be careful with their stores since it had become apparent that the makeshift community might have to last for several days on what was currently stored in the kitchen fridges and pantries. Provisions could be delivered by helicopter, but they consisted of dried or processed food and Mrs Honeycutt, the head chef, would not serve it as a matter of professional pride.

As Marcus finished his final mouthful, he thought that she was doing a fine job; the vegetable curry was delicious. He rose, levered himself onto his crutches, firstly putting his plate and cutlery into a plastic supermarket bag for ease of carrying, and started to swing towards the small set of steps that led down to the Assembly hall. A large bucket had been placed at the bottom for dirty crockery.

Afterward he could never properly explain what happened next, apart from to say that it felt completely unnatural, but as a sense of unreality often accompanies such accidents as these perhaps one should not read too much into it.

He had just placed the rubber feet of his two crutches on the top of the stairs, and had moved his body so that the whole of his weight had transferred to them, when it seemed like the whole world shifted. The feet of his crutches slipped as if they stood on ice instead of dry wood, and had been given a sharp kick to the side at the same time. He fell badly; he was in mid-swing and so his foot was off the floor. The crutches impeded his arms, and he had no way of controlling his descent. He landed halfway down the steps, hit his head and, as he faded into the blackness of unconsciousness he thought, " my God now Karl is on his own."

The bang resounded around the hall, and everyone looked up, saw Marcus crash to the floor, and fall down the stairs in a jumble of flesh and wooden crutches. Karl watched, frozen at first, and then recovering he rushed over to where Marcus lay in a tangle by the bottom step. Blood seeped from his hairline and flowed across his forehead; his face was pale and greasy in the glow from the overhead lights. He was unconscious.

Karl looked up the steps and on the very top one he saw a large puddle stretched along where Marcus has slipped. It was odd he thought there would be water there. The hall was quite warm, it had not rained for days and anyway the roof did not leak.

Someone had called the nurse and a few seconds later she pushed through the crowd that had formed around Marcus. She bent down her hand feeling for a pulse at his throat. He stirred at her touch groaning.

"Well he can still move that's one thing." muttered the nurse.

Marcus tried to sit, but fell back again as he turned green. He could not speak and his eyes were unfocussed.

"Concussion ... probably. I'll need to check but I dare say he'll be like this for a few days. Another one for that helicopter tomorrow morning I think. He needs someone properly qualified to look at that head of his. Can someone please go and get the stretcher for the Captain ... yes from the ward."

People started to disperse, and as they did so, Karl caught a glimpse of someone he had been looking for several days. Iona Skane stood by the main doors to the Assembly Hall. At first Karl thought that she must be looking towards the prone figure of Marcus - probably surveying her work he thought bitterly - but when the crowd thinned a bit more he saw that he was mistaken. Iona Skane was not looking at the sprawled figure lying at the bottom of the steps, but actually a little to the left.

It was with a sinking emptiness in his stomach that Karl tracked along her line of sight. There was no doubt who it was Iona Skane regarded with that horrible hungry aspect. Sat at the foot of the stairs, playing with a plastic snake, and totally oblivious to Iona's scrutiny was Aimee Clarence; and all of a sudden Karl felt very alone and exposed.

Chapter 4

No helicopter. Missing people.

Early the next morning, as soon as he had woken, Karl went straight to the hospital room to see Marcus and Rosetta before they were taken away in the helicopter. To his surprise he found the ward as he had left it last night with the exception of the nurse who now looked anxious. There seemed to be no preparations for any imminent departure and no sign of Rosetta's mother.

"Haven't you looked outside today?" she said when Karl enquired why this was. "Fog, thick as pea soup. The helicopter can't come. I haven't seen the girl's mother this morning. She's probably heard about the helicopter.

"Luckily these two look mostly OK ... she is stable and staying that way. The Captain has a broken arm but I'll keep him sedated and splinted up and he should be safe here for a couple of days." She indicated Rosetta and Marcus as she said this. Rosetta seemed not to have moved since yesterday. She still lay on her back as if asleep; but looked pink and healthy. Marcus did not have the same easy feeling about his immobility. His face was grey, rough stubble already was starting to form around his chin. Occasionally he stirred restlessly and muttered in his sleep. His arm was strapped up with bandages and pieces of wood stuck out from either end of the bandages indicating the presence of a rough splint.

"However I am quite worried about Mrs Doyle here, I think some infection might have got into that ankle of hers. She needs to be in hospital soon or there might be some problems." She shook her head. Marcus looked over at the old lady who had been so chatty just yesterday. She lay quiet on a low camp bed, which had been pressed into service in the hospital, and she was somehow made more vulnerable by her silence. She looked thinner and frailer than yesterday. Hearing her name she opened her eyes and smiled at Karl, then she closed them once more and lapsed into sleep again.

※ ※ ※ ※ ※

The nurse was right about the fog Karl decided. It rose seemingly from within the earth and smothered everything. Nothing could be seen or even heard, as it muffled all sound, and the world became an alien place in its eerie white embrace. Karl stood at the bench by the cliffs and looked out to the place where his village should have been visible and wished fervently that he knew what he should do. Iona Skane had the complete run of the school and there was nothing he could do to stop her. She probably did not even think him worth disposing of he thought bitterly.

These grim thoughts were disturbed by a sound, one he had not heard from the school before. A bell tolled dully through the fog. It came from the main school buildings to his right. He remembered that the school did have a bell tower - it was quite visible on top of the main school buildings - which was to be used in case of emergency. He turned towards the sound and by instinct made his way towards the Assembly Hall.

By the time he arrived there was already a good crowd gathered at the foot of the steps to the reading room. Miss Eastville stood on top of the steps looking distracted as she waited for everyone to arrive. A few minutes passed, and then Miss Eastville took a deep breath, clapped her hands and addressed the crowd.

"We have a serious development, and as we are cut off from outside help I must ask everyone who can do so, to try and help." she said. She paused obviously finding the next part difficult to say. "We have one, perhaps two, children missing. Both were seen late last night, though not together, and extensive enquiries have not led to their discovery. One is of great concern because she is young and particularly vulnerable. The second child is much older and more capable, but I am equally concerned for her for, as we are all aware, the valley is particularly dangerous at his time. The children of which I speak are Aimee Clarence and Iona Skane."

At these words Karl looked around for Mrs Clarence who he could not see; her absence was immediately explained by Miss Eastville's next words.

"We already have search parties out looking, but as conditions are difficult we need as many pairs of eyes as we can. So I am asking all who are able to make their way to the front of the building where teachers will be forming some more groups of searchers. Please do not go off on your own, we do not want to have to search for any more people. Just report to the teachers and join organised groups, so we know where you are. The teachers will be able to provide descriptions and other relevant information.

"The situation is most urgent so if you can help please do," and with those words she walked down the steps, making her way through the crowd towards the door.

Karl walked behind mechanically following the crowd his thoughts a whirl. This was his fault he was sure. He had seen Iona Skane watching Aimee last night, and he had known that there was something wrong, but he had done nothing. Now they had both disappeared and Karl was sure that it was no coincidence.

He did not allow himself to be distracted by his guilt though. It might have been his mistake that had led up to this, but he would try to make up for it, he owed it to Rosetta. And he already had an idea about how to do it.

Once he was outside Karl waited in line to talk to Mr White. There were other teachers who had groups nearly ready to set off, but Karl had his idea and he needed to talk to Mr White to make it work; other teachers did not know him so well, and might well refuse.

"Ah Mr Bastion. Now we are intending to form a line and work our way down towards the main entrance. Only way to be sure we are not missing anything you know?"

"Thank you Mr White, but I have an idea that I might help in a different way."

"Oh... well, in what way? But please be brief, you know time is short."

"I have a boat ... at the school I mean and it occurred to me that it might be useful to have someone looking on the water. Along the foot of the cliff and so on."

Mr White looked very grim at these words. He sighed and said "You are right of course, but I am not happy with you going alone. I remember it is a canoe you have? It has just a single seat? The school boats are all in the boathouse which as you know is currently six feet under water, so you will have no company on your search."

"I know the river very well sir. I've lived in the Vale all my life and have spent most of my summers in my canoe on the water. I would just search the waterline along the foot of the cliff. If they have fallen down they might need help now. I'd say it is just as risky to not send someone as to do so."

Mr White looked long and hard at Karl, looking over his glasses as he did so, until he said after some seconds "Very well I'm trusting you because I know you to be responsible. I will be out with the search parties and will not be able to check. So one search along the foot of the cliff, and then come out of the water to help with the land search. I want your word on that."

Karl gave his promise.

"Good. Now look for a bright red raincoat, or a yellow top. These are the clothes that Mrs Clarence thinks Aimee is most likely to be wearing. It is good that they are both bright colours, so we might have a chance of spotting them even in this fog."

Karl nodded to acknowledge that he had heard, and ran toward the Gym to pick up his canoe. As he ran he thought that Mr White need not be concerned; he had no intention of going alone.

※ ※ ※ ※ ※

"Musty ... Musty!" Karl half shouted as stood by his canoe near the small marshy inlet where they had first seen Marcus fishing all those months ago.

He hoped that the sensitive ears of the badger could catch his shouts as they travelled through the fog, all the way up the cliff and through the tunnels to where Musty slept these days. After a couple of minutes he heard a rustle from above, and then a short time later a black and white muzzle appeared through the slowly drifting mist.

"Karl!" said the badger sounding relieved. "What has been happening? I have heard nothing for the last two days. Marcus has not been down to see me and I don't have any news of Rosetta. How is she; have they removed the poison?"

"She is alright, I think. It looks like she flushed away, or somehow destroyed the poison. The nurse thinks her body is just recovering. Marcus is not so good I think. That is why he has not been down," and he related the story of Marcus' fall and injury.

"That will be Iona Skane's devilry or I'm a fox," said Musty. "She will have somehow put that water on the step."

"Yes, but there is more. Aimee, Rosetta's sister, is missing, as is Iona Skane. Everyone is looking for them, but I think we can look better if we have your nose to help."

"Again I think this is no accident. I fear it will be hard to find them if they are deliberately hidden."

"Yes but we have to try. I've said I'll look along the cliff shore in my canoe and I wanted you to come with me so you could ... you know sniff."

"My nose is of little help in a fog like this, and I am not sure about going out in this contraption." He went over and sniffed the canoe. "But never the less you will find it hard to stop me coming. Another day sat in that tunnel, with no information and I would go mad I am sure."

Karl pushed the canoe the last few yards until it rested in the water next to the bank, held it steady so that Musty could scrabble over the edge and then got in himself. Musty sat between his legs his front paws resting on the lip of the canoes cockpit.

"So Musty, what I am going to do is push off and paddle toward the flow of the river. Once we are there I am just going to drift with the current keeping as close to edge as I can. The current is pretty strong so that may take a lot of my attention. I'm relying on you to keep an eye out for anything unusual that may need investigating ... and don't do that." Musty had just flung himself to one side of the cockpit to investigate some splash he had heard, and had caused the canoe to wobble alarmingly - "Keep still or we will be both in the water and they'll be looking for us!"

"Apologies! This is quite worrying to me. If badgers had been meant for travel by water then we would have been made with fins."

"Just keep still and keep your eyes, and nose, peeled for anything."

They moved out into the disturbed flow of water that showed where the riverbed lay so far below the surface. The fog was so thick that the bank and cliff of Oldmere Knoll became just a blur if they drifted even a few yards away. So Karl had quite a job in keeping the canoe close to the bank and keeping its progress slow in the fast flowing current, both necessary tasks if Musty was to keep an effective watch on the banks and rock walls as they drifted by.

After about five minutes they came close to where the cliff had exploded a few days before. A mass of earth and rock lay piled in a smooth brown heap below the new hole in the knoll. From the school it had been difficult to see the extent of the breach in the rock face as a lip of rock and earth hid it from an observer looking from above. But the view from the river showed what a spectacular collapse it had been. A black maw, half hidden by fog stared out at them, the only movement the steady stream of water that flowed out from its depths.

"Wow." said Karl. "I'd have liked to have seen that one go. Mary in our class claimed to have heard it in the night, but ..."

"Quiet!" said Musty in an excited voice. " Take me there quick."

"Why, what have you seen?"

"Smelled, not seen. It may be nothing. Just see if you can get me ashore near that hole."

Karl turned the boat and moved with difficulty across the current toward a fallen tree. It had been pushed over by the weight of the landslide above and stuck out some way into the river. He brought the canoe alongside so the current pushed the boat against the tree and kept it steady. Musty hopped onto the front covering of the kayak and ran along his paws sliding a little against the slippery plastic until he reached the end where he scrabbled off onto a waiting rock.

"Stay here. It will be easier for me to look alone. If there is something then I will return." and with that he disappeared into the fog.

He was soon back. "Get out of that boat, and come with me. We have something very interesting here."

"What have you found? Aimee?"

"No, but I think that this is worth the time we will spend. It could be very important."

Karl thought of his promise to Mr White, but then remembered that he had said he would make one pass along the banks at the foot of the cliffs and that any detours he made would not really break his promise. "After all," he thought to himself. "I have to make a thorough search after all."

"OK. Can you pull that rope so I don't slip?"

Musty grabbed hold of the small wooden toggle that dangled from the front of the boat with his teeth, and leant back digging all four paws into the soft earth. With one hand holding on to the tree, and the other on the canoe, Karl shuffled across the decking on his hands and knees until he reached the bank.

They climbed up the cliff towards the new hole in the cliff, passing to one side of the pile of debris cause by the landslide which was too soft to get a good purchase. As they approached the source of the landslide, Karl noticed something slowly emerging from the darkness and fog. Beneath the overhanging rock left by the collapse, Karl could now see where the stream of water, which came from the hole, actually originated.

"Is that a tunnel?"

"Yes it is, and what is more I can smell something very interesting coming from there."

"What?" said Karl.

"Many things, but two caught my attention. Firstly I smelt my nest, the one in the Ancient Library, where I have been sleeping recently. It is very faint, but you cannot mistake the smell of your own nest."

"And that means, that if you can smell the scent coming from that tunnel, then it must join up somewhere with the tunnel where you sleep."

"Yes, and there are no other doorways or passages in the tunnel that leads from the cliff face to the Ancient Library, which means that there must be one that we do not know of. This tells me that there must be a secret entrance from the Ancient Library which leads somehow to this tunnel in front of us."

"Gosh," said Karl his mind suddenly alive with possibilities. "You said there were two smells. What is the other?"

Musty's ears went flat against his head. "Yes. The other one also cannot be mistaken. It is the scent of death."

Karl went pale and said, "Could we have found Aimee or Iona Skane?"

"I do not know. It is faint. Whatever causes it lies a long way down that tunnel."

Karl thought hard. What should he do? The temptation to just go and get a teacher to come and sort the whole thing out was great, but that might expose the whole of the Ancient Library and everything else to the eyes of the head teacher. "She'd probably turn it into a theme park, whilst all the time the Morrigan remained hidden and dangerous. I have to know what this tunnel is all about before I bring in any outsiders. What's more Aimee could be hurt or in danger in there, and any delay might just make it worse."

"Well," Musty interrupted his thoughts. "What do we do? I can go in alone in needs be."

"No, we go together."

Karl went down to make sure the canoe was not going to come loose whilst they were away. "The last thing we need is to get stranded and have to be rescued by a load of teachers," said Karl when Musty complained about the delay that this meant." An empty canoe floating past would get a swarm of people all over the cliff and they would be sure to find the tunnel."

When he was back they climbed up the last few meters to the entrance to the tunnel. The landslide had torn away many of the rough stone blocks that lined the tunnel, but some iron fittings still clung to one side indicating that there had once been a door connecting the tunnel to the world outside. The resemblance to the other tunnel in the knoll was clear; the size, shape and nature of the stone in this one made it a twin with the one that led to the Ancient Library.

"I wonder why they sealed this," said Karl, his interest roused. "when they left the other one open?"

"Who knows? Come, there will be time to answer such questions later, when everyone is safe and the Morrigan back in chains. For now we must move on."

Karl had a key ring torch, which fortunately had new batteries. He switched it on and pointed it into the blackness. After a few yard the tunnel veered to the right.

"Let's go then," said Karl, and they moved off into the darkness.

Chapter 5

Rosetta wakes, and finds things have changed somewhat.

Rosetta drifted into consciousness. As she did so the memory of that night, the night she got cut, slowly bubbled to the top of her mind. At first she was not sure if it was a dream; it seemed as unreal. Such things did not happen to her, Rosetta Clarence a normal school girl from Oldmere. But then she felt the ache in her hand, and the bone weary fatigue brought on by her body's fight against the poison, and she knew that it had all happened. She forced her eyes open.

She recognised a classroom she used for mathematics from a large fireplace, but it had changed. The desk was covered in cardboard packets of pills, bandages and other medical equipment. She looked to her right and saw an old lady she recognised from around the village. She did not look well. Her face had a thin film of sweat over it and was a strange colour. She bent her head backward to look at the space behind her bed and saw something that made her sit up.

The school nurse was curled asleep in a chair, which was no surprise, but in a camp bed in front of her lay Marcus. His arm was bandaged and splinted. Rosetta's movement woke the nurse.

"Oh hello you! I've been expecting you to pop up for a while now." she said brightly at first. Then she seemed to think of something and paused. " Now lie back - I have to get the head teacher. She needs to talk to you …"

The nurse picked the receiver of the telephone that lay on the desk, dialled a short number and waited a second.

"Hello. This is Mrs Brennan. Miss Clarence is awake now ... you wanted to speak to her. OK yes I'll see you in a minute."

Rosetta looked on with some nervousness. She had expected the call to be to her mother, not Miss Eastville. Why was that?

What is more she had never spoken directly to the head teacher before and was unsure what to say. She could hardly come out with the whole story. Talk of Celtic demons and possessed prefects would only make her seem delusional. She should at least tell her about Iona Skane's attack, but she was reluctant somehow. Iona was not really responsible for her actions; the Morrigan infused her, influenced her and brought out the worst aspects of her character. If they could defeat that creature then Iona Skane could go back to being her normal self. If she just blurted out an accusation then an attempted murder charge would hang over the rest of Iona's life - it would ruin her.

The head teacher came in looking strangely nervous. She sat and motioned for Rosetta to do so also.

"Good afternoon Miss Clarence. I'm pleased to have you looking well."

"Hello Mrs Eastville," said Rosetta, she glanced over at Marcus. "What has happened to Mr Vates?"

Mrs Eastville looked a little surprised at the question, but just said. "He fell down some stairs. I believe he will get better ... I'm afraid I need to talk to you about something else Miss Clarence." She sat on a stool that stood nearby, and said, "I'm afraid that we have some worrying news for you. Your little sister Aimee.... she is missing."

"What! Since when ... how long have I been unconscious?"

"She has been missing since this morning, and you have been out for two days. We have search parties looking – your mother is among them - but the weather conditions are very bad and this makes it difficult. The fog makes it impossible for any helicopters to land and so we are very much on our own.

"I was hoping that you might be able to help us. We thought you might know of any likely places, special hiding places and so on, where Aimee might go and hide. Anything might be important."

"No, she always stays with Mum... er you said fog?"

"Yes it came down overnight, very thick. So you can give us no clue as to any possible location?"

"No ... nothing"

Mrs Eastville sighed, and then said. "I also have to ask you something else, something difficult, something about what happened to you Miss Clarence, which given... everything, might be important for the welfare of the missing people."

"People, what is there more than one!"

"Oh yes I did not say. There is an older child missing also, disappeared about the same time. A prefect, we are less concerned about her as she is generally quite sensible, but are of course also searching for her. Her name is Iona Skane."

Rosetta's head whirled and Miss Eastville continued. "If there is someone dangerous out there, it makes the disappearance of these children particularly worrying. If you can help us find the person who attacked you it would be of great help. So can you remember anything about the time when you got injured; I'm guessing it was an attack of some sort? There is plainly a knife cut on your hand."

Rosetta thought quickly and made her decision. "Yes it was an attack, but I can't really remember much about it; it was dark and the memory is very hazy now. I might get better after a while I suppose." She tried to look like she was dredging her memory. In reality she remembered all too well what had happened that night, but she thought that Iona Skane deserved a chance; the real Iona Skane not the creature possessed by the Morrigan. She was sure that the real Iona still lay within, controlled and supressed by the power of the Morrigan. She had caught a glimpse of that girl by the Archaeological dig.

If it really became necessary, she could 'remember' the night of the attack, and Iona could be dealt with.

"What about Aimee?" continued Rosetta. "What are we doing? You do know she can't look out for herself very well, she..."

"Your Mother has told us all about Aimee," said Miss Eastville. "There are search parties scouring the whole of the area. It is difficult in the fog, but we are doing our best. Your friend Mr Bastion has even gone out in his canoe. We are leaving no stone unturned I can assure you."

"Can I go and search?"

Miss Eastville glanced over at the nurse, and said "I'm afraid not ... Miss Brennan says you are not to go out after being so sick ... and I must admit that I am inclined to agree with her, not least because we know that someone has attacked you once, and there is no guarantee that they will not have another go. So I'm afraid I cannot allow you to join the search. What is more I believe your mother would agree with me."

Rosetta was about to argue, but she saw that Miss Eastville looked quite determined, and resolved to stay quiet; the more fuss she made, the more likely she was to be watched and prevented from sneaking off to help.

Something of these thoughts must have showed on her face for Miss Eastville looked a little suspicious and said, "If I see you out there will be trouble, so mind you stay indoors." And with those words, she stood up smiled absently at Rosetta and left.

Rosetta stayed seated trying to think. The nurse sat across from her so there was no way she could sneak out to help with the search. She was stuck, unable to do anything but wait; an unbearable thought, given the danger that Aimee was almost certainly in. It could be no coincidence that Iona Skane had gone missing at the same time as her sister. She had taken Aimee for some unknown purpose, though it was certain to be unpleasant, and Rosetta could do nothing as she was stuck indoors.

A sudden thought struck her at this moment, and she sat up in her chair. "I would like to do some studying if that is OK ... as I'm stuck inside," she said to the nurse.

Mrs Brennan looked a little flustered, "Well, as long as you do it here, then I've no complaint to make."

"Well it's not very good for studying here, but I could go into the Reading Room and work there. I'd still be inside and you could come and check on me quite easily."

"Well ... yes. It would get very tedious for you here with just me, and a couple of poorly ones for company. I'll take you through"

She nurse got up and escorted Rosetta though the short corridor which connected the makeshift hospital room from the Assembly Hall. Picking up some paper and a book from her cubicle in the hall, Rosetta made her way to the Reading room and settled down at one of the tables. The nurse smiled and turned as Rosetta pretended to settle down to make her way through some of her holiday work.

It was a twenty-minute wait until she spotted the nurse pop her head round the corner of the Assembly Hall to check on her. Pretending not to see her she put her head down further into the book of algebra. When the nurse disappeared this time, Rosetta waited a few seconds and then darted from her table round to the back of the Custodian's desk, where she dropped down.

She waited for a few seconds anticipating some kind of cry of discovery. When there was none she peeped over the top and saw that her disappearance had gone unnoticed by the one or two people who still occupied the Assembly hall; those too old or young to take part in the search for the missing schoolchildren.

Satisfied, she dropped down again, turned and pushed at the door that led through to the Antechamber. Much to her relief she found it unlocked. Marcus must have been in no position to lock it the night before. She opened it a crack and quickly squeezed though the gap. Once inside the room beyond she pushed the door to, turned to the room behind and then gave a small gasp as she saw what had become of it.

Every bookshelf, every drawer at Marcus's desk had been turned out, leaving complete chaos behind. What was worse was that the door to the Ancient Library was wide open. Rosetta had intended to use the secret entrance out into the cliff to sneak out to join the hunt for her sister, but now looking at the scene spread out before her she was certain that there was little point her doing this; Iona Skane had certainly taken Aimee through here. She must have found a mention of the hidden door in the folio - it was no secret to The Custodians after all - and come looking. The door behind the bookcase was not particularly well hidden, particularly if the searcher knew it was somewhere in the room, so it would not have taken her long to discover it.

Rosetta approached the passage and listened, but she could hear no sound drifting up the winding staircase that led down to the Ancient Library. They must still be somewhere in the passages that lead to the gate in the cliff face. It would be locked - Marcus never left it open as anyone could then wander right into the ancient library - so they might be back any second. She would have to be extraordinarily careful.

She grabbed one of the torches that Marcus kept hidden in a corner of the corridor near the door, and as quietly as she could she crept down the stairs, listening all the while for any noise or other signs of an intruder. As she descended she kept her torch hidden under her jumper so that only the tiniest amount of light leaked out to show her way. This made it easy for her to see if there was light ahead and harder for anyone ahead to notice her approach. But she saw no light and she heard no sound; at the bottom of the stairs she switched off her torch and was met with complete darkness.

They must have gone across the cavern to the tunnel that winded out through rock to the cliff face; perhaps Iona Skane could now open locked doors, and they had simply used the tunnel to get out of the school unnoticed.

She switched the torch back on and moved forward, thinking that she must investigate the tunnel, even if it was just to satisfy herself that they were not there, when she noticed something lying on the floor by the one of the bookcases which lay shattered against the one of the walls. It was the colour that caught her eye at first. A vivid redness shone out amongst the multitude of greys in the Ancient Library, and a closer look made her realise that she knew what it was, and as she did so her heart gave a leap.

It was Aimee's favourite toy; her red plastic snake. It lay on the floor half hidden by a bookcase which Rosetta now realised had been dragged from it s original resting place. Rosetta bent down, lifted the bookcase slightly and pulled the snake out. She held it and the memory of Aimee playing with it overwhelmed her. She felt panicked again at the thought that she might lose her forever, and the desire to find her welled up in her heart uncontrollably. As these feelings came so did the light in her hand. Somehow surprised even now by her power Rosetta dropped the snake and fell back onto her backside. The light faded as she did so leaving her with only the torch light, muffled by her jumper, to see by.

The long time unconscious, followed by the shock of discovering her sister gone, had made Rosetta forget that she had other resources to call upon. She thought quickly to what Marcus had said about the powers of a Glyph:

" .... *they can sense deception, and things that have been hidden* ..."

Both apply here thought Rosetta, and she stood up, grabbing the snake as she rose. Holding the toy with both hands she imagined her sister and the finding of her with a determination born of fear for Aimee's safety. And as she did so the light came again, but this time tinged with red - it shows my anger Rosetta thought - and it shone upon a patch of wall near where the snake had fallen. The light grew intensely bright for a second, Rosetta heard a sharp click, and it flashed into nothing.

It took some minutes for Rosetta's eyes to adjust once more to the dim light from the torch, but when it did she saw to her amazement that a section of the wall had broken away leaving what was plainly the outline of a door.

Of course thought Rosetta, the doorway to the sacred place of the Morrigan has been known and used by the Custodians for centuries; it would not be in the main school building, which after all is relatively new. Nor would it have been outside where it could have been found by anyone. No the Ancient library was located in this particular cave in the knoll, not only because it was a good place to keep books, but also because it also hid the place which the Custodians wanted to keep close to them; the prison of the Morrigan of Water.

Rosetta walked to the door and stood in front of it. Switching off her light she waited for a minute and saw the outline of the door coloured with a flickering light, despite the fact that the cavern should be pitch black. She reached out her hand and pulled at the edge of the door. It took a great effort to move even a small amount and Rosetta realised that the door must be actually made from rock, not just made to look like it was. She leaned back, pulled with all her strength and slowly the door moved. As it did so she saw a tunnel, carved from the primeval bedrock; there were no bricks or masonry here to give a comforting feeling of civilisation. The tunnel dropped down steeply and from below there was a flickering light. It was a light whose origins could not be mistaken. It spoke to the cave dweller that lies dormant in all of us;

It said "Fire"

Chapter 6

The Morrigan

The light from Karl's torch bounced and bobbed along the rough stone blocks which lined the walls. He glanced back towards the tunnel's entrance. The eerie light produced by the fog outside cast a strange sheen on the waterlogged surfaces near the entrance. He turned and moved on with Musty padding silently by his side.

After a minute he stopped to examine the walls, his curiosity piqued by a memory from a school visit some time ago. Feeling the stone he said "This looks like the stone they have in some of the Stone Age barrows I've seen over in Wiltshire. That means it is very old - older than the Romans, and probably even older than Marcus' ancient druid ancestor."

"Less of the learnedness please," said Musty pushing urgently at his legs with his snout. "We have a job to do here remember ? And time is short."

Karl lowered his hand and shook his head. "Sorry you're right. We must carry on."

They moved on and turned a corner leaving the last view of the outside world behind them. Shortly afterwards Karl felt the ground change beneath his feet, and he pointed his torch down to see what had changed. The packed mud of the tunnel had ended and a new surface of tightly fitting cobbled stones sprung from the ground. Marcus pointed his torch at the wall and saw that its construction had also changed. The stone was now dressed, constructed by a skilled mason and Karl was sure that this section of the tunnel was roman, but did not say so in case he was told off by Musty again for being a Smart Alec.

As they progressed, the tunnel wound seemingly randomly through the knoll. Once it even turned dramatically through a right angle, presumably to avoid some obstacle that would have been too difficult for the tunnelers to move aside. And it was after this sharp turn that they were forced to a sudden stop.

The passage seemed to disappear into a void; the walls and floor of the tunnel seemed simply to vanish into black nothingness, making further progress impossible. Leaning out Karl shone his torch around and the cause of this situation became plain. The tunnel entered a room about the size of a classroom, or would have done so except for the fact that this room had no floor. Instead a pit fell down over the whole of the area where the ground should have been.

On the other side Karl could see the passage continue following the exactly same line as the tunnel at their end. Karl shone his light down to see the bottom of the hole, but the beam of his torch could not reach; it faded to nothing as blackness overtook the beam. He picked up a small rock and dropped it. It took several seconds before the sound of a water splash came back up from the depths.

Karl cast the beam of his torch around looking for a way to cross the chasm. As he did so Karl noticed that the walls of the room were not made from stone blocks as the tunnel was. Instead the walls were made from the rock of the knoll, but smoothed and flattened by the chisels of ancient masons. The reason for this endeavour was made plain as he focussed his torch on one part of the wall.

The flat surface of the walls was covered with carvings - with what seemed to be words. They were gathered into small groups, and looked like a collection of poems or verses. He flashed his torch about and every part was the same. The letters were written with Roman letters, and carved in the Roman style, but Karl was sure that the language being spelled out in this room was not Latin. It was like a Roman was writing out a language he had only heard, just as it sounded to him.

Something caught Karl's eye as he flashed the torch about the room. At the level where the floor ought to be, attached to the wall on all sides was a ledge or path. It was wide enough for a child to pass walking forward, but an adult would have to pass crabwise facing the wall. Whatever the reason for such a strange arrangement it did provide a means for Karl and Musty to cross the room.

"Well this is a strange place," said Karl to Musty "Shall we go on? What is your feeling?"

"I will go first," said the badger. "My weight is less likely to break the ledge or set off any traps. We certainly must continue for the smells I felt outside are getting stronger ... both of them; we cannot stop now."

Musty stepped from the main passage to the left hand ledge and walked forward cautiously, his head swaying from side to side as he tried to smell any possible danger. Karl waited until Musty had turned the first of the corners before setting off so that each section of ledge did not have to bear the weight of both himself and the badger. Despite his confident assessment standing on the safe platform of the main passage, it was not so easy to walk forward in a normal manner; the knowledge that to his right lay a great depth and that one misstep would send him falling into it, made him cling to the wall on his left somewhat. But the ledge seemed strong, being cut from the rock, and before long Karl found himself stood beside Musty in the passage on the other side.

Without a word they passed along this new passage that continued in much the same manner as the old one. But before the pair had gone more than a dozen yards Musty pulled at Karl's trouser leg and muttered "Here ... wait"

Karl cast his torch ahead and saw what seemed a large bundle of clothes lying against the wall some ten meters ahead in the gloom. To his relief they were nothing like the clothes that had been described to him by Mr White. They looked like a tweed jacket and pair of leather shoes.

"I will go," said Musty. "Stay here and I will call." Karl nodded.

Musty approached the shape and sniffed at it. After a second or two he called back. "You can come. We have both a mystery solved and a tragedy here I think."

Karl approached and soon saw that what lay in the passage must be a body, one of an adult. He slowed involuntarily. He had never seen a dead person before and was scared. He forced himself forward and stood before the body feeling a little weak at the knees.

The corpse was that of a man. He sat on the floor with his back against the wall, like he had simply stopped for a rest on a hot summer day. Remarkably he had not decomposed at all. His skin, where exposed, looked grey and lifeless, but was otherwise smooth and unbroken. He wore a white shirt and a tweed jacket, with grey trousers. His hair was black and grey, worn long in a ponytail.

On closer inspection Karl saw that the man's shoulder had been injured. The jacket on the left side was stained with blood. Steeling himself Karl lifted the lapel of the jacket to have a look and saw there was an impressive amount of dried blood soaked into his shirt underneath. Looking up the body Karl saw a small cut just below the man's shoulder that seemed to be the wound responsible. Karl did not think that such a small wound could have killed him, and looked about for any other injury that could possibly explain his death.

There did not seem to be any - there was no more blood, nor was there any apparent bruising or other problems on his head - and Karl was about to put it down as mysterious when a thought occurred to him.

"Musty, can you have a good sniff at that shoulder of his and tell me what you think."

Karl held the jacket open and Musty put his front paws onto the man's stomach so his nose could reach his shoulder. He snorted in surprise and dropped to the ground.

"Monkshood!" he said.

Karl nodded knowingly. He was about to say something when he spotted something poking from the inside pocket of the man's jacket which he was still holding open. It looked like a piece of paper. Lifting the jacket he gingerly put his hand inside and lifted it out. It was a letter, a long one; the envelope bulged. Turning it over Karl read the address.

"It's for Marcus," he said. "The address is that of his regiment I'd guess. This must be that letter, the one that he never received from his father, which must mean that this person is ..."

"Atticus Vates," finished Musty.

Karl looked at the face again. He had never seen the man in life, but now he knew who he was he could see the family resemblance. The eyes were shut, but Karl could well imagine that in life they were the same sharp blue colour as his son's.

"So now we have the solution to the mystery of what happened to Marcus' father. It looks like he had an encounter with Iona Skane's poisoned knife the night he disappeared, and somehow ended up here, where the Monkshood finished him off. He never had the chance to send the letter he wrote to Marcus, but did have time to put the note into the secret compartment in the Antechamber."

"Yes, but now we must press on," said Musty. "We have an urgent task which needs to be done to prevent another tragedy. This one has happened and cannot be helped."

Karl nodded and carefully pocketed the letter. They passed the remains of Atticus Vates and moved further along the passage into the centre of the knoll. After just a few minutes Musty stopped and said "Turn off your torch, there is light here" and when Karl did so he could also see a faint red glow lighting the passage ahead.

"It is fire," said Musty.

Rosetta paused at the top of the passage staring at the flickering shadows, suddenly nervous. How long she waited there she could not later say, but it was the object that she held in her hands that snapped her out of it. She looked down at the red plastic snake and memories of Aimee flooded into her mind. Finding new resolve Rosetta set off down the steeply descending tunnel towards the firelight.

The tunnel ended after a short but steep descent with a blank wall of stone which simply cut across the passage. Just before this blockage a square hole had been cut into the stone wall on the right hand side of the passage, providing an exit out of what would have been a dead end. It was from this entrance that the flickering light came. An ancient looking wooden door, which would have normally blocked the entrance, was pushed against the wall next to the doorway. Rosetta could not see into the room from where she stood. So she crept down the tunnel until she could peer around the corner.

The door opened into a large cavern lit by a large fire, which burned, smokeless, in the centre. This blaze was isolated from the main cave by a low circular wall that hid the source of the flames from view. They simply rose high and undisturbed to the roof, which was bizarrely unstained by soot or scorch marks. To the right of this flame, taking up all of one side of the cave, stood a large lake. It lurked black and still; not a ripple disturbed its surface. A slight trickle issuing from the cavern wall over in the semi darkness to the right seemed to be the source of water for this underground lagoon.

In the middle of the room standing between the water and the fire was a large square stone box, which reminded Rosetta of a sarcophagus. It stood waist high and was covered in inscriptions. The carvings looked very much like Latin to Rosetta.

In contrast to the right, the left side of the cavern looked simply like a cave. It was strewn with a field of debris. Broken rocks, some as large as a man, lay everywhere. Half hidden beyond these boulders Rosetta could just make out a black hole in the far wall which indicated another tunnel must lead out of this strange place.

Lying on top of the carved box was Aimee. She lay on her back, dressed in a red jumper and appeared to be asleep. Her chest rose and fell slowly in the flickering light.

Rosetta rushed forward, all thought of stealth gone. Dashing down the few stone steps that led from the tunnel to the floor of the cavern, she started to sprint over to the box. She skidded to a halt as Iona Skane stepped out from behind the tower of flame, her small, deadly knife in her hand.

"Hello Rosetta, I really was not expecting you today," she said lightly, and quickly stepped across from the fire until she stood directly next to Aimee, her knife held loosely in her hand. "You should have died you know. I loaded enough aconite on that blade to kill a fully-grown man, and believe me I do know how much that is. An eleven-year-old girl should have been gone in an hour. You really have got some hidden depths Rosetta Clarence and it is such a shame that all those surprising abilities of yours do not count very much in this particular situation," and with those words she moved the knife over and held it next to the skin of Aimee's throat.

"I doubt very much that your remarkable talents of recovery are reflected in your sister here. I mean given she is inadequate in almost every other way. It really was very tedious having to deal with her on the way here. Whining all the time. At least as far as I could tell, since she cannot even speak. She is really very stupid."

Rosetta anger getting the better of her started to move forward at these words.

"What I mean," said Iona, her voice hardening, "is that your sister will not be able to survive even a prick from this knife, and so you had better be very careful about how you behave.

"Firstly you will move away from me, back towards the door. You may sit on the steps but if you try anything at all, including those special things that come from you being a gyfrinllythyr, then I will kill your sister.

Rosetta stopped and backed away back towards the doorway where she had entered. The moment Rosetta had sat down on the stone steps. Iona Skane dashed back behind the flame, and before Rosetta could even think about moving she was back with a small black rucksack held in her free hand. She placed it next to Aimee and watching Rosetta all the while, rummaged inside until she brought out a small figure. It was very crude, made from fired clay, but despite the lack of finish you could make out that it was the figure of a woman.

"This," she said seeing Rosetta's attention move to the statue, "is the start of it all for me. I found it sticking out from beneath that Christian monument outside the school. That moment changed my life. Before that I was just an ordinary school child, bothered by exams and how I could not keep up with Emily Watson," and as Iona Skane said the name of that unfortunate girl an unpleasant smile spread over her face. "But as soon as I clutched this statue I felt my mistress's presence. It both comforted me and made me realise that I was better than the other fools in my year. It changed me, made me powerful.

"It contained only the weakest trace of my mistress; a hint only. But that was enough, given our shared.... soul. She came to me that night in my dreams and said that in order for me to fulfil my potential, to become great, she needed to be free from her prison. She explained that many hundreds of years ago an evil sorcerer had trapped her within the knoll. This sorcerer in fact," and she ran her hand across the stone box. "This sarcophagus contains the remains of that man, kept here as a symbol of her imprisonment for the last two thousand years.

"She also told me that the descendants of that

sorcerer had remained in the valley, determined that she should stay trapped forever. Several times she had nearly escaped, just to have them slam the door in her face once more. What is more she said that this gaoler could be found in none other than the Custodian of Oldmere School.

"As I lay on my bed with my mistress's' statue together we formulated a twofold plan. My mistress knew only that her prison lay somewhere in the depths of the knoll, but not the precise location. She was in a prison without a window, and could see the outside world only through my eyes. But if I could find a way to get myself to the sacred lake then she could instruct me in rites on how to make her truly free. But the knowledge of the way to the lake was a secret known only to the Custodians so I must somehow drag that secret from those people.

"Also my mistress told me that, previously on the occasions when she had nearly escaped, she had been given the opportunity because there had been some great disturbance in the knoll; digging or other such activity and that gave me an idea.

"I told her that I knew that, if I showed her statue to the new head teacher, she would likely start excavations in order to uncover the secrets of the knoll. And that might give my mistress some freedom, and in doing so provide me with some of her power."

As Iona spoke, Rosetta saw to her astonishment a shadow flick for a second amongst the rocks on the other side of the cavern. There was someone else here! She tried hard to keep her attention fixed on Iona as she spoke, whilst still watching the rocks for any further movement.

"So at the end of last year I showed the statue to my fool of a father and he, predictably, went to the headmistress. She ordered an archaeological excavation to start over the summer. And so all was in place for this year; they would dig and my mistress would pass at least some of her powers to me."

"When did you decide that it would be a good idea to remove your competitors for the Archer prize?" said Rosetta playing for time and scanning the rocks every chance she got. There! A small animal flicked between the rocks. It had to be Musty. Why did she not think of him before she came alone down that passage? He must have heard her in the Ancient Library and followed.

"Oh my!" said Iona in mock admiration. "You have been a good detective, haven't you? Well my mistress was most interested when I told her of the Archer Prize. She knew that if I won the prize, and she was free once more then I could take her with me to Munsford University. And there, we would have future leaders of the world at our mercy. Before long they would be our creatures."

Then Rosetta saw Karl. He inched, using the cover of the rocks, towards the central flame. He caught her eye but she dared not reciprocate; Iona Skane was watching her too closely.

"But before I could proceed we needed to find

the way to the sacred lake. For this I needed an ancient manuscript that my Mistress thought might hold all the secrets of the Custodians - she had seen them holding it many times as they wandered around this chamber. All of last July I searched the Custodian's quarters and the Old Library, but with no result. Eventually the old Custodian became suspicious and caught me one night as I searched the room behind his office. We fought and I struck him with my knife, but I fell and knocked my head in the struggle and was knocked senseless for some minutes.

"When I awoke he could not be found but I did not fear exposure for I knew him to be a dead man already. During the summer my Mistress had taught me much including the uses of herbs and ancient medicine."

"Poisons you mean!" Rosetta burst out.

"Including some poisons," said Iona unperturbed by Rosetta's anger. "I expected him to be found in a ditch or in the grounds of the school. But when I returned to my room my Mistress told me he had come to the sacred place, but had merely passed through on his way to death. Imagine my frustration when I discovered that he had died in the very place for which I searched. That he must have gone there whilst I lay insensible, and had I been conscious then I would have been able to follow, to free my mistress."

From the corner of her eye Rosetta saw that Karl had reached a large rock close behind Iona. He lay on the floor and poked his head out from behind it.

"Now, at last I may perform that service. Just the blood of an innocent, spilled in this place and it is done." Iona looked down at Aimee lying asleep on the slab and smiled. Rosetta, realising her meaning, and once more, unable to control her self started towards the sarcophagus.

"Will you keep still!" said Iona Skane with a meaningful twitch of her knife. "I can bleed her just as well dead, as alive. I do not believe it matters to the ceremony which one. Fear not, if you keep still, then your sister will survive. Though I wish I could say as much for yourself."

It was as she spoke these words that Karl and Musty struck. They both dashed out from behind the rock. Musty, lowest to the ground and best able to move from a standing start, went straight for Iona Skane's ankles and reached her before Karl. He sunk his teeth into the lower part of her leg. Karl just behind made to try to rugby tackle her, to drive her forcibly away from Aimee. Rosetta frozen in surprise did not move.

Iona Skane spun around in shock. The point of her knife waved around in front of Aimee's face before being driven away by the momentum of Karl's attack. As her hand swung away it knocked the stone statue, which fell to the floor with hash clink, audible even above Musty's growls and Karl's shouts.

As she recovered her balance Iona dropped her knife and raised her hands to the ceiling as if appealing to some higher power. As her hand went up, everyone else in the room felt a force, and invisible weight driving them to their knees. Even Rosetta felt it and she staggered unable to move forward to try to help Musty and Karl. But even as the Morrigan drove her down she felt her power respond from within her; she knew that even deep in the stronghold of this Devil Woman she was stronger.

But it was too late. The delay had given Iona Skane the time to reach down for her knife. She stood, her eyes fixed on Aimee. But as she stood she revealed Karl.

He had been pushed onto all fours, by the crushing weight of the Morrigan's will, but this had brought him to within reach of the fallen statue. He reached out, grabbed a fist-sized rock and with an effort raised it up and then drove it down. His hand, aided by the crushing power that suffused the room, came down fast and hard. It struck the statue square in the middle and it exploded in a shower of rock.

Iona Skane collapsed with a cry of pain, falling in a heap by the foot of the stone sarcophagus. Instantly everyone was released; the weight vanished and all could move freely. As they stood they instinctively backed away from the fallen girl, for a bizarre mist, black as ink had risen from her body and drifted - it almost could be said to move - towards the lake that lurked smooth and opaque nearby.

Iona Skane groaned and sat up, leant with her

back against the sarcophagus and her head in her hands, as if she had been knocked senseless. Musty and the children stood watching her, and suddenly they no longer hd any concern for their safety. It was somehow clear to them that Iona Skane was no longer the same person as she had been just a few seconds ago. The influence of the Morrigan had been smashed with the statue.

As they watched they saw another transformation take place; at the same time more human, and more terrible, than the departure of the Morrigan. As Iona Skane pushed her hands through her hair you could see the memories of the last six months flood back pure and clear, unstained by the influence of the Morrigan in her mind. Her face went blank as she remembered what she had done and her mouth went slack; her hands stopped their sweep through her hair. Rosetta fought an urge to go and comfort the girl as a look of horror descended over her face; she no longer looked magnificent, no longer beautiful, that glamour had gone. But now she looked like Iona Skane, schoolgirl of Oldmere School Rosetta found that she could feel sorry for her.

Iona rose unsteadily and raised her hands up in front of her eyes. Her face looked shocked at the sight of them, like they were covered in blood. She looked around her.

"No ... no. What has happened to me ...what have I done... how could ..." she said. Again she looked around and as her head turned she caught a glimpse of the lake. At the sight of it she seemed to make her mind up about something. She swooped down picked up her rucksack and ran. She ran not towards the main door, which was blocked by Rosetta, but towards the blackness of tunnel from which Karl had emerged just a few minutes before.

Musty and the children rose feeling strangely weak. Karl recovered first and after a few seconds dashed after the schoolgirl with Musty close on his heels. Rosetta thought to follow until her train of thought was interrupted by the sound of a child crying.

Looking over she saw Aimee sitting up on the cold stone, tears flowing down her face. And it was not only tears which flowed. To Rosetta's horror she saw a line of red rivulets flowing down Aimee's head from a long cut across her forehead. A cut that she had no doubt had come from the venomous knife of Iona Skane.

All thoughts of pursuit disappeared from Rosetta's mind and she rushed forward to the crying child.

"Rosy! Rosy!" said Aimee - she had never learned to say "Rosetta" as she found the word too difficult - and relieved she tried to sit up when she saw the familiar form of her sister crossing the room to comfort her. Rosetta leant over the stone of the sarcophagus, the lake to her back, so she could grab her and give a hug. Aimee looked at her smiling absently, the tears dying as quickly as they had started. Then before her eyes Rosetta saw Aimee's face change. A look of confusion spread, and she raised a hand up to her cheeks and face uncertainly, fingers probing her own flesh. Rosetta remembered the effect of Monkshood and knew that her sister now felt the spreading numbness that was the poison's first effect.

As she reached over to grab her sister, a crash made her jump and the noise made Aimee cry once more. The tears flowed, silently this time; her fear was beyond her to express. Rosetta looked over and saw that the heavy wooden door that was the way out of the chamber had slammed closed. Simultaneously she felt a horrible sensation run along her back like iced water. Somehow she just knew that something was rising from the black waters of the lake behind her.

Karl ran following the bobbing gleam of Iona's light through the dark tunnel. He had lost his torch in the brief struggle in the cavern and found it difficult to keep himself from tripping over hidden obstacles. Musty however, using his badger's senses kept pace with him, and guided him where possible. They passed the corpse of Atticus Vates, giving it barely a glance as Iona's light disappeared around a corner. Soon after they heard a small scream from ahead, and Karl remembered the pit that they had encountered on their journey from the river. He slowed down and as he walked forward the light from the torch ahead grew steadily stronger.

Around the corner he saw what had caused the scream. Iona Skane rushing forward in a panic had come to the pit at speed and taken by surprise had tumbled over the edge. But she had not fallen in; her torch lay on the floor just before the pit together with her bag, and Iona herself struggled at the edge of the pit, her legs dangling over the drop, her hands slipping as she tried to pull herself up.

Without thinking Karl rushed over, grabbed her wrists and pulled, helping her up over the edge. It was a quite a struggle as Iona was much older and heavier. Musty rushed up and helped by pulling on Iona's belt with his teeth, and with a lot of scrabbling of feet they eventually got her onto solid ground where they all collapsed to the floor chests heaving with the exertion.

After a few seconds Karl glanced up and saw that Iona stared across the passage, looking straight at him with a strange expression upon her face. Karl scrabbled with his hands and feet and pushed away from the girl until his back struck the stone wall.

Iona looked shocked by Karl's fear. "It wasn't me you know, who did those things ... at least I think it wasn't," said Iona. And now Karl could identify the look on Iona's face; it looked like she was holding back tears; it was a face of despair. Iona banged the floor in frustration. "I couldn't help it," she cried out. "And now everything is ruined. All my time at school, my work.... all gone."

Karl just looked at her not knowing quite what to say. It stayed like that for some seconds until Musty swiped at his sleeve with his claws distracting him. He looked down. As ever the badgers face, though essentially inexpressive, managed to convey what he felt. He was worried.

"I must go - Rosetta is in danger!" Musty quickly licked Karl's face in a farewell, before he ran back along the tunnel they had just come down, paws flying.

Karl looked up and saw that, whilst he had been distracted Iona had got up and was already halfway around the edge of the pit. Karl stood unsure of what to do. He stayed like that for a few heartbeats, until he realised that Iona had taken the only torch and that unless he followed her he would be stuck in the dark, and so with his mind made up for him, and with many misgivings about leaving Rosetta, he set off around the edge of the pit.

Iona, with a speed born of desperation, was already off the ledge and running down the main passage, before Karl had made the second corner around the pit and he redoubled his efforts to catch up. When he reached the entrance to the pit room there was only the last flash of light from Iona's torch to show him the way forward. The darkness grew around him, but Karl was not worried. He knew that it was only a minute or so until the light from the outside would make his progress easy. So he walked steadily forward his hands stretched in front in just in case, until the cold light of the fog-drenched world outside meant he could speed up to a shuffling jog.

He turned a corner and saw the silhouette of Iona Skane ahead. She was scanning the ground ahead, and Karl thought that it was likely she was looking for a way down to the river - she might even have seen his canoe. And it was the thought of the loss of his boat which made him shout aloud.

Iona spun around in surprise - she obviously had not expected pursuit - and the sudden motion made her slip on the wet rocks in the entrance. She waved her arms around in a desperate attempt to regain her balance, but it did no good and after an endless moment when she just seemed to hang in mid-air she disappeared from view.

Karl ran up as quickly as he dared to the entrance. He looked down. It all looked as it had done before. The fog was thick, his canoe remained tied to the tree and there was no sign of Iona Skane. He scanned the ground below the tunnel entrance. She would have fallen directly onto the pile of rubble below and now he looked carefully he could see a line of disturbed earth that started halfway down the pile ... and ended by the river. As his eyes scanned this area he noticed a rock near the start of the trail that gleamed black-red. An empty feeling welled up in his chest - he knew instinctively that this stain was blood.

He moved his attention to the river, and now he knew what to look for he saw it straight away. A line of waterlogged clothing topped by a mop of wet black hair floated in the brown swirling torrent that showed the path of the river. Iona Skane lay face down in the river. She did not move.

Karl thought about dashing down to try to save the girl, but realised almost straight away that it was hopeless. It would take minutes to get down to his boat and by then Iona would have disappeared into the fog - she was becoming hard to see even now - and even if he found her she would be too hard to drag onto his boat. As he watched the object float into the mist on the river Karl realised that Iona Skane was already dead.

He sat down strangely overcome by emotion at the death of his enemy. Then, coming to his senses he realised that, though he could do nothing for the schoolgirl in the river, he could help Rosetta. He stood, grabbed the torch that Iona had dropped, and headed back into the hill.

※ ※ ※ ※ ※

"Get down!" Rosetta looked right into Aimee's eyes and needing no further encouragement, the child crawled weakly to the edge of the stone lid and dropped behind the sarcophagus and crouched down there shaking. Rosetta turned to the lake.

A black mist, the same as that which had risen from Iona Skane when the statue had smashed, hung in a black cloud over the surface. It continued to rise and as she watched Rosetta imagined she saw it burst from a series of slowly rising bubbles emerging from the very centre of the lake. The mist thickened until it obscured the back wall of the cavern completely. In a matter of seconds the cave grew cold and Rosetta's breath became fog.

The blackness stopped growing, and after a short pause started to thicken and shrink. It coalesced into a pillar of darkness which itself then changed, becoming more distinct. Features formed, and before long the figure of a pale woman with jet black hair hovered over the lake a few meters from where Rosetta stood transfixed.

The Morrigan stood tall, much taller than even a tall man, and was dressed in a black cape. It wrapped around her, covering every part from her feet to the very top of her neck in a single sweep of material. Her face, white as snow in shocking contrast to the darkness of her dress, was fabulously beautiful, but expressionless. Her hair was jet black.

"I am pleased to meet you Rosetta Clarence," the figure said looking into Rosetta's eyes. As their eyes met Rosetta felt a pressure on her mind, like something was gently squeezing it; how someone would check a fruit to see if it was ripe for picking. Her voice was light and calm, like a teacher's. "Yes very pleased. I have been waiting for this meeting since I had that run in with the very first Custodian of Oldmere Vale." Her eyes flashed to the sarcophagus for a second before returning to Rosetta.

"When he put you back in your box you mean; defeated you and saved the world a great deal of trouble."

"*He did not defeat me*," snapped the Morrigan her eyes going hard. "Here I stand, and where is the custodian of Oldmere Vale?" She looked around in mock astonishment. "*In bed!*" she snapped in answer to her own question. "He is in bed whilst his inheritance, the legacy of thousands of years falls around him.

"But I see you have already been turned against me. Perhaps I should enlighten you as to the true story of Oldmere Vale." As she spoke Rosetta felt the pressure build a little on her mind. She resisted, but found it hard to concentrate; to bring forward her power.

"I have lived in this island since time endless. I existed before even then, but was formless thoughtless - I cannot remember it well. There are four of us now, but then, at the beginning we were one - a single animal. But then men came and their thoughts and desires woke us, and as we woke we divided. We became the four eternals - creatures of water, fire, air and earth. But beneath the surface we are still linked, still the same as in the beginning; we are one mind; one will. As long as one exists we all endure somehow.

"As we awoke we found men - those whose thoughts first awoke us - and we were disappointed. Their minds were crude and we decided that they needed to be guided. We taught them and they, seeing our wisdom, worshipped us. We were known as the Morrigan, and men advanced because of us. Kings vied for our favour, because of the victories in battle we could bring. War brought them wealth and glory and we were masters of war.

"But then came the druids. They came from over the sea, and they were immune to our power. They hated us, preferring a life of peace farming the soil, and had great power of their own. They spread over the land and trapped us, sent all four of us to sleep in their places of power so we might never again influence the world of humans.

And it might have stayed that way had not the Romans come. They destroyed kingdoms. They hated and feared the Druids and killed them all, until all that remained of them was in the mountains of the west. In the end the Romans came even here, and in their desperation the Druids of the west woke one of the Morrigan. They woke me; as they faced defeat their high values of peace and harmony were forgotten. They only remembered that we might bring victory in battle. In the end they were like all men before them."

She laughed at the memory. "I gave them victory, but in the end they were defeated by one of their own. A traitor. He sold his people to the Romans. But he did not count on the blood lust of his new friends. They killed the druids who had raised me, meaning that I could not be sent fully back to my sleep. Alone he could not do this, but he what he could do was to trap me in this lake, and to set a constant guard upon the place. He created the Custodians, that have guarded me ever since. This creature, this traitor lies in the casket in front of you as a constant reminder to me of my powerlessness."

The Morrigan paused again contemplating the stone box. Rosetta felt her mind drift with the story. She began to think anew about the role of that first Custodian - no better than a traitor to his own. Yes she could see that perhaps he was no better than the Morrigan. Unnoticed by her the pressure on her mind intensified a little.

"But then again he also was helpless. The Romans killed all the druids, also their helpers the Glyphs, and alone he could not send me back to my slumber. I existed and could return at any stage by some accident of fate. As he died in old age, a vision came to him. A prophecy, which said there would come one last Glyph, one that could destroy us four sisters. Destroy us, not just send us to sleep. He wrote the prophecy down and died. That prophecy is written on his tomb. A last delusion from a traitor riddled by guilt."

The pressure inched up, and Rosetta began to see that perhaps the world did need a strong leader, someone who might remove all the evil in the world, by force if necessary. After all what could be worse than the weakness and indecision that governments and leaders showed these days?

"So my imprisonment started. I was not dismayed however. I knew that eventually chance would favour me, and indeed several times I nearly escaped. But each time the Custodians frustrated me.

"In the end it was a chance find by Iona Skane

that gave me my opportunity. She found an offering from an age-old follower. The statue still had the power of belief given to it from that ancient worshipper. And so great was that power, it gave me a way in to her mind even though she was not close to the sacred lake. Her thoughts, though subject to the usual human failings, so fitted my own that it was hardly any effort to control her. Such frustrated ambition! I gave her the desire to take what she needed and she gave me the chance of a way out. A chance I have taken."

With those words The Morrigan moved over the lake, paused by the edge and with a satisfied smile took a single step on to the shore.

"I am free! The blood of an innocent has broken my chains as I knew it would."

The pressure on Rosetta's mind increased tenfold as the Morrigan's power waxed with her new freedom. As it did so Rosetta could feel the true substance of the Morrigan leak though into her thoughts, and her mind recoiled at the evil in the touch. At the same time she heard a whimper from behind the tomb of the first Custodian, and she remembered her sister.

At this the power in her rose like a tidal wave, uncontrollable. The Morrigan felt it and looked over in alarm.

"You are free. But free to be destroyed. I have tasted your world, creature of dark and I reject it!" Rosetta spoke without thought. The words came from deep within her; from the same place that held her power. "You have used the small freedom you have enjoyed in the last months to destroy lives, to kill the innocent, just so you may be free... free for more pointless destruction."

The power now filled Rosetta so fully that it was hard to contain - she felt she would explode. However now she knew she could control it, and that the decision to destroy the demon before her was hers. That she, Rosetta Clarence, was the one who would decide the Morrigan's fate.

She looked at The Morrigan. It stood defiant, hatred on its face; it knew that it was defeated, that it could not match the power it felt emanate from the young child before it.

Rosetta made her decision.

A beam of light shot from her forehead towards the Morrigan. It raised its hand as she did so, but not in defence for it knew that none was possible against such power. From its hand came three shapes made of black mist. They looked like birds, ravens perhaps, and they shot in three different directions towards the walls of the cavern where they disappeared.

The beam hit the Morrigan in the chest and she screamed. Her human form disappeared and she became a formless blob. The mist boiled and the screaming stopped. A strangely distorted voice came from the boiling mass.

"I am destroyed Glyph of Oldmere Vale, but it is you who are defeated. My sisters now begin to wake. They will rise and enter the world of men once more. We shall ..."

But then the boiling mass of mist vanished and as it did so the whole of Oldmere Knoll shook. Lumps of earth and small pieces of rock fell from the ceiling. Rosetta was just starting to become alarmed when, just as suddenly the shaking stopped.

Rosetta watched the space where the Morrigan had stood, until a whimper from behind the druid's tomb snapped her out of her reverie. "Aimee!" She ran until she could see her sister.

She lay in a crumpled heap, her face grey and sweaty, her breathing laboured. Her eyes flickered and she smiled a weak smile at Rosetta.

"Rosy." she said; more of a sigh than word, and she closed her eyes.

"No! This will not happen!" said Rosetta and she threw herself down beside the girl placing her hands upon her heart. She delved deep within her for the feeling she had before when, unknowingly, she had managed to heal herself from the effect of Monkshood. She could not find it. It felt like her abilities had disappeared. She looked down helplessly at her sister, and as she looked into the child's face in despair her powers at last reappeared in a surge.

Rosetta felt hope flicker and pushed her hands down, willing her sister better with all her heart and mind.

"Get better ... just get better" she muttered under her breath. She ripped the power up from her gut and pushed it into the tiny body beneath her. Her hands glowed purple as she felt a vast surge of energy flow down her arms into her sister's torso. Her sister's body actually lifted off the ground as the power flowed into her. She gave a splutter and opened her eyes again just for a second before she fell to the floor and lay there. Rosetta leant closer and examined her sister's face. She was breathing, her chest rising and falling in an easy steady rhythm.

"Rosetta," Karl had just emerged from the shadows with Musty at his side. He looked slightly awed "Did you just do what I thought you did?"

"I don't know what I did, or how" said Rosetta looking down at the sleeping form of her sister. "I'm just pleased that I did." She looked up and looked at Karl's face. It looked pale and streaked with dirt.

"What's happened, where is Iona?"

"Dead..." and as he said it his voice choked. "She fell and drowned. I couldn't do anything. Musty had said you were in danger and so I started back ... I changed my mind and turned about. I thought that I might have been mistaken about saving Iona, but then the whole of the tunnel collapsed behind me and I couldn't go back any more. What about you? Were you really in danger?"

Musty spoke up. "She faced the Morrigan, and defeated her," he said, pride in his voice.

"What! She was here?"

"She came from the lake," said Rosetta. "Whatever Iona was doing to free her worked, and she could leave. But I think it was her downfall. If she had stayed there then I don't think I could have destroyed her; the Custodian's prison also protected her."

Musty trotted up and licked Aimee's face. She smiled in her sleep. "Well done Rosetta," he said his black eyes eying her intelligently. "And now I think we should go and relieve your mother's anxiety. And do so before we are left in the dark"

Now that Musty spoke, all realised that over the last few minutes the central column of fire had started to drop lower and lower. It was now just one quarter of the height it had been when they entered the cavern, and was still dropping.

Refusing Karl's offer of help with a shake of her head, Rosetta picked up Aimee from the ground. Still asleep, she rested her head on Rosetta's shoulder, wrapped her legs around her waist, and in a group they walked towards the door that led to the Ancient Library.

For the first time in weeks Rosetta remembered Christmas.

Chapter 7

Several farewells.

The children sat with Marcus by the back door, hidden from casual observation by the overhanging hawthorn bush. It was two days since Rosetta had walked from the cavern carrying Aimee asleep in her arms. Karl and Musty had left the tunnels separately through the back door, in order to try and get back to the canoe by trekking along the riverbank. After much struggling through undergrowth they had made it and had discovered that the entrance to the underground caverns, uncovered by one landslide, had now been disguised by another.

Rosetta had told the agreed story to Miss Eastville when questions were asked; she had found her sister asleep hidden under a shelf in the Old Library. Wide eyed, she explained she had looked there because she thought no one else had yet, as they were all aware of the rules against entering. And as it turned out no one had. There were several mutual looks of astonishment amongst the searchers at their oversight.

They had taken her out into the suddenly clear winter day - the fog had inexplicably vanished just half an hour before - and someone had been sent to look for Mrs Clarence, who still searched for her daughter out amongst the school grounds. A short time later Rosetta's mother had appeared, seemingly from nowhere, grabbed her second child and cried silent tears of relief. Rosetta stood and watched with a smile.

♣ ♣ ♣ ♣ ♣

In the distance the three watchers could see a yellow digger working at the entrance to the blocked road tunnel. The weather had improved and the flood in the valley was receding. In a day or so the road from the school would be clear and the villagers could start to make their way back to their houses. In the meantime helicopters had made it through, now the fog was gone, and taken home all those who had an urgent need - this included Mrs Doyle, the old lady with the broken leg - and the school was now nearly empty of students. Marcus had refused to be evacuated and remained despite his injuries. One of the helicopters had dropped a new leg - courtesy of his old army regiment - and he was now fully mobile once more; his broken arm hardly hindered him now his leg was back. The school nurse, armed with new supplies had provided him with a plaster cast.

A distant explosion boomed along the valley.

"They will have the blockages near the ford clear at this rate," said Marcus looking up towards where the landslides had cleared the valley, "and then the water will drain even quicker."

"Things won't be normal though," said Karl feeling morose despite the beautiful weather. "I don't think the school will quite be the same ever again." Searchers had found Iona Skane's body just the day before. It had caught under a fallen tree, which had just emerged from the floodwater, and Karl's guilty feelings about his lack of a rescue attempt had resurfaced. They persisted despite everyone telling him that there was nothing he could have done for the girl; the doctor investigating had said the wound to her head would likely have been fatal by itself, even if she had not fallen in the water.

"It may not seem like it now Karl, but things will feel normal again," Marcus sighed. "I fear that things were not normal for Iona Skane for some time." He reached behind him into his rucksack and brought out two books. One was instantly recognised by the children.

"The Folio!" they cried simultaneously.

"Yes," said Marcus. "Last night I went back through the cavern to the passage that you found,

Karl. Just before the pit I found a small bag and next to it, lying in the mud, these two books."

"Iona dropped it when she nearly went over the edge," said Karl looking sad once again.

"Yes, and don't forget who pulled her up," said Marcus giving Karl a significant glance. "One of these books is the Folio, which incidentally mentions the room with the pit. The writing on the walls is a transcript of Celtic spells. The idea being that if an enemy came through, then they would have to shuffle along the ledge passing close to the spells designed to bring disaster to those with evil intent; quite clever really.

"The other book I found is Iona's diary. She must have always kept it close, for if its contents had been read by someone else, then there would have been a lot of explaining to do. Personally I found it an extremely sad read."

"What does it say?" asked Rosetta.

"It starts at the beginning of last year, and was what you would expect a diary from a girl of Iona's age to be like. There is talk of the Christmas just gone, and various pieces of gossip from her home town - a place on the west coast of Scotland. Then when she came back to school its tone changed.

"She was not very happy at school was Miss Skane. Always just behind the very clever pupils at the top of her class, she was never satisfied. She wanted to be top - this was driven from home I think - and every time one of the other pupils beat her she became deeply unhappy, much more than was warranted by her achievements. She was chosen to be one of the competitors in the Archer prize, but even that just made her sad; I think she knew inside that she would not win. And that is what she wanted to do most of all - win in all things.

"Then about May this year the tone of the diary changed again. This was about the time that she found the statue, the discovery of which she mentions. After that she becomes very different. Now instead of unhappiness at any perceived failure at school she started to emphasise how the other pupils must have had some sort of unfair advantage, and started to use these fictitious sleights to justify her own cheating.

"Interspersed among these twisted jottings are places where the influence of the Morrigan becomes very clear. Direct reference to the secret role of the Custodian, which she could not have found by herself, and talk of her 'Mistress' start to come into the text. She becomes more and more confused and deluded until it is clear that she no longer sees the Archer Prize as a thing to be achieved for its own sake. She now must achieve it so her Mistress can be become powerful.

"It is also at this point in the diary that two new things come in. Firstly she starts to plot to free her mistress; to actively work against the Custodian, to gain access to the sacred lake and perform rites that will mean that the Morrigan may be free, free to possess her physically and to leave the vale. She starts to search the Antechamber for example, looking for clues or secret passages.

"Secondly - and when you actually see this set out in the diary it really gives you the shivers - on occasion it is clear that the Morrigan has complete control over Iona. The writing changes - it becomes old fashioned, as does the language - and you know that a different brain is shaping the words, that the person writing here has nothing to do with Iona Skane." Marcus stopped, breathed heavily and said, "It is just after the first passage written like this that Iona described the murder of my father."

"Is it Iona who wrote it?" said Karl. "I mean was it not the Morrigan directly."

"No I'm afraid it is Iona who wrote the words, and who performed the act. Though the person who writes has very little to do with the insecure, frightened and desperate schoolgirl who started the diary in January. The Morrigan had used her desires to twist that child into the monster we all saw in the last few months, though from what I understand, at the very end her old self came back.

"The death of my Father made very little difference to her efforts to free the Morrigan. School tradition demands that, on the death of a Librarian, the antechamber and old library are locked with a set of padlocks owned by the head teacher. Presumably to prevent the ransacking of these areas when they are undefended.

"When I arrived she was unconcerned. She saw me as some sort of crippled child, unaware of the secrets of the custodian, and unable to reveal the secret of the location of the Morrigan's prison. I was at best a nuisance; quite insulting, but in many ways accurate.

"She was, however, very concerned when you arrived Rosetta, though at first she did not know who you were and what you could do. The Morrigan had sensed your appearance and instinctively felt that you could be a threat to her plans. The power of the Glyph presumably gave you away and forewarned her, though at that time she did not know the details of what you were.

"From that moment onwards your confrontation with the Morrigan became inevitable. Musty was 'born', I became involved guided by the prophecy and your power started to stir.

"The Morrigan and Iona went on with their plan regardless. They found vulnerable children who were in the shortlist for the Archer prize and started to play with their minds, following a two-fold strategy. Firstly if, using their power, they could destabilise these children's minds so their work would suffer then they would be soon out of the running for the Archer Prize. That would leave the way open for Iona to win; for that was part of their aim in the end. They wanted Iona Skane, possessed by the full power of the Morrigan, in amongst the students at Munsford University. From there she could influence and control people who would become future leaders of this country and perhaps even other nations.

"But to that she must also free the Morrigan, and

that is where the second part of their plan came in. They already knew that disturbances to the earth could loosen the Morrigan's chains somewhat. So if they could get these students to somehow open the crack in the ancient sacred lake that lay in the archaeological dig, then perhaps the Morrigan might be released or at least have more freedom to work towards her ultimate liberty.

"In the end they abandoned that plan, because it became apparent that the Custodian, the one they thought so useless, was becoming aware of the situation. And what is more he had teamed up with the enemy that the Morrigan has sensed for so many months; the one she feared the most. Again their guesses were correct. They also thought that perhaps that the location of the Morrigan's prison might be known to the new Custodian or at least might be inferred from something in the folio. And in that they were correct. Once they had discovered the Ancient Library, then Iona could feel her mistress's presence close by, and she simply followed that feeling until she found herself by the sacred lake.

"The diary ends with Iona Skane, having discovered the Sacred Lake, planning to kidnap Aimee to use her as sacrifice in some ancient rite. From what is written in the diary, it looks like Iona believed that a mere blood sacrifice would be enough, but I personally think that The Morrigan deceived Iona. I think that in the end the Morrigan would have forced Iona to deliberately murder a child, an innocent. As it was Iona Skane performed that deed by accident - the cut Aimee received was not intentional - but it was enough to break the spell that held the Morrigan prisoner." Marcus fell silent.

After a minute or so Karl said. "If you have been through to where Iona dropped the bag then you will have ..." He paused seemingly unsure of what to say.

"My father," said Marcus. "Yes I found him."

It was that evening when they buried Atticus Vates. Marcus had decided that it would be best if his fate remained a secret. If they told the authorities they had found his body then there would be all sorts of questions. Iona Skane's part in his death would have to become public knowledge, and also that the location of the secret lake would also have to be revealed.

"I think Iona's parents have suffered enough without the added burden that the knowledge of their daughter's crime would bring, and I am quite sure that my father would not want the secret of the knoll revealed and this place to become some sort of curiosity for tourists. His death will have to remain a mystery to most."

They decided to bury him in the sarcophagus that held the body of the druid, the druid that started it all, those thousands of years ago. There was a symmetry to it that would probably have pleased Atticus Vates, Rosetta decided. The Morrigan was finally gone and it was somehow fitting that the last of the Custodians should rest in the same tomb as the first.

They were all there when it took place. Rosetta, Karl, Musty and Marcus. It was Marcus who opened the tomb. He shifted the stone lid to one side with a crowbar and looked inside. After a few seconds he called the children over.

The dry air so good at preserving books had done the same to the body of the ancient druid, mummifying his body. His skin had turned a deep brown and had become like leather. There was no smell. He was encased in a white shroud, also well preserved, which looked something like a toga. Entombed with him was a long sword, untouched by rust, and a tall staff topped with an ornate silver statue; a statue of a badger.

Rosetta picked up Musty, who had been gently nudging her feet, to show him. "There you go my brave man," she said. " He knew you were coming to help us"

With some difficulty they pushed the lid until it lay crosswise across the lower end of the tomb, and gently they slipped the body of Atticus Vates, also wrapped in a shroud, next to the body of his ancient ancestor. They all stood there for a moment until Rosetta gave Karl a nudge and together they slipped away leaving Marcus alone with his father.

It was just after this that they started to notice a change in Musty. He spoke less and was more Badger-like in his behaviour. He started to yip and half-bark between words. More and more frequently the badger would not come to meet them by the old playhouse. He moved out from his nest in the tunnels under the knoll, to where they did not know.

"He goes back to his true nature," said Marcus, when Rosetta came to him crying over the change in the Badger. "A Glyph's familiar comes only when it is needed, like the power of the Glyph itself. Musty the badger just held the force that is your familiar; he is not the familiar itself. If that power is ever needed again then he will come back, perhaps as a different animal. Musty must go back to just being a badger."

Musty himself sensed the change and one day in January he came to the children who were playing in Rosetta's garden. He ran up to them and they bent down. Rosetta looked into his eyes and felt a faint echo of their connection. "Musty," she said. "Hello."

Musty looked back and struggled to speak." He opened his mouth, but no words would come until he finally forced something out, seemingly by an act of pure will. "Goodbye, my children," and with that Rosetta felt the already weak connection to Musty snap inside her, and the badger turned and ran back through the hole in the hedge where she had first seen his snout appear all those months ago.

They did see Musty after that. He still came with his family, who seem to have accepted him back, to forage in Rosetta's garden, but he never spoke to them. Traces of the old Musty still remained though, Rosetta always thought, for he would stay, when the rest of the animals had scattered at the sight of one of the children. And if a tin of cat food were available he would be quite happy to sit and eat it, squatting just a few feet away from the children as they watched.

※ ※ ※ ※ ※

Christmas was something of a relief for Rosetta after all the excitement of the last few weeks. Karl's parents wanted to have the Clarence's over as thanks for looking after their son during the flooding of the valley, but it was decided after some discussion that the Clarence's should host, as Aimee was much more comfortable in the familiar surroundings of her house.

Karl's parents, him a sculptor and her a teacher, were in the living room talking to Rosetta's mother, with Aimee playing on the floor, when Karl said to Rosetta "I've got something for you - Christmas present if you like. Come into the kitchen."

Karl went to his bag and pulled out a parcel carefully wrapped in Christmas paper and said, "Here, I finally finished it last night."

"I haven't got anything for you," said Rosetta suddenly anxious.

"Never mind. I have got plenty. The parents are still overcome with gratitude for getting the outside scholarship ... go on open it."

Rosetta tore away the wrapping paper and revealed a shoebox. Raising the lid she saw a flash of wood peeking out from amongst some screwed up tissue paper.

She plunged her hand in and pulled out a beautifully carved wooden badger. It shone golden brown in her hand. Looking at it Rosetta remembered the day all those months ago when Karl had taken her for a walk around the grounds of Oldmere School. Looking carefully she realised that it was the same statue that Karl had roughly cut out from the fallen branch during that summer day, but now it was unrecognisable.

"Oh ... it's lovely. It even looks a little like Musty," said Rosetta smiling.

"Well I got to know the way he looks very well," said Karl his voice a little strange, and when Rosetta looked at his face she felt sure there might be a tear hiding in the corner of his eye. "Let's go back. They'll be putting the TV on soon. " He said.

When they arrived back Rosetta showed the parents her new present which they all admired greatly. Karl's father was particularly proud Rosetta thought, but it was when she showed it to Aimee that Rosetta and her mother received something of a shock.

Aimee picked up the carving, and Rosetta tensed ready to take it from her in case should she start to chew it, which is what would happen in the normal course of events. But this time Aimee just looked at it with a serious attention then looked around her and said quite clearly "Dog".

Rosetta and her mother looked at each other astonished. And though the Bastion family smiled and looked charmed they could not have possibly realised the significance of what they had seen; that Aimee during the three years of her short life had never before uttered a single intelligible word beyond the names of her family.

"No Aimee," said Karl, smiling like his parents "That's a badger."

Aimee looked at him seriously. "Bageee ... Bageee," she said.

Rosetta's mother, recovering herself a little, started to excitedly explain to everyone about Aimee, and the new treatment in Denmark, and how it, magically seemed to be working when so many other things had failed.

But Rosetta looked at her sister and, seeing for the first time the new understanding in her eyes, she wondered if it came from Danish doctors or from the vast surge of power, driven by a desire to heal, that she had pumped into Aimee in that cavern deep in Oldmere Knoll.

Epilogue

Marcus looked across his desk in the antechamber at the children. A letter consisting of many pages lay spread on the wooden surface in front of him. Karl knew the letter to be from Atticus Vates; the one he had found on the body of the old Custodian, and had delivered to its intended recipient just a few days before.

"As you may guess, this made very interesting reading," said Marcus indicating the letter with an open hand. "It is indeed an attempt by my father to anoint me as Custodian by post. There are several things that are now clear to me, two of which stand out.

"Firstly I have been made aware by the contents of this letter that, though the Morrigan of water is gone - destroyed completely by Rosetta - there are three more of these creatures that exist. Remember, legend has it that the Morrigan had four aspects, each associated with one of the elements; earth, air, fire and water. We have only removed one of these and so there are three more which remain.

"Each of the others is in a dormant state, rather like our one was before those ancient druids woke it in that desperate attempt to protect their valley all those centuries ago. But each may now have been woken, and if they are then they will be free to wander the world and cause chaos. What happened by the sacred lake that night makes me very much afraid that, as she died, the Morrigan of water made a desperate attempt to wake her sisters so that she could have some form of revenge on the human race.

"The other thing that the letter tells me is that each of the places that hold these Morrigans has its own Custodian. Oldmere Knoll is just one of four places where the ancient Druids set a guard on these ancient demons, though it was considered the most important as it had a "live" prisoner to guard. The others, as far as they know, were just guarding against the faint possibility that their Morrigan may awake."

"We must warn them," said Rosetta. "They may be in great danger."

"Yes," said Marcus. "But there is a problem. My father tells me that there has been no contact between most of the Custodians for many hundreds of years. The Custodians of Oldmere knew the location of the other Morrigan sites in a general way only. We have no idea of their exact locations, or, apart from one, who is the Custodian of each site."

"But that means we cannot warn them, and, the other Custodians will be taken by surprise when the Morrigans awake," said Karl.

"Yes," said Marcus. "And I fear that they may not

even believe that what they guard is real. It has been so long since any of the Morrigans were awake, that they may think it is some silly tradition, or superstition. That was the case here in Oldmere, remember, in Victorian times."

Rosetta looked very worried. Karl said "Who is the Custodian we do know about, and where are the other Morrigans imprisoned?"

"The locations of the others have only a vague descriptions in the letter. The Morrigan of Air is somewhere in the Lake District and the Morrigan of Earth in East Anglia. That is not much to go on.

"What we do know is the rough location of the Morrigan of Fire and, most importantly, the identity of its Custodian"

"And who is it?" said Rosetta.

"We don't know the name, but at least from 1826 until the Second World War the Custodian in charge of the Morrigan of Fire has always been the Provost of University College London, and it is a good guess that they still are. It is also reasonable to assume that the Morrigan of Fire is held somewhere in that city. I would guess near the University. If that that is still the case, and the Provost knows the identities of the other Custodians, as well as the exact location of the Morrigan of Fire then we will at least have a start.

"Well," said Karl. "Can't you organise a school trip for half term? I suddenly feel the need for an educational visit to London."

"Just what I had in mind," said Marcus.

The Venomous Knife of Iona Skane

About the Author

Bob Cregan lives in the county of Somerset, UK with his wife and two daughters. He likes cycling and guinea pigs.

Check out his webpage at http://www.bobcregan.co.uk/

If you are interested in new work, updates and random chat then you can join his mailing list also to be found at http://www.bobcregan.co.uk/

Printed in Great Britain
by Amazon